THE YEAR'S BEST

BEST

MYSTERY & SUSPENSE

STORIES

1982

THE YEAR'S BEST

MYSTERY & SUSPENSE STORIES

1982

Edited by Edward D. Hoch

WALKER & COMPANY

NEW YORK

First published in the United States of America in 1982 by the Walker Publishing Company, Inc.

Published simultaneously in Canada by John Wiley & Sons Canada, Limited, Rexdale, Ontario.

Book design by Laura Ferguson

ISBN: 0-8027-0713-0

Printed in the United States of America

10 9 8 7 6 5 4 3 2 1

ACKNOWLEDGMENTS

"The French Lesson" by Asa Baber. Copyright © 1981 by Asa Baber. Reprinted by permission of The Sterling Lord Agency, Inc. as first appeared in Playboy Magazine.

"What You Been Up to Lately?" by George Baxt. Copyright © 1980 by George Baxt. First published in Ellery Queen's Mystery Magazine.

"The House on Plymouth Street" by Ursula Curtiss. Copyright © 1981 by Ursula Curtiss.

"The Chalk Outline" by Brian Garfield. Copyright © 1981 by Brian Garfield. First published in Ellery Queen's Mystery Magazine.

"The Hours of Angelus" by Jonathan Gash. Copyright © Jonathan Gash, 1981.

"Camford Cottage" by Michael Gilbert. Copyright © Michael Gilbert, 1981.

"Suspense" by Ron Goulart. Copyright © 1981 by Davis Publications, Inc.

"Sweet Baby Jenny" by Joyce Harrington. Copyright © 1981 by Joyce Harrington, reprinted by permission of the author and her agents, Scott Meredith Literary Agency, Inc. First published in Ellery Queen's Mystery Magazine.

"The Problem of the Octagon Room" by Edward D. Hoch. Copyright © 1981 by Edward D. Hoch. First published in Ellery Queen's Mystery Magazine.

"Mexican Triangle" by Clark Howard. Copyright © 1981 by Clark Howard. First published in Ellery Queen's Mystery Magazine.

"Won't Daddy Be Surprised?" by Clements Jordan. Copyright © 1981 by Clements Jordan. First published in Ellery Queen's Mystery Magazine.

"A Token of Appreciation" by Donald Olson. Copyright © 1981 by Davis Publications, Inc.

"Coyote and Quarter Moon" by Bill Pronzini & Jeffrey Wallmann. Copyright © 1981 by Renown Publications, Inc. First published in Mike Shayne Mystery Magazine. Reprinted by permission of the authors.

"The Absence of Emily" by Jack Ritchie. Copyright © 1981 by Jack Ritchie. First published in Ellery Queen's Mystery Magazine. Reprinted by permission of Larry Sternig Literary Agency.

"Ask a Silly Question" by Donald E. Westlake. Copyright © 1981, Donald E. Westlake. Originally appeared in Playboy Magazine.

For Madge and Jim McMahon

CONTENTS

INTRODUCTION

THE FIRST ATTEMPT TO COLLECT THE YEAR'S BEST detective stories between the covers of one book came in 1929 with the publication of *The Best English Detective Stories: First Series* (1928), edited by Father Ronald Knox and H. Harrington. The book is still famous for Father Knox's introduction, in which he laid down his ten commandments for detective story writing. The twenty authors he chose included a number of familiar names—Marie Belloc Lowndes, Maurice Leblanc, E. Phillips Oppenheim and Baroness Orczy—but only one of the stories is still widely read today: Agatha Christie's "The Tuesday Night Club," which marked Miss Marple's first appearance in print.

A second volume followed in 1930, covering the best of '29 and including another all-time classic, Anthony Berkeley's "The Avenging Chance." But no editor was credited for this volume and no subsequent volumes were published, at least in England. The scene shifted to America, where mystery writer Carolyn Wells edited *The Best American Mystery Stories of the Year* for two years, covering the best of 1930 and '31. Two stories by Dashiell Hammett were the prizes of these collections—"The Farewell Murder" and "Death and Company."

After that followed fourteen years of silence, until David C. Cooke began editing *Best Detective Stories of the Year* in 1946. His first volume, covering the best of '45, included Q. Patrick's "White Carnations" along with thirteen other stories and authors now mainly forgotten. But it was the beginning of a long series that continued, under the editorship of Cooke, Brett Halliday, Anthony Boucher, Allen J. Hubin and myself, until last year.

So this volume is, in a sense, both a continuation and a new beginning. The years from 1928 to 1982 have seen great changes in the short mystery, and some of those changes are reflected here. Only a few of my fifteen choices are detective stories. The others fall under the much broader heading of mystery and suspense. Thirteen stories are from magazines and two are from anthologies which appeared originally in England. One of these is published here for the first time in America.

I make no excuse for the fact that nearly half of my fifteen choices come from one source, *Ellery Queen's Mystery Magazine*. In an age when magazine fiction of all sorts continues to decline, *EQMM* remains the one bright hope of the mystery short story, as it was when Frederic Dannay began editing it more than forty years ago. The British novelist Desmond Bagley recently wrote, "The standard of American crime writing is exceptionally high, due in great measure to the work of Fred Dannay, who has done more for the genre in the English language than any other single man. He has taught two generations of writers by wielding a meticulous editorial pen."

In a declining magazine market, the year 1981 did produce a few bright spots. A new weekly magazine, *Women's World*, began using a mystery short-short in each issue. When the policy was discontinued at mid-year, reader response forced its resumption in the fall. And there was a growing trend toward semi-professional magazines in the field. Publications such as *Mystery, Skullduggery*, and the Canadian *Black Cat* began to build a following, using a mixture of well-known and beginning writers.

For their help in producing this book I wish to thank Frederic Dannay, Eleanor Sullivan, Allen J. Hubin, Al Nussbaum, and Martin H. Greenberg, who contributed the listing of the year's best mystery novels at the back of the book (with a few additions from my own reading). A final word of thanks to my wife, Patricia, without whom none of it would have been possible.

Edward D. Hoch

ASA BABER

THE FRENCH LESSON

Asa Baber is a new name in suspense fiction. A contributing editor of Playboy, *where this story first appeared, he writes here of the early days of war and intrigue in Southeast Asia, when even murder could seem to have its justifications. A powerful story, and winner of* Playboy's *annual award for the best short fiction published in its pages.*

"THIS FRENCHMAN IS A TERRIBLE PERSON, GENE," Chen said. He rocked back and forth in the bamboo rocker.

I remember Chen clearly, even though it was 20 years ago. I thought of him as a puppet, a small Chinese puppet. I assumed he was at least 50, possibly older. He was bald and full-faced, and he wore steel-rimmed glasses that complemented his rumpled linen suit and vest.

Like the country of Laos itself, Chen was full of contradictions. He fancied himself a banker, and he tried to dress like one, but he wore shower clogs instead of regular shoes and a red bandanna around his throat rather than a tie. Chen had a habit of fingering black worry beads while he talked. Listening to his English, his London School of Economics English, only deepened the conflicting presence of the man.

I sat on my bed drinking Beefeater gin without ice. I drank a lot in those days, and while I preferred my gin with ice, I took it any way I could get it. The hotel refrigerator had broken down the day before the monsoon began. I was, by definition, left with warm gin and a trapped feeling: tropical claustrophobia; something like being stuck in an elevator that is also a steam bath.

Chen had taken to coming in and talking with me whenever he found me in my room. He gossiped idly while the rain poured down on Vientiane, on the muddy Mekong River and the tin roofs of the storage sheds, through palm fronds and flame trees, a rain so hard that sometimes it obscured everything except the vines that framed my windows.

It was a violent rain and it drove the gecko on my ceiling crazy: He darted from corner to corner and talked to the rain in his lizard language.

"Let's go smoke some dope," I said to Chen.

"The den's probably flooded," he said, waving my suggestion aside. It was clear that he wanted to talk to me at some length about something. He was busy setting me up, and he did not want his train of thought to be interrupted. Of course, I did not understand that at the time.

"This Frenchman takes ears when he kills," Chen said.

"He doesn't sound nice," I said.

"Simply not to be trusted," Chen sighed. "He's a madman, I'm sure of it." He sighed again, and it struck me that he might have been speaking of a failed marriage or a bankruptcy.

Chen was a money-changer who used his tailor shop as a front for a black market in currencies. He tended to speak sadly about many things. He was particularly morose about people who did not honor deals. I had seen him come to tears, for example, about a minister of finance who could not pay the interest Chen had charged him on a personal loan. To that extent, Chen had a tragic sense of life. Coincidentally, the person in question was found drowned on the bank of the Mekong a week later. People said it was the work of the Pathet Lao, and Chen did not disabuse them of that notion.

"Simply not to be trusted, those French," Chen said.

"That's what Gunny Nadeau used to say," I said, "and look what it got him."

Gunny Nadeau had been my second-in-command. He and I had brought a special team out from Camp Pendleton. We hooked up with Sergeant Sutton at Tachikawa and Tony Allard at Kadena. On paper, we were attached to Task Force 116. In fact, we spent a lot of time around the Plain of Jars.

Until everybody got snuffed except me.

While Chen and I watched the rain outside my windows, I

drank as much gin as I could to forget that Gunny Nadeau's charred body was lying in my poncho, brown side out, on line to be shipped back to Travis Air Force Base. The bodies of Sutton and Allard had made it out before the rains hit, but Gunny Nadeau was waiting for me.

I knew that all three men would be listed as killed in training exercises in California. That is what happens when you die in a nonwar.

"Your Sergeant Nadeau was French, wasn't he?" Chen asked.

"Cajun," I said. "Louisiana French. Same as Allard. Sutton was Canadian. There wasn't a real frog among us, Chenny. Isn't that something?" I asked.

"I'm sorry about your friends, Gene," Chen said. "Perhaps they paid the price for freedom."

I did not reply to that. The rain had a hypnotic effect on me. I did not want to analyze history or talk politics or listen to a chubby Chinese tailor define life and death. I was sorely pissed at the war I saw shaping up, and I wanted to get out of Vientiane as fast as I could. I had resigned my commission and was waiting for the rains to lift long enough to catch the next transport to Bangkok. Things had not turned out the way I had hoped.

"I was talking to the Indian air attaché yesterday," Chen said. "He says he thinks this Frenchman may have brought in a surface-to-air missile." He dropped that into the conversation like a marble into a water bucket. "This Frenchman amazes me," he went on. "You cannot believe the stories I've heard recently. Last month, this Frenchman supposedly came into town dressed as a woman. A woman, of all things. He walked into the W.C. downstairs and shot one of your cultural-affairs people right in the face. And then, to make matters worse, he took one of her ears, too." Chen clucked his tongue. "Leaving his mark, do you suppose?"

"They take ears all the time incountry," I said.

"Yes, I know, but here in Vientiane? And a woman, to boot? I think that's going a bit far, don't you?" Chen asked.

"Yes," I said.

"The French are your allies, after all."

"Listen, Chenny," I said, "the French are on their own side.

Period. Just like everybody else out here. The French figure this is their territory. They were here before us, and some of them think they'll be here after us. Maybe they will; I don't know." I paused. "Sometimes they have advisors down to patrol level with the Pathet Lao, I can tell you that," I said.

"How terribly confusing," Chen sighed again. "I don't understand any of it at all. Perhaps I'd better leave while I can."

"Be my guest," I said. "Take your money and split. Go back to Hong Kong and start a real bank."

Chen tried to light a cigarette. His matches were too damp, so I threw him my lighter.

"Someone should take care of this Frenchman, Gene," he said.

I rubbed my jaw. I hadn't shaved for a week. "Does he have a name?" I asked.

"I think it's LeGault."

"LeGault," I repeated. The gin burned in my throat.

"Yes. His father owned a string of rubber plantations. Large ones, too. LeGault was brought up near Luangprabang. He went to the Sorbonne for a few years. His older brother was killed at Dien Bien Phu, and LeGault came back to run the family business. You'd think he'd be angry with General Giap for his brother's death, but evidently not. I hear he hates Americans."

"Some people never get it right," I said.

"Yes, but what I don't understand is, why is he allowed to wander all around the countryside, doing terrible things, shooting people in the face, setting up missile sites, just generally mucking about, while you Americans act as if there's a picnic going on instead of a war? It doesn't make sense. Why doesn't someone take care of the rotten apple?"

I laughed. "Who are you working for, Chenny?" I asked.

"Absolutely no one," he protested, "except myself."

Nothing was said for a time. I was fighting with a vision I kept having in my days and nights: a chopper spinning down, out of control, a bright magnesium star burning into the earth.

It was as if Chen could read my mind. "You know, Gene," he said, "LeGault might have been responsible for that accident your people were in."

"Accident my ass," I said quietly.

"You know what I mean."

"I was there, Chenny. I was talking to them on the radio. I had the panels out and they had us spotted. It wasn't rotation problems. Don't buy the press release. They were hit by the first SAM in Laos. You think I don't know a hit when I see one? Somebody upped the ante. Maybe it was your boy LeGault."

"He's not my boy," Chen bristled like a terrier.

I remember how hot my body felt at that moment, almost feverish. "Maybe somebody should take him out," I said.

"Now, now," Chen pretended to warn, "you'd have to play your cards very carefully if you decided to do that."

"So?" I asked. "You think I can't do that?"

"LeGault has lived here all his life," Chen said.

Looking back on it, I see how obvious this all was: the pattern, the hints, the coy preparation, the construction of argument and evidence. But I was angry at the time, or I let myself be wooed into anger, and I heard only what I wanted to hear. I understood at that moment that LeGault was mine if I wanted him and if I could get him. He was being handed to me on an unofficial platter without one incriminating thing being said.

I was 25 years old, three years out of college, a Marine officer who was one month past the disappearance of his buddies in a bright ball of fire. I thought about that as I vaguely took in my hotel room: chipped plaster walls and rusted plumbing and old editions of *Le Figaro* torn up for toilet paper and my seabag stowed in the corner and the mosquito netting rolled up like a royal canopy above the rickety wooden bed.

"May I buy you a pipe?" Chen asked after a long silence.

"You sure can," I said.

"Whatever you are thinking about, forget it," Chen said casually.

"OK," I said. I snapped my fingers. "Gone."

Chen laughed. "Very good," he said.

Chen drove me through the rain in his small Citroën down to the opium den near the river. He went in with me and I watched the young girl heat the brown ball of goo on the end of a long needle. When the opium was ready, she placed it in the bowl of the pipe and clicked the needle on the pipestem. She handed the pipe to me without smiling. Chen paid her, but he did not stay to take a pipe with me.

I am not sure how long I stayed there, but I do remember that later in the evening, after my second pipe, I thought Gunny Nadeau was in the lower bunk. He was telling me war stories again about how he had been captured on Wake Island at the beginning of World War Two and how he'd lost a toe to frostbite at the Chosan Reservoir in Korea.

"Lieutenant O'Hair," the Gunny laughed at me in my opium dream, "they can take this next war and shove it."

"Happy new year, Gunny," I said. "Happy 1961."

I went into a deeper sleep, and when I woke up, the Gunny wasn't there anymore. I could taste earth, violets, autumn leaves. My lungs were burning and my head ached, but my body felt light, almost immaterial. It was wonderful opium.

"*A bientôt,*" I said to the girl as I left. "*Ca va mieux.*" I did not know if she spoke French, but I had been sent to Laos because, among other things, I spoke French, and I was damned if I was going to speak English to the people.

There was a light under Chen's door, but I felt too peaceful to see him. I went into my room and sat down in the rocker and sipped some gin. I was almost relaxed. That lasted for less than five minutes. There was a knock on my door and I knew it was Chen.

"Gene." He rushed into the room, "I just got a call. LeGault is over at Tiger's."

I took another swig of gin. Nothing settled in my mind and I eyed Chen coldly.

"He's there, don't you see?" Chen clapped his hands and turned in a circle.

I belched. I was not feeling warlike.

Chen moved around my room like a moth. "What luck!" he smiled. "What marvelous luck."

"The luck of the Irish," I laughed. "Eugene O'Hair, at your service, Mr. Chen, sir."

"Gene," Chen said, "I don't think you understand. LeGault is over at the baths."

"You think so, huh?" I asked. I thought I saw the face of Gunny Nadeau nodding at me from nowhere in particular, from my mind's eye. "Maybe it's not LeGault. Maybe it's somebody else."

"It's him!" Chen protested. "Tiger called me. She knows him. Tiger knows everybody."

Reading this as I have just written it, I have to laugh. I was being steered like a boat in a channel, and I took direction willingly, because I wanted to kill, I wanted to even things up, and I carried in the jumbled baggage of my consciousness the idea that vengeance was mine, that I had earned it through my contact with drill sergeants and football coaches and politicians and professors and all the other men I had tried to mold myself after. Vengeance was manly and clean, sharp as a whalebone, and I was God.

"Maybe I should just take a look-see," I said slowly.

"Absolutely," Chen said in a low voice. "You should at least know what this man looks like. He's quite dangerous. He might decide to come after you."

"That would definitely not be nice," I grunted as I kneeled down and unzipped my Val-a-Pak. I took my .45 out of its plastic wrapper. As I loaded the magazine, pushing the fat cartridges down on the magazine spring, I could smell oil and metal and brass casings. I checked the slide, admiring the precision of the machining, the beauty of the grooves. I could feel myself start to salivate. That may sound insane, but it is a fact: I was in love with small tolerances, colors of metal, gunpowder, the fit of the pistol butt in my hand, the weight of the weapon, my knowledge of it.

"Let's us go take a look at this frog," I said to Chen. I tucked the .45 into the belt of my slacks. I was in civilian clothes. There were no white men in uniform in Laos at that time.

Chen did not go with me, of course. People like that never do. He ducked out from under my arm and went into his room. "I'll be with you in a minute," he said, but I knew he was lying. It did not matter. My pulse was racing and I felt alive for the first time in weeks. The thick air did not tire me and the rain was no hindrance. I gave one last yell for Chen and then took off for the bathhouse, Tiger's Place. It was a few blocks past the American mission house.

Tiger was one of those Oriental women of indeterminate age who carry a tough beauty with them all their lives. She wore silk dresses with high collars and slit skirts. It was hard not to watch her legs while you talked with her. She wore gold rings and pearl necklaces and expensive perfume, and I suspect she was on the payroll of every secret service in Laos.

"Gene, I can't let you in," Tiger said when she saw me standing at her desk. "We're full."

"Where's LeGault?" I asked. I had the gin bottle in one hand and the .45 in the other. I took a last long hit of gin and put the bottle down on a table. "Chen told me he was here."

"You're drunk, Gene," Tiger said calmly.

"I just want to see him, OK? I got to know what he looks like. He took out some of my buddies."

Tiger said a very strange thing. In a wooden and noncaring voice, she asked me, "You are forcing me to tell you where LeGault is?"

"Yeah," I laughed. I pulled the slide back and let it slam forward. "There's a round in the chamber now."

"In that case, he's in number five. With Valerie."

"Thanks, Mama-san," I smiled. I slipped through the beaded curtain and crept down the long corridor, down the dim hall in a crouch that I thought was professional as hell.

It was all very stupid, of course, because I was just being used without my knowing it. There were any number of governments that wanted to be rid of LeGault. I did not recognize it at the time, but I was in a ballet, being choreographed by unseen forces, and I was too dumb to know it.

I listened at the door of number five. I heard water running and a woman's low, happy voice. Steam floated out of the half-open transom. I cannot explain it, but I felt as if I were standing in a dingy hotel hallway in a small town in Illinois. I expected, for the moment, to see my grandmother behind that door.

I opened the door a crack without being heard. Valerie was scooping bowls of water from the tub and pouring them over a man's head as he lay back in the water. She was cooing like a pigeon, the way she always did with me. She held a red washcloth in her other hand and she rubbed it across the man's chest.

They probably felt the breeze from the door at the same time, because they turned toward me together. I was standing in the firing position, arms extended, legs apart, both hands holding the .45 and pointing it straight toward them.

"Allez-vous-en," I said to Valerie. She was wearing bathing-suit bottoms but no top. Her hands went to her mouth in fear. I gestured with the pistol and told her to get out again. She did, running past me like a slim spirit.

I was watching LeGault's eyes. They moved once toward the mattress on the massage table. So it was there that I sat, and I thought I could feel the bulge of a pistol under my thigh.

It was a strange conversation, because I spoke only French and he replied in English. We were each insulting the other that way.

LeGault was a thin man. He wore the scraggly beard of a professor and he had a narrow face, middle-aged, with a certain Gallic disdain in the pitch of his mouth. He spoke as if nothing meant much to him, nothing at all.

"It goes well?" I asked him in French.

"It goes," he said in English.

"Marvelous," I said.

"What do you want?" he asked casually after a silence.

"I'm not sure," I said.

He toyed with the red washcloth. "Valerie?" he asked. "You are jealous or something?"

"No," I laughed. "I'm not jealous, believe me."

"Good," he said with finality. He splashed water lightly across his shoulders.

I kept the pistol leveled at his forehead. I was only a few feet from him. "I adjusted the spring on this yesterday," I said. "Very light trigger pull. Less than a kilo."

LeGault's mouth formed an ironic grin. "I hope you aren't nervous," he smiled.

"Don't worry," I said.

We sat there for a time: no conversation, each waiting the other out, conscious of water dripping and rain on the corrugated roof and occasional voices from other rooms.

"You are LeGault, aren't you?" I asked with a laugh.

He spread his hands. "I am whoever you wish me to be," he said.

"They say you French are everywhere."

He looked at me, then the ceiling. "How can that be?"

"I ask myself that," I said. I leaned against the tile wall. "I ask myself what in the hell the French are doing in a secret war against the Americans.''

LeGault was inching his way up out of the water. I let him do it. I knew what was going to happen. I saw the whole thing before it actually happened.

"Well, life is very confusing, isn't it?" he smiled. He had crooked teeth.

"I agree," I said.

"Your French is quite good," he said. "Where did you learn it?"

"I lived in Paris for a couple of years," I said.

"Yes, it's a Parisian accent."

"Yes," I said, "and where did you learn your English?"

"Here and there," he said. There was another silence. "Did you like France?" he asked.

"Most of the time."

"Good."

"But the French can be very cold, very snotty," I said.

"I'm sorry to hear that," he said.

"Oh, yes," I said. "The French can be the most selfish people in the world. They always assume that they know more than anybody else. About everything."

"I don't think you met the right people," he said.

"Probably not."

"I have only been to Paris a few times myself," LeGault said. He was playing for time, thinking that someone would come and save him. He did not realize that he had taken too many things into his own hands, become too uncontrollable, and that he was off everybody's white list.

Something told me I did not have to rush. I was enjoying the power I felt, enjoying it immensely. "Tell me about yourself," I said. I laughed at the politeness of my query.

"There's nothing to tell," LeGault offered.

"You grew up in France?"

"No. Here. Indochina."

"The son of a plantation owner?" I asked.

"My father was a farmer."

"You went to the Sorbonne?"

"You know all about me?" LeGault grimaced.

"I'm learning," I said. "What's your full name?"

"Jean-Claude LeGault," he said quietly. He sat up in the water, pulled the washcloth around his neck, made a production of splashing and smiling. "You already know that."

"I didn't know your first name," I said.

"Well, then, I am sorry I gave it to you."

"No, no," I smiled falsely. "I appreciate it."

"*Merde*," he said. It was the only French he would speak to me.

"You're down here from the north?" I asked.

"No," he said. "Saigon. I'm sure you know it."

"I know Xam Nua," I said.

"Ah, then you are not a tourist." He laughed. "So you have to be what? CIA?"

"Not exactly," I said.

"Well, you're not the Red Cross," he said.

"No, not the Red Cross," I said.

"You won't tell me?"

"Marines," I said.

"No," he said in that French fashion of dropping the jaw in disbelief. Faked disbelief.

"Yes!" I said brightly.

"But look at you. You are not in uniform."

"No. Neither are you."

We both laughed at that one.

"I think of you Marines as, you know, very fancy," he said.

"Bellboys?" I smiled.

LeGault looked at the ceiling again. "Marines are good fighters," he said.

"Yes, when they have a chance." I said. "When they aren't shot down by your SAMs."

"SAMs?" LeGault asked. He perverted the word, drew it out with a jutted jaw, made it sound unfamiliar.

"Surface-to-air missiles," I said.

"I do not know these SAMs," LeGault said.

"Nobody else did, either. Not around here. Not until a month ago. But somebody brought some SAMs in. They happen to be very effective against helicopters," I said.

"I wouldn't know," LeGault said.

"Really?" I said. I pulled the hammer of the .45 back with my thumb. The small sound reverberated in the room. That noise was chilling, even to me, and I was on the right side of the weapon. "Yes, you do. You know."

LeGault talked more rapidly. He tried to seem angry. "You're going to shoot me?" he asked. "For what? I don't know what you think I've done, but I can hardly defend myself this way."

"It's funny that you never heard of SAMs," I said. "I heard you and your crew were unloading the launchers at the airport and trucking them right up the Royal Road." I was amused at my own improvisation on Chen's brief story. I thought it was brilliant.

"That's absurd," LeGault said. He moved to a kneeling position. I let him do that, too.

"I heard you take ears when you kill," I said.

"Don't be ridiculous," LeGault said. "Who is telling you such things?"

"A little bird," I laughed.

"Well, none of this is true," he protested. He sank back on his haunches, but I could tell he was still ready to spring. He reminded me of a tiger, a tired tiger.

"Tell me more about yourself," I said.

"Me?" he laughed. "I have an export-import business in Saigon. I play tennis. I swim at the club. I waste my life. Really, you must believe me. The business pays my bills and I don't have to lift a finger. I fly to Bangkok and Hong Kong and Pnompenh and here, and I might take some opium with me sometimes, but can you blame me? Do you know what I can sell a block of it for in Paris?" He assumed he had struck a rich vein of autobiography and he built on it. "I thought you were a narcotics man at first. I've had some trouble here. I buy from the tribes. Other people are interested in the same territory. It's a risky business."

I let him wind down. I listened to him with my eyes half-closed. Then I laughed.

"It doesn't check out, frog," I said. "You don't play tennis—you're pale. Look at you. You've got bites on your neck. You don't eat well. You've got that three-thousand-yard stare.

You're a jungle bunny, LeGault. Just like me. You think I can't figure that out? We've been snooping and pooping in the same places, my friend. But you raised the stakes. You broke the rules. You brought in a little toy that we didn't expect. And you blew up three of my buddies. Three guys just doing a job. Coming in on resupply. And you blew them out of the sky. Poof. Just like that. Place your bets; nothing more goes; poof." I was conscious that my anger made me a better linguist. My French was impeccable, filled with argot, and I spoke rapidly, like an angry waiter.

"That's absurd, what you have just said," LeGault objected. Still in English, of course.

"Right near a hill called Phu San," I said. "Near the Plain of Jars."

"Don't talk nonsense," he said. "I have never been near the Plain of Jars."

I spoke my first English. "Yes, you have," I said. "You grew up there. It was your back yard."

There are moments when time slows down for me. It loses momentum. I can see myself watching myself. Indeed, I am a little bit outside myself, and I know what's going to happen, what each person will do. And it is done. It is a powerful, addictive perception, as good as opium or gin.

LeGault pushed off in a swan dive toward me, but he didn't do it very well and his feet slipped on the bottom of the bathtub. He rose in an awkward arch, his arms flailing like a scarecrow's.

I pumped one round into his chest. I did it very coldly, without thought. It was as if an invisible hand had slammed against him and tackled him in mid-air. His dive was broken and he crumpled outside the tub. Only then did I realize that my ears hurt from the explosion.

There was a lot of blood. LeGault's face was pale as alabaster and his eyes were empty. I knelt by him, patted his cheek with my pistol. "That's for Gunny Nadeau," I said, "and Sutton and Allard." I paused, trying to think clearly. "From Lieutenant O'Hair, 075718." I stood up. "I don't take ears," I said.

It was all very manly and brave and dramatic, or so I thought

at the time. I had just made the world safer and myself
stronger: justice, vengeance, all that good shit.

I walked back to the hotel in a daze.

No one can kill without thinking about it.

I sat in my room until dawn, playing solitaire and wishing
that Chen were around to talk to. He seemed to have disappeared.

I drank more gin, but it made me nauseated, so I smoked a
couple of pipes of hash. It was not opium, but it would do. The
gecko liked the smoke and he moved where it drifted. The rain
had eased and the gecko had less to worry about, so he got
stoned with me.

By the time the AID station wagon came to get me, with orders so recently cut that the mimeo ink smeared on my hands
and trousers, I was too wasted to appreciate the irony of my
leaving. The mission house had commandeered a special
Caravelle with MATS markings from Bangkok; a French crew
and a French steward who asked me idly if I'd heard about the
murder of a Frenchman in Vientiane the night before.

I tried to answer the steward in his language, but I found that
I could not speak French anymore. The words stuck in my
throat. I simply never spoke French again. Not ever.

"I hope they get the bastard who did that," I said finally in
English.

The steward stared at me as if I were an epileptic. *"Bien
sûr,"* he said to me with a contemptuous salute. *"Moi aussi."*

"What was that?" I asked with a stupid smile. I watched the
steward's eyes glaze over with that disrespect the French have
for people who do not speak their language. I was not in the
best of moods, because I had just supervised the loading of
Gunny Nadeau's coffin into the hold of the Caravelle. That had
been my only demand when the consul came to tell me that I
had to leave Vientiane immediately. So my tolerance was low
and I made a production of leaning on the steward as I climbed
the steps into the aircraft, acting like an American country
bumpkin.

"Looks like the monsoon's lifted long enough to get us out
of here," I said to no one in particular. The passenger cabin was
empty. The flight was for me alone.

"Would you like a drink?" the steward asked me.

"You got any American beer?" I asked.

"We have wine," he said. "It is not American, but it is decent enough." His English was fluent.

"You got any German wine?"

"No," he said, turning his back on me.

"I sure like German wine," I called to him. He did not answer me.

Gunny Nadeau and I flew back to Bangkok and Saigon and Kadena and Tachikawa. We changed planes in Japan and then flew on to Wake Island and then Hickam and then Travis. We were on Priority One orders, the same way we'd gone out, and the Pacific Ocean was as dull as ever. The Gunny's coffin was off-loaded at Travis, but I didn't get to see it, because I was being hustled onto a DC-3 that was waiting on the runway to take me down to El Toro.

Although I had resigned my commission, I spent another few weeks back with the First Marine Division. Most of the time I was being debriefed, talking into a tape recorder in a barracks in Camp Pendleton. I knew it was a polite version of custody and that they were wondering what to do with me. Sometimes they let me jog the firebreaks, and once they let me go into Oceanside to swim and shop. But there was always someone with me, and I felt very trapped.

They gave me tests and asked me to write up reports, but I could tell that they were waiting for something, some signal that said it was all right to release me and let me back into civilian life. That signal eventually came, though I have no idea what it was.

I can only testify that the scars are there in strange patterns.

If you met me, you would never guess that I killed so coldly. I seem like a nice person, if somewhat tense, and I put on a good act of being civilized. The disability lies deeper, in a place not charted, and it surfaces in private forms that only people like me can recognize.

For example: I don't read Ronsard's sonnet about age and beauty and sleep, the one that inspired Yeats, and Villon's Middle French written in frozen ink is not mine anymore, and Proust is out, as are Camus and Simenon and Sartre.

And if I were in your home, and if you were to play the songs of Brel or the recordings of Piaf, or if you were to brag about your best Château Lafite-Rothschild or your richest Beaujolais, you might not notice any change in me, but I would be thinking, very briefly, about killing you.

GEORGE BAXT

WHAT YOU BEEN UP TO LATELY?

George Baxt burst upon the mystery scene in 1966 with a revolutionary first novel, A Queer Kind of Death, *highly praised by Anthony Boucher and other critics. Author of screenplays and television scripts as well as several other novels, Baxt was born in Brooklyn and has lived in England and Los Angeles. He presently resides in New York, where he's been turning out short stories like the following, a fine satiric view of life and death in today's Hollywood.*

RICHARD WEILER CAREFULLY MANEUVERED HIS wife's Mercedes Benz along Sunset Boulevard. The traffic wasn't particularly heavy in the early afternoon, but he was anxious to avoid any dents or scrapes. It was known to his friends that he respected the car more than he did the woman. Elissa had been a beautiful bride, her family's wealth easily enhancing her attractiveness, but twenty years ago when he watched her coming slowly down the aisle on her father's arm, he was very much in love with her. Today he loved nothing, just the feel of the magnificent vehicle as he idled along and the exhilarating sense of a newly discovered freedom that had blossomed a few hours earlier.

Elissa was gone, leaving behind the Mercedes, a bored husband and, somewhere out there in the world, a nineteen-year-old son and an eighteen-year-old daughter who had flown the nest with what Richard considered unbecoming alacrity. He repositioned the mirror for a good look at himself. After a moment's careful consideration he decided he looked better than he had in months. The face familiar from numerous television commercials ("Diabolica will kill your crab grass!" —"Ahhhh, the smooth, easy taste of decaffeinated Bolluta!" etc.) now reflected a somewhat sheepish grin revealing magnificent white teeth against a background of carefully shaded tanned skin. Oh, yes, thought Richard, I feel like a new man.

I feel like a new life. I need a new world. I could use a drink. He kept his eye out for a bar. He couldn't decide which was shabbier, the few pedestrians or the palm trees. He remembered a charming bar he used to frequent years ago when he was a struggling young actor. Come to think of it, that's where he was first introduced to Elissa, in that charming bar across from the bus terminal. Behind the building that housed the bar had been a small theater where a German refugee held acting classes. Richard didn't learn much about acting, but he perfected a superb German accent. And he made friends. And he met Elissa and they were married and now they were parted and there straight ahead was the bus terminal.

So shabby, Los Angeles is so shabby, he thought. The bus terminal looked filthy and unloved and there was no bar across the street. There was a bench in front of the bus terminal with a solitary occupant, a man who appeared to be Richard's age. Memory of an earlier friendship began to nag. There was something familiar about this man sitting on the bench. He was hatless and the shock of hair hanging over his ears reminded Richard of the one good friend he had made in acting class, Augustus Locke. The cavalier and devil-may-care Augustus who aspired to Shakespeare and Ibsen and all things esthetic and beautiful, all things alien to Hollywood. Augie the original, the madman who once climbed the old Hollywood sign and then hung by his knees from the H.

"Now *that's* macho," Richard remembered saying to Elissa.

And Elissa said with a sniff of disinterest, "Macho do about nothing."

My God. Oh, my God. Richard remembered. Elissa had been Augie's girl!

He pulled over to the curb for a better look at the man on the bench. It was at least ten years since he had last seen Augie, but he could never forget that face, those beautiful classical features that cried for matinee-idol acclaim but were in the wrong city. Richard rolled down the window and shouted, "Augie?"

The man leaped to his feet. His right hand went to his inside jacket pocket.

"Hey, Augie, it's me! Richard! Richard Weiler!"

Slowly Augustus Locke lowered his right hand. He seemed to move slowly toward the Mercedes with caution, as though he distrusted even the sound of a familiar voice. He squinted against the glare of the hard harsh sun.

Richard conjured up the ugly guttural German accent from the bowels of memory. "Iss nod enuff to be secksy, Herr Locke, muss also sprechen zer dialock zo awdience hunderstands, fahrshtay?"

"Fahrshtay," said Augustus softly and now approached the automobile with confidence. He stuck his hand through the window, meeting Richard's and shaking it with vigor. "Of all the people I never expected to run into today."

"You looked as though you didn't want to run into any people. I thought for a minute there you were going to pull a gun on me."

Augustus said nothing but found a smile.

Richard continued, "What you been up to lately?"

"Well, right now I'm waiting for a bus to San Diego."

"Where's your car?"

Augustus looked sheepish. "I totaled it yesterday. It's a miracle I'm alive."

"I'm glad you are. I've thought a lot about you lately. If I'd known where to reach you . . ." He heard himself sounding like almost everyone else in his profession. *"We must get in touch sometime." "I've been meaning to call you." "I swear I never got your message."*

Augustus roared with laughter. "That old Hollywood jazz! Well, I see you're doing great! A Mercedes yet! You seem to be in every commercial on the tube." His voice softened. "How's Elissa?"

"How's about a drink?"

Augustus thought for a moment. "I really have to make that bus."

"What's so urgent?"

"Well . . ." he seemed to be fumbling for an explanation. "You see, there's this guy I need to connect with in San Diego and then we're driving into Mexico. I got this deal going."

"Come on. There are lots of buses to San Diego but not enough old friends. Come on, Augie, let's go talk a while. Let's indulge, get corny over the old days."

Augie thought a moment, looked warily over his shoulder to the bus terminal, and then got into the car.

Ten minutes later they sat at a bar Richard found at the foot of Fairfax Avenue. Maggie the barperson brought them two beers, set a plate of peanuts between them, and crossed to the kitchen.

"Had I know you and Elissa were finished," said Augustus as he scooped up some peanuts, "I'd have shown up sooner. That's the girl I should have married, but you beat me to it."

Richard chuckled and then sipped his beer. "Say, what happened to that dreary dame who used to make up our foursome? You know, the one who was all art but no craft. I can see her like she's standing in front of us. Blazing red hair pulled back and tied in a tight bun. A big pearl earring attached to each lobe. Sweater and skirt, always sweater and skirt. Nice hips but no bosom to speak of. God how I disliked her. Now what was her name again?"

"Madeline. Madeline Longley."

"Madeline! That's it, Madeline. I wonder what became of her."

"I married her."

Richard's face reddened as he stared at Augustus. "Hell, I'm sorry. I mean I—"

Augustus was laughing uncontrollably. His head was flung back and his chest was heaving. Maggie, returning from the kitchen and carrying a tray of clean glasses, wondered if he was having a fit.

"Oh, God," gasped Augie, "oh, my God, that was funny." He wiped the tears from his eyes with a paper napkin. "How I wish I had heard that description eighteen years ago before I decided to marry her."

Richard stared hard at Augustus. He sensed there was something wrong with the man. He kept looking over his shoulder and every so often he patted his jacket where the inside breast pocket would be, as though seeking reassurance from something the pocket contained. The laughter was almost maniacal. From the ferocity with which he had chomped on the peanuts, Richard expected to see blood come trickling from Augie's mouth.

"That last time we met—in Grauman's lobby, remember—"

"Sure, it was at least ten years ago, but I remember."

"That wasn't Madeline you were with."

"No . . . can't remember that one's name. Some bimbo I picked up somewhere." Augie's face hardened as he stared into his beer. "Madeline and I weren't much of a marriage. I didn't make it as an actor. That was her first disappointment. Then we couldn't have any children—that was her second disappointment. Then she found out I was steadily unfaithful. So she turned to religion and illness. When she wasn't in church, she was in the hospital."

"You still married?"

Augie was watching Maggie carefully giving the glasses a second polish. She was fastidious. He liked that in people. She took pride in her bar. He could see in the way it was all so neatly laid out. She was what his father would have called a fine figure of a woman, for sure. Her eyes caught his. He felt something stirring and was astonished. She was not his type at all. He winked, she smiled, and he turned to Richard.

"Funny us running into each other like this today. I wish it had been last week."

"Oh, yeah? Why?"

"It would have been different, that's all." There was an awkward silence, and then Augie asked, "Where are your kids?"

"Gone. Flown. My son's in New York, or at least he was when he last sent a postcard. He was in some drug rehabilitation program. I hope he stuck it out."

"And the girl?"

"I don't know. I'm not sure. She always liked kids. Maybe

she's working with kids somewhere." Richard was sounding morose, and that was not what he had in mind for himself. He was free of Elissa and he'd been driving around trying to find a new avenue for himself. He tried to explain this to Augustus who kept nodding his head but was actually retaining little of what he heard, his mind now containing an olio of his next sip of beer, Maggie behind the bar, and getting to San Diego.

"Augie?" asked Richard.

"What? What is it?" His eyes were wide and he was sneaking a quick look over his shoulder.

"You're not listening to me."

"Sure I am! Anyway, listen old buddy, I got to get back to the bus terminal." He was toying with Richard's car keys. Richard had placed them on the bar between their drinks.

"I'll drive you back as soon as we finish our drinks. Unless you're in that big a hurry—"

"Oh, no, no. It's great running into each other like this again."

"When do you get back from Mexico?"

"I'm not sure."

"I just thought we'd get together again."

"That would be great. Believe me, I really have missed seeing you, shooting the breeze the way we used to, rehearsing our scenes together . . . and those times we'd do nothing but compare poverty."

They both laughed and Maggie smiled. She liked the actor she recognized from the television commercials. He was suave and smooth and obviously a gentleman. And she'd been very impressed by the Mercedes when she noticed Richard pulling into the adjoining parking lot. But his companion made her nervous and uneasy. His eyes had what she would later describe as "a very haunted look, like the banshees were after him." And there was something unsettling about the way he kept looking over his shoulder and patting his jacket as though maybe there was some weapon hidden there.

Richard was staring at the ceiling. "Old Meyerbeer?" Augustus had asked him if he knew what had become of their German drama instructor. "Well, I'll tell you. Last I heard he went back to Germany where he directed a new translation of

King Lear in which Lear not only does not go mad but throws those rotten daughters of his into exile.''

"You're putting me on."

"I kid you not. Elissa saw the production in Munich. She was traveling with her mother. She couldn't wait to get home to tell me about it." His voice softened. "Those were back in the days when she couldn't wait to get home to me."

Maggie had turned on the radio on a shelf above the glasses and was worrying the tuner.

Augustus said, "I'd sure love to see Elissa again. That beautiful blonde hair, that white white skin, that gash of red mouth. By God, she was a looker! Has she changed much?"

"Elissa was rich enough to afford not to change much. Still blonde, skin still white, still the red gash of mouth, but the eyes got steely."

"I'd sure love to see her." Augustus sounded as wistful as a small penniless child with its nose pressed against the window of a candy store.

"Well, if I thought she was back at the house, I'd drive you there. But I don't think she's there."

Augustus clapped a hand on Richard's shoulder. "Man, I think it's time we started making tracks."

"Sure, sure." Richard raised his stein to drink it.

Maggie found the news on the radio and was listening intently. The announcer was reading carefully and without emotional commitment. Richard and Augustus stared at the radio. They had heard a familiar name. ". . . the brutally battered body of Madeline Locke was found in the bedroom of her Topanga Canyon home this morning by a neighbor who said she had seen the victim's husband drive away early yesterday morning. Augustus Locke is wanted for questioning in his wife's murder. Late yesterday morning a wrecked car found near Mr. Locke's home was identified as belonging to the suspect—"

Richard was staring at the snub-nosed revolver Augustus had taken from his inside jacket pocket and was pointing at Richard's chest.

"Augie," whispered Richard.

Augustus got to his feet and with his free hand took the keys to the Mercedes. Maggie held her breath and silently prayed to

the Jesus she loved to deliver both herself and the handsome actor. "I'll try not to total the Mercedes." Augie was backing
away to the door. "Don't follow me out."

For reasons he would never be able to explain to himself,
Richard restrained a wild urge to burst out laughing. *What you
been up to lately*, he had asked Augie earlier. Well, he certainly
found out.

Augustus was smiling as he ran out the door.

"Jesus, Mary, and Joseph!" cried Maggie as she rushed to the
phone.

"Wait!" The mixture of harshness and urgency in Richard's
voice stopped her. "Not yet," said Richard. "Let's give him a
head start."

"But—but he's a murderer."

"They'll catch him. He won't get away. But let's give him
this break. He's never really had a decent break in his life."

What a magnificent car, thought Augustus, what a truly
magnificent car. Now if *I* had married Elissa, this would have
been *my* car. And the marriage would have worked. That's
what was wrong. Elissa and I were meant for each other until
Richard came along. Beautiful, beautiful Elissa of the blonde
hair, white skin, and red gash of a mouth. Ugly whining sickly
Madeline. How did I put up with her under the same roof all
these years?

The Mercedes was headed south for the San Diego freeway
when the patrol car spied it and gave chase, siren screaming.
But Augie's mind was elsewhere. It was dwelling on the un-
fairness and inequity of life and what a rotten shuffle he himself
had got. His foot pressed the accelerator and the Mercedes
seemed to be fighting him. He began losing control of the
steering wheel and soon he was in the wrong lane with a truck
bearing down on him. He swerved to avoid the collision and instead sent the car plummeting over the edge of the road into a
ravine that lay hundreds of feet beneath.

The Mercedes rolled over and over. First, the roof was torn
away, and then both right fenders wrenched free with sickening
groans. Augie's door sprang open and he tried desperately to
hold on to the wheel, but blood was streaming down his face

and his right arm was broken and he knew both his legs were shattered and he was nearing the end of the tragi-comedy known as the life of Augustus Locke.

When the Mercedes hit the bottom of the ravine, the door to the trunk was flung open and Augustus, thrown from the car, and just a few moments away from death, stared with pleasure at the person he had so longed to see once more. She had fallen out of the trunk, her head hanging loosely, the neck broken. But the blonde hair and the white skin were still beautiful, though the red gash of lips was now a large ugly stain caked with blood. Elissa, my beloved, my beautiful Elissa.

What you been up to lately?

URSULA CURTISS

THE HOUSE ON PLYMOUTH STREET

Ursula Curtiss, daughter of the late mystery writer Helen Reilly, has carried on the family tradition with a fine series of mystery novels beginning in 1948. Her infrequent short stories are equally good, and this one from Cosmopolitan, *about a woman in search of a new house, is especially memorable.*

*I*F MRS. TYRELL'S COMPETENT HUSBAND HAD BEEN *home, the terrible episode would never have taken place. She would have been able to eat turkey stuffing as before; she would not have been jerked out of nightmares with frequency, months later and in an entirely different house, trembling, crying.*

But Neil Tyrell was in London at a conference of aerodynamic engineers, and although Mrs. Tyrell was good at a number of things in spite of her airily decorative appearance, remembering about the changeover from daylight saving time was not one of them.

It was, accordingly, two o'clock instead of three when she drove up to the new house and found its former owner still in possession.

She had found the house by herself, that cold October day in the quiet countryside south of Boston.

The two-chimneyed white clapboard house, shuttered in gray and clearly very old, had a settled air as it stood on its slight rise well back from the road under elms. Mrs. Tyrell did not have the boldness to knock on doors and ask about properties for sale

. . . but here there was a tall young girl, bundled into a blue parka and raking desultorily under a bronze-gold burn of hickory tree in a corner near the road.

Mrs. Tyrell had Bonnet with her, the large Airedale of whom the current babysitter was ridiculously afraid, but not his leash. She closed the car door against his expectant whiskers and approached the girl, who leaned on the rake and watched her come.

For her age, somewhere in the mid-teens, she had a colorless and surprisingly dreary face. "Hello," said Mrs. Tyrell, against her will as sprightly as a dental nurse. "My husband and I are house hunting around here—Cresset seems like a very pretty town—and I wondered if by any chance you knew of a place for sale with a few acres?"

Something wrong about the eyes, as if the light blue irises had mended imperfectly after a shattering. Retarded, thought Mrs. Tyrell with the twist at the heart of any woman with two healthy, clear-gazing children. And not all that young: at least nineteen or possibly twenty.

"I'll ask my mother," said the girl, letting the rake fall into the pile of brown leaves, and began to walk toward the house before Mrs. Tyrell could demur.

Which she had intended to do, she realized bemusedly fifteen minutes later. "Oh, no, please don't bother," would have been off the tip of her tongue if there had been even a half-second to spare.

Diners occasionally bit down on a pearl along with the oyster, somebody always won the Irish Sweepstakes—and this place, with six acres that included a stretch of woods, was for sale at approximately the price the Tyrells had been prepared to pay.

The woman who introduced herself as Helen Wadsworth delivered the information with some reluctance, standing on the walk and gripping a coat about her in the biting air. "It's all been very unexpected. My husband's company transferred him out to the West Coast with practically no warning, and the house isn't quite in condition to be shown yet. If you'd like to come back later on in the week—"

Mrs. Tyrell, looking at the cold yet handsome features, almost challengingly bare of makeup and framed in dark hair with uncompromising threads of gray, was sure that this was no coy reference to unwashed lunch dishes or a day's delay in the dusting of table tops. Equally, standing so close to the front door, which had a great burst of honeysuckle beside it, she was convinced that if she drove away she would return to find that the house had been snapped up in her absence.

She said cajolingly, "Mrs. Wadsworth, I've looked at so many houses in the last couple of months that I've stopped seeing anything but the absolute basics. I'm not shopping, honestly. We know exactly what we want, so I'd only take up a few minutes of your time."

It was far more than that.

Mrs. Wadsworth opened the door, stepped aside, followed her visitor over the threshhold, said after a second's hesitation, "Excuse me," and walked rapidly deeper into the house. Mrs. Tyrell, who had absorbed with delight the wide floorboards, the deep fireplace, the views through five crisply white-silled windows, listened unabashedly.

She heard sounds from a refrigerator and then the snap and rustle of a paper bag and, "Why don't you take these over to Mr. and Mrs. Hopkins? I'm sure they skip lunch if nobody reminds them."

More order than suggestion, it was acted upon at once. Mrs. Tyrell was obscurely relieved at the faint click of a door latch. Mrs. Wadsworth, coming back, said briefly, "My daughter knows I'm selling the house, of course, but not how soon. Well, this is the living room, obviously . . ."

If she had been honest about the state of the house, and almost every room was in some degree of upheaval, Mrs. Tyrell had been equally truthful. Weeks of viewing had trained her eye to forget paint, strip off wallpaper, empty out furniture so that only the underlying space and proportions remained.

Downstairs, along with the dining room—also fireplaced— and kitchen, still warmly scented, were the master bedroom and bath and a slip of a room, which would accommodate three-month-old Damon comfortably for some time to come. Upstairs—Mrs. Tyrell deferred the attached barn for the moment; in her mind it would be of interest chiefly to Neil and perhaps five-year-old Annie—were a corner bedroom with fireplace, bath, and a very large guest room with a trestle table against one wall. A door at its back opened on a long narrow attic.

It was an accepted fact that real-estate agents preferred not to have owners on hand; in their eagerness owners were prone to such utterances as, "We just love this place, we wouldn't dream of selling if the doctor hadn't insisted on a dryer climate for my wife's arthritis."

They need not, thought Mrs. Tyrell, have worried about this owner. Mrs. Wadsworth, opening doors, was as noncommittal as if judging strange territory herself. It was a surprise when she said, apparently of the trestle table, "My mother lived with us when we first came here, and raised African violets, but then she moved to Dedham."

For some reason it sounded like mischievous incising on a tombstone. They were standing on the upper landing. Mrs. Tyrell glanced curiously at the other woman, and then craned out the window at the sound of a nasal bawl.

"That's the Pattillos' calf, next door." Mrs. Wadsworth nodded at a trim red barn visible beyond trees. "They're from New York. At one time they had pigs and turkeys, too—living off the land was the idea, I suppose, although you'd never know it to look at them."

Now a corner of the marble mouth did flick up—in amusement? Mild contempt? "Since then they've opened a gift and book shop and only raise one calf at a time and keep a few chickens. We get all our eggs there."

Back to business. "Would you like to see the barn?"

Mrs. Tyrell didn't really care about the barn—she had made up her mind even before mounting the stairs that they must have this house—but she said yes because Neil would want all the details when she called him in London. "First, though, I have our dog in the car. I ought to let him—"

"I'd much rather you didn't," said Mrs. Wadsworth, pleasant but edged. "My daughter is extremely allergic. Oh, I know, there are dogs just down the road, and in fact when Nancy feels that one of us needs punishing she goes there and exposes herself deliberately. It's days, sometimes a week or more, before she can breathe easily without pills."

It was stated without rancor or even censure, as a lived with fact of life. "I can't stop her, and I can't control stray dogs, but I do do what I can."

"I can certainly see that," said Mrs. Tyrell with a pang at the vision of the pale, joyless face. "I'll be quick, then."

The barn, its sliding door closed on a gray Ford, its only source of sunlight two small windows high up in the loft area, was extremely cold. In addition to the expectable tools and paint cans, it housed a gas-powered garden tiller and a riding lawn mower at which Mrs. Tyrell cast an ignorant but speculative eye. There was close to a half-acre of grass in front and a deep swath in back before the field, separated by dwarf fruit trees, gave way to woods.

At the rear of the barn a Dutch door ajar on a wooden ramp led down into a stable area, which Mrs. Tyrell, by now shivering, declined to investigate. Nor was there any point in her looking at the cellar. The furnace (gas, she learned) was obviously working, and she wouldn't have known what else to ask about.

As they walked back along the passage to the kitchen, Mrs. Tyrell said "that in her husband's absence abroad, and as a formality, she would like his uncle to see the house. Would tomorrow morning be convenient?"

"Certainly," said Mrs. Wadsworth. That would give her time to locate the appraisal and the builder's report, the bill of sale and maintenance contract for the new electric pump—all the cellars in older houses in this area had water in them during the spring—and any other relevant documents from their own purchase a year ago.

Her air of calm indifference worried Mrs. Tyrell. What if she were already finding this paper search a nuisance and planning to sell instead to a friend who already knew the particulars? Fingers nervous with the momentousness of the occasion, she wrote a check for $100, adding on the line provided, "Binder on 849 Plymouth Street." Mrs. Wadsworth wrote her a receipt.

A growing awareness of Bonnet's undoubted predicament in the car kept Mrs. Tyrell's further queries to a minimum. She and Neil had already acquired information about schools in a number of South Shore towns, Cresset among them. She noted down the amount of the mortgage and the bank that held it, the taxes, and—Neil would be proud of her—the zoning.

At the kitchen door, she turned for a final glance out at the distant woods, a weave of deep gray stitched here and there with red and yellow. She said compulsively, "I hope your daughter won't mind too much."

"Oh, no. Nancy is actually very fond of her stepfather. It's the idea of having to make new friends," said Mrs. Wadsworth in a forthright way, "but she'll adjust."

Mrs. Tyrell walked to the car then drove away at a slow cruise, looking for a safe place to let Bonnet out. She passed the Pattillos' house, shingled in smoke-colored cedar, and, farther along on the opposite side of the road, the dogs Mrs. Wadsworth had mentioned: a pair of Dobermans coming alertly to their haunches in deep grass at the tentative sound of the car engine. Presumably, they guarded a remodeling in progress at the corner, although at the moment there was no sign of workmen. Mrs. Tyrell, contemplating the long watchful heads and sculptured muscles, was glad of the chain-link fence: Annie, having grown up with an Airedale, had an innocent trust in all dogs.

A right turn onto a road drifted with yellow leaves presently provided a clearing at the edge of a woods for Bonnet. Part of *their* woods, Mrs. Tyrell realized with pleased surprise. A few minutes later, putting off an inspection of the town center because she had told the babysitter she would be back by four, she was on her way home.

Damon slept unconcernedly in his crib, fortified by a gourmet meal of formula and saltless strained squash. Annie, as rosy-gold as he was dark, knew all about her mother's quest and was full of excited questions. Stalled by, "I think so, but we'll see," she sat on the edge of a chair while the call to London was put in.

Mrs. Tyrell had done some concentrated thinking on the return trip. It was probably true that the house would still be available when Neil returned in just under two weeks. A lot of people didn't want that much space, inside or out, or automatically distrusted anything two hundred years old, or, increasingly, preferred to huddle in the elbow-reach safety of a development.

But it was equally true that any real-estate agent who got wind of what was going on would urge upon Mrs. Wadsworth some judicious painting and grounds-manicuring. An outlay of perhaps five hundred dollars would be reflected in a two-thousand dollar increase in the asking price.

Neil, given a detailed description, agreed. They were totally at one about the kind of house and surroundings they wanted, which was why he had left countersigned checks on a joint money account.

"You really like it, don't you?"

"Oh, Neil. Remember that place in Cohasset we thought about but it was at the far end of nowhere? It doesn't *compare* with this."

From the particular to the general—the children, the conference, the London weather. The barman at the Little Mayfair remembered Mrs. Tyrell from a trip made when Annie was three and had asked about her. Then: "Have Charlie take a look at the house before you sign, will you?"

"I was going to. Say hello to Annie, she's sitting here like an image, and I'll call and let you know."

Charlie Tyrell was Neil's uncle, blithely retired at sixty from a number of successful careers, including one as builder. He would know all about the points of stress in an old house, septic tanks, and other exotica. Reached at seven o'clock that evening, he said that he would be delighted to drive down to Cresset the next morning but that he had an unbreakable appointment in Boston at one, so what about taking two cars?

In the morning, Annie pleaded to go along. She was an extraordinarily good and companionable child, but even the best of five-year-olds could grow difficult with fatigue, and Mrs. Tyrell promised to bring back a picture instead. "It's just going to be long business talks and there wouldn't be anything for you to do. Besides, you have to be here to see that Bonnet is very polite to Miss Coates."

Both of these arguments had validity. Under them was something of which Mrs. Tyrell was so ashamed that she covered it up swiftly, even to herself.

She was not surprised to see Charlie's rakish dark green Jaguar there ahead of her on Plymouth Street; it was his habit to drive as though headed for the next pit stop. She had braced herself for a feeling of letdown, even of severe doubt, at this second view of the house. Instead she took in with appreciation and the pride of near-ownership details that hadn't registered exactly before: the separate front door, which opened directly onto the stairs, the black banding of the white chimneys—to keep out witches, according to one New England legend.

Nancy let her in. The hair concealed by the parka's hood the day before was in thick glossy dark braids, wiping away two or three years, and her rather heavy face shone so from soap and water that it took on a faint glow from the cherry pull-over she wore with jeans.

She dropped into a chair with no accompanying invitation. "My mother said to tell you they're down in the cellar."

"I'd only get in the way," said Mrs. Tyrell, compromising on an arm of the couch, "so I think I'll wait here if you don't mind."

The starred gaze riveted itself upon her with open curiosity. "Did you bring your dog?"

"No, he isn't really that fond of the car." It was a lie, which would have made Bonnet grieve into his whiskers.

Feet could be heard below, crunching on cement and then mounting the stairs, which led up to the door in the dining room. Nancy frowned at the rug as if, having used up her two utterances in prodigal fashion, she did not know what to do next. Her brow cleared with relief. She said, firm and confiding, "I'll like California."

"I'm sure you will." Again Mrs. Tyrell felt a wrench of compassion; this had been dinned into the girl like letters of the alphabet. "I've only been to San Francisco, but it's a beautiful—"

The cellar door had opened, and now Mrs. Wadsworth and Neil's uncle were in the room with greetings. "Sound as a nut," remarked Charlie of the house's underpinnings. Lean and weathered, with a debonair little gray mustache, he looked like a man who enjoyed life. The glance he shot at Mrs. Tyrell said that although professional caution was going to keep him from any real encomiums he approved wholeheartedly of the venture.

"Nancy dear—" Mrs. Wadsworth was almost unrecognizable from yesterday afternoon in a dark wool dress with a strand of

pearls, her chiseled lips the palest of rose "—have you picked
up your room? Mr. Tyrell has seen all of the downstairs and the
barn, but I'm sure he'll want . . ."

"No housework necessary," said Charlie, smiling at Nancy
—too late; obediently on her feet, she headed for the door of
what would be Damon's abode and disappeared.

"Now—" With a gesture at the couch that included both her
visitors, Mrs. Wadsworth sat down in a chair beside a low table
and picked up papers and a bankbook. Her left hand wore a
diamond like a diminished ice cube. "I talked to my husband
last night, and he said that although there'll have to be a title
search these would serve as proof of ownership . . ."

The business discussion that Mrs. Tyrell had described that
morning to Annie had begun. The terminology now falling on
the air was enough to damp any real excitement, but the wheels
were in motion, and she was grateful for Charlie's expertise.

She emerged from a semidaydream about living-room curtains to discover Charlie looking purposefully at his watch. It
was the time of late morning when he liked someone to ap-
proach him with a Bloody Mary, and Mrs. Tyrell herself would
have accepted one with alacrity, but any such offer here was
unlikely as the sudden appearance of a marching band.

Instead of suggesting any adjournment, however, Charlie
asked if he could use the telephone and came back with an air of
almost hand-rubbing enjoyment that could only have sprung
from the deferral of his unbreakable appointment. If he hurried
his exploration of the upstairs, he said, and if Mrs. Wadsworth
thought he could be of any help, there would be time for him
to go with her to the title company.

Mrs. Tyrell had a sensation of being picked up and swept
along, but delightfully so. Although he was fond of his nephew
and by extension his nephew's wife, Charles Haywood Tyrell,
widower for a dozen years, was not a man to discommode himself except in what he considered to be an extremely good cause.

It was a bare twenty-five minutes later that, having handed
Mrs. Wadsworth out of the Jaguar in front of the title company
office—it was his plan to proceed directly to Boston from there,
leaving Mrs. Tyrell to do the chauffeuring back to Plymouth
Street—he said kindly, "I have all the figures you gave me, and

you don't sign anything until the closing. Look around, why don't you, and meet us here in half an hour?''

Cresset was not the kind of town in which all business was conducted behind Colonial fronts, but its tree-lined residential side streets opened up cleanly on a long and curving main street whose sidewalks would also be shaded in summer. In Mrs. Tyrell's immediate radius were a flower shop, a grocery-plus-liquor store, a pair of discreetly curtained windows, which said Dressmaking on one side and Alterations on the other—and, just beyond those, two wooden signs, creaking in the wind and separated by a single entrance. Books. Gifts.

The Pattillos, the ex-New Yorkers who would be their neighbors. Mrs. Tyrell opened the door and went in.

It was a deep, pleasant place, ivory-walled, divided for three-quarters of its length by Wedgwood blue lattice work supporting occasional vines and hung at intervals with odd items: a saucy black Raggedy Ann, a bath sheet with hearts and flowers around an embroidered "Ours," a webbed golden bag holding the sparkle of two champagne glasses.

There were customers on both sides. Mrs. Tyrell devoted herself to a revolving stand of earrings in the gift area and bided her time.

A few feet away, a large woman in a toggle coat was debating over a pair of crystal salt and pepper shakers.

"They're awfully small."

"They are delicate, aren't they?"

The second speaker was presumably Mrs. Pattillo, small and lithe in what were probably designer jeans, well-faded, with a turtlenecked burgundy top. Her short bell of hair was like mushroom silk, her makeup frankly and entertainingly just a brush of silver on her eyelids, lashes like tiny black whisk brooms, lipstick the color of rose wine.

The toggle-coated woman made her purchase. Mrs. Tyrell turned with a pair of dangling glass triangles. She said, "I'd like these, if I may," and introduced herself. "We're buying the Wadsworth house, and I thought it would be nice to come in and meet you."

Mrs. Pattillo's eyebrows flew up. "Really? Let me call Donald, he'll be thrilled. I'm Tracy, by the way, like twenty-three million other females born that year. Donald? Come over here a sec.''

The man who sauntered around the end of the lattice work was tall but as supple as his wife, with fiery dark eyes and a short, immaculately clipped black beard. He said when he had welcomed Mrs. Tyrell, "Well, that was fast. We didn't even know anyone was looking at the house."

Mrs. Tyrell explained the unlikely dovetailing of circumstances. "It's expediting matters that Mrs. Wadsworth is anxious to join her husband out on the Coast."

Neither of the Pattillos turned a head or even a hair, but something passed alertly between them. The customer patchily visible on the bookshop side uttered the kind of cough that spoke of patience wearing thin, and Pattillo excused himself. Mrs. Tyrell paid for her earrings and departed thoughtfully.

"You're in luck," said Charlie in an aside five minutes later. "The house is in her name, so there won't be any delay. The closing will be the day after tomorrow, and I think you've got a gem."

Mrs. Tyrell had known it, but it was nice to have his seasoned endorsement. Her swift and second trip upstairs had revealed two bonus details—an extra linen closet and the fact that the attic had a narrow back stairway. Dormer-windowed on both sides, it could be painted and turned to other purposes if they decided to use the barn loft for storage instead.

Charlie sped off in his Jaguar, and Mrs. Tyrell drove Mrs. Wadsworth back to Plymouth Street. Apart from, "Mr. Tyrell was so kind and very helpful," her passenger had nothing to offer. She was clearly not a woman of small talk; still, the car seemed to buzz actively with silence.

The Dobermans were not quiet today. They raced and ranged behind the chain links like a pair of powerful whips, growling with the collected menace of thunder before erupting into sound. As if afraid they would give a buyer pause, Mrs. Wadsworth said, "They never do that at night. I think children poke sticks in at them, just because the fence is there."

And then, astonishingly, "Will you come in and have a drink? This has all been so . . . I could certainly use one."

An explanation of the startling offer wasn't long in coming.

The house breathed emptiness at them when Mrs. Wadsworth used her key. She asked if Scotch would be all right and came back with two glasses clinking lightly with ice. When she had sat down, she said, staring with fixity through one of the windows that overlooked the front lawn, "I didn't talk to my husband last night. I haven't the slightest idea where he is. He's left me."

Mrs. Tyrell, who had been geared to something more in the way of a toast, thought transfixedly that her Scotch was going to go down the wrong way. She managed, "Oh?"

Mrs. Wadsworth acknowledged this choked syllable with a certain aloofness of her own. "It isn't the kind of thing one cares to advertise from the rooftops, but the Pattillos will undoubtedly tell you, and I thought you might as well hear it from the source."

She was remembering the interval at the title company. Mrs. Tyrell was irritated at the rush of warmth to her face, as if a perfectly natural interest in neighbors-to-be had suddenly turned into snooping.

"My husband is a few years younger than I am and very attractive to women. I accused him of an affair, perhaps wrongly—" into Mrs. Tyrell's head flashed an image of silvery eyelids and clear-rose lips "—and there was a quarrel. We were outside at the time and I imagine it was highly audible next door."

Hard to imagine the composed voice raised, and only possible to guess from the measure of rigidity how much this was costing her. "It wasn't the first such quarrel, naturally, but it turned out to be the last. Even if I could manage a place like this by myself, which I can't, I wouldn't care to stay on in Cresset."

No, thought Mrs. Tyrell; in spite of changing standards it would be intolerable for a woman like Mrs. Wadsworth. There were a few poisoned tongues in any town, and it was even possible that Nancy would be speculated about as a cause of dissension.

She said simply, "I'm sorry," and Mrs. Wadsworth dismissed that with a shrug and a remote smile. "The California part is true, anyway. I do have friends there." Then, with understandable brusqueness—privacy unlocked for casual inspection by a stranger—"Unless there's anything here you want, I'm going to put up a Garage Sale notice this afternoon and get rid of everything."

And, unspoken, make a fresh, stripped-bare start. Mrs. Tyrell finished her drink and rose. She said, making the allusion with a trace of awkwardness, "I'll ask my husband about the lawn mower and garden tiller. How much are you asking?"

She had started the car before she remembered the picture promised to Annie. She got out again and snapped it, inspected the Polaroid print, and then drove off.

"I think children poke sticks in at them," Mrs. Wadsworth had said of the Dobermans—but it was Nancy who was doing just that. At the sight of the recognized car she averted her face as though oblivious and dropped her prod in the same way she had let the rake fall to the ground, although Mrs. Tyrell could have sworn that she saw a flash of silver at the prod's head.

It was not an incident worth notice—unless the dogs ever got loose and had a chance at their tormentor. The very young, and Nancy certainly qualified as that whatever her chronological age, liked to provoke reaction for its own sake; there needn't be intentional cruelty involved.

Still, Mrs. Tyrell wished that she hadn't seen it.

Annie was rapt at the photographed pair of upstairs windows that would be hers. Standing in the small back garden, which in summer supported three tomato plants, a rosebush, a dwarf peach tree, and a row of hollyhocks, she gazed around her with daring. "Is it five times as big as this?"

How to explain acreage in terms a child would understand? "This would all fit in half the front lawn," said Mrs. Tyrell.

From then on it was an afternoon of telephoning. First Neil, in London. The conference was being cut short because its president had collapsed and died of a heart attack in the small hours, so that he would be home in six days. He said yes to the mower and tiller—"I don't want to spend all my weekends looking like the *Man With a Hoe*—" and, "Better call the storage place, our stuff may be at the bottom of the heap, and get hold of Bill McGinnis."

The stuff was antique furniture left to him by a great-aunt, for most of which there had been no room in this little starter house. Bill McGinnis, a colleague of Neil's, was their own would-be house buyer.

Mrs. Tyrell was far too excited to read after dinner. She watched a made-for-television suspense movie instead, and that was a mistake. Perhaps because there had been rain tapping at the cellar window, which was the camera's frequent and suggestive focus, and there was now real rain driving against the window at one side of her bed, she came awake with a single stark question in her mind.

What if Mrs. Wadsworth's second version of her husband's abrupt and permanent departure had been as false as the first, with an air of forced-out truth simply because it had come second?

That could mean that he had never left at all. Not . . . upright, at least.

The question, having sidled in, settled down, and gave birth to a few ugly young.

Marital quarrels frequently ended in violence rather than a mere walking out. A sharp signal had passed between the Pattillos at the mention of transferral to the West Coast. Mrs. Wadsworth was a strong woman, but even so—

There were two vehicles in the barn.

At this point, savingly, an imaginary voice said in the portentous tones of a low-budget-film sheriff, "Fan out, men. I want every square foot of these woods examined for signs of recent disturbance."

Mrs. Tyrell switched on the bedside light. It was four-thirty, and although Damon was inching toward a more civilized hour he would soon be demanding his bottle. She got up and put it on to heat, eager as much for his company as for purposes of circumvention. Presently, his tiny hands curled with pleasure and his perfect, threadlike black eyebrows registering little flickers of which only he knew the cause, he was sanity made absolute.

The closing went off without incident on a cold and soaking day. For an occasion of such import it was surprisingly brisk and brief; perhaps, thought Mrs. Tyrell, not unlike getting married at city hall. When they were all on their feet one of the spectacled men said to Mrs. Wadsworth with a glance out at the glistening street, "I'll bet this rain and cold makes you look forward to sunny California."

"Yes, I must confess it does."

"Roy likes it out there, does he?"

"Oh, very much," said Mrs. Wadsworth.

It had been agreed that she and Nancy would be out of the house by three o'clock on Sunday, leaving the second set of keys on the living-room mantel. Although it wasn't a day to linger in the open, Mrs. Tyrell held out her hand. "I won't be seeing you again, so good-by and good luck."

"The same to you, and thank you for being—discreet." Mrs. Wadsworth hesitated a moment in spite of the rain. "If you happen to meet a couple called Hopkins, it's all right, they know, too."

Mrs. Tyrell had turned her ignition key when there was a tap on the car window: Tracy Pattillo, looking like an exotic child in yellow oilskins. "Does this mean the deed is done?"

"Yes, I'm going to start bringing things down on Sunday."

And that was the day when, even enjoined by Saturday's six o'clock news, she had forgotten to adjust her clock.

She brought the entire household with her: Annie, Damon in a bassinet, and Bonnet. It was finally the kind of day that October was supposed to bring, crisp, leaf-scented, with an occasional chase of white clouds across a sky of brilliant blue.

The barn stood open and empty. Damon was oblivious in his nest on the back seat. Leave him, for the moment; warm and fed and lulled by the trip, he was in the deepest part of his afternoon sleep. Mrs. Tyrell closed the car door gently, walked across the lawn to where Annie and the Airedale waited and used the front door key for the first time.

The living room, now furnished only with a shift of tree shadows on walls and floorboards, seemed to have grown in size. It greeted them with a warm, familiar aroma—poultry seasoning? Maybe the quarrel hadn't been about a woman at all, thought Mrs. Tyrell, giddy with ownership; maybe it had started out with, "Do you have to put that damned stuff in everything?"

And there with suddenness in the doorway to the dining

room, causing a fast slam of fear in the throat because she had come so silently, was Mrs. Wadsworth.

She had undergone another of her transformations and wore trim gray slacks and an open-necked white shirt with the sleeves rolled up. "Mrs. Tyrell. I thought when I heard the car that you were Nancy. She's doing a few last-minute errands, and we'll be ready to leave as soon as she gets back." She added pointedly, "It *is* only two o'clock."

Mrs. Tyrell, her error explained to her, felt strangely stung and self-conscious. "I'm so sorry, I don't know how I did that. I've brought a few things to put in the barn, and then we'll be around outside. Please, take your time."

Mrs. Wadsworth had retreated a step into the dining room when she said with sharpness, "Your dog."

Bonnet, having completed a speedy investigation of the bedroom to the left of the hall, was advancing toward them on his tightly fleeced, pillar-y brown legs.

Mrs. Tyrell checked him with a hand on his collar. Two days ago, before she had seen Nancy at the fence with the cane, she would have offered to incarcerate him until the Wadsworths' departure. Now she said, "I'll see that he stays with us," and ushered them all out the door.

Bonnet rushed off at once to search for a stick; an otherwise mature six, he lost his head at the sight of any kind of running space. Damon hadn't stirred. Mrs. Tyrell opened the trunk, and between them she and Annie carried brushes, an old sheet, and cans of paint—a glowing white to replace the living room's yellowing cream—into the barn.

Annie was captivated by the echoing hollowness and the smells of earth, old wood, long-gone hay. She called from the stable area, "Did the horse live here?"

"Once, I suppose." Mrs. Tyrell walked down the ramp toward where the child had positioned herself solemnly at the back of a stall as if to get a horse's-eye view of things. "We have to go outside awhile, Annie, until the people leave."

Annie's navy coat was caught on what turned out to be a nail. Mrs. Tyrell freed her, heard the lightest of sounds from the layering of dusty straw, and put a hand to her ear. She had considered the glass triangles somehow appropriate for this day, and one of them had dropped off.

She was fond of the earrings, which shone with icy clarity inside the curve of her hair, once the color of Annie's but now turning darker. She moved the straw carefully and experimentally with the tip of her shoe: Glass would drink up and reflect even this filtered light.

But what she was looking at, and what gradually revealed itself to be a great stain, almost torso-sized, was blood. Not very old blood, because it was still readily identifiable as such.

The bottom half of the stable door clicked shut. "He was going to do something dreadful to my daughter," said Mrs. Wadsworth, standing behind it. There hadn't even been a warning gather of drum rolls; she was simply there. "Just because she got out of temper and tried to . . . He was going to put her away."

At the first words, the past-tense words, Mrs. Tyrell had reached for and was gripping Annie's hand; it shivered through her head like lightning that unless Mrs. Wadsworth had gone right up to the car she couldn't know Damon was there. The same flash showed her the source of the shame she hadn't wanted to examine before. Mixed with her compassion, from the first, had been a slight recoil from Nancy. Had the similarity of names troubled her? Certainly she had not wanted her child exposed to the flawed gaze, which, translated into terms of sound, would be a steady, busy drill.

Not retarded, but unbalanced and dangerous.

As if she hadn't grasped what she had been told, Mrs. Tyrell got words past a heavy, hard-beating pulse. "My husband's uncle is meeting us here. In fact, I think—is that his car?"

Mrs. Wadsworth didn't trouble to turn her head. "Nancy will be twenty-one in the spring, and then she comes into the principal of her grandmother's inheritance—such a dear little thing she was, when she was three. I couldn't have court-appointed people prying around after all these years."

The years when she had had control of the income—and the prospect of the years ahead. In consequence, the ultimate action taken, here in an old New England barn, with Mrs. Tyrell stumbling into it like a rabbit into a snare.

Her unconscious had suggested more than she knew during those rainy small hours. It presented her now with the trim red

barn so readily to hand, its owners away all day, which undoubtedly contained things like cleavers, because who could
cope with whole steers or pigs?

But then what had been done with Roy Wadsworth? Any ex-
tensive digging would soon betray itself in wet ground, and the
Pattillos were already dubious about the transferal to the West
Coast.

A remembered smell of poultry seasoning, not once but
twice, mingled with a few remembered words and caught
sickeningly at the back of Mrs. Tyrell's mouth. She said, taking
a bold two steps closer to the stable door, "I haven't the
slightest idea of what you're talking about, but whatever it is
it has nothing to do with me. I'd like to show Annie the back,
so—"

It had had to be tried, and of course it failed. Mrs. Wadsworth said in an appallingly conversational voice, "Nancy will
be here any minute."

And if Nancy comes, if there are two of them, we are lost.

Mrs. Tyrell measured her as she imagined men in a fighting
mood measured each other. She was outtopped by two inches
and outweighed by about twenty pounds. And there was
Annie, not quite comprehending but holding her hand very
tightly, to think about.

And, in the car, Damon. So very small, so—disposable.
Bassinet wicker burned up in a flash.

Mrs. Tyrell moved her gaze, craning for a view of the lawn.
She saw Bonnet, beside the car and gnawing at a stick clasped
between his forepaws even though nobody had played with
him. She said with an air of vindictive triumph, "You'd better
take away that thing my dog has, before he runs out in the road
with it."

The clear fear of a dog on these premises, with the according
tale of severe allergy. How sure could a spur-of-the-moment
killer be that the tidying had been complete?

Mrs. Wadsworth half-spun and went crashing down against
the tiller as Mrs. Tyrell, up the ramp in less than a blink, sent
the stable door flying at her with the desperate strength of
knowing that this chance could not be achieved again.

Her chest hurt. "Annie, run and get in the car, quick, and

lock your door. No, you don't," she gasped to Mrs. Wadsworth, struggling to rise with a beginning trickle of blood at one side of her chilly white forehead. *"No, you don't."*

She had never in her life inflicted deliberate harm on another human being, and even at this moment it was difficult to get down on one knee, seize the shirted shoulders, bang the gray-threaded dark head against metal with a force that terrified her. Then she was up and running across uneven planks—*dear God, don't let me trip*—toward sunlight.

She reached the car, shaking so that she had to wrench twice at the door, and somehow got in. With what felt like the last of her breath she called to Bonnet who, believing that a game had finally begun, had pounced across the lawn.

And out of the barn came Mrs. Wadsworth, lurching, horrifying, with a lawn edger grasped like a javelin.

Leave Bonnet—after his years of nursemaiding Annie, his vigilant new station beside Damon's crib? Carry away the memory of the stick sprouting hopefully out either side of his whiskers?

"Bonnet, come!" shrieked Mrs. Tyrell, and at the last possible second he dropped the stick, bounded forward, and scrambled into the car.

By the sheerest providence and because the house had looked so empty, the keys dangled from the ignition. Mrs. Tyrell was backing without so much as a glance over her shoulder when the lawn edger struck the windshield with a force that would have cut flesh to the bone. Damon woke up and gave a tiny querulous bleat, but they were out of the driveway and safely on the road.

Annie said an awestricken, "Mama—" and Mrs. Tyrell said tensely, "Wait, Annie," because it took all her trembling concentration to reach the corner, turn right, pull off at the clearing beside the woods. (A single and necessary trip made to the Wadsworth part?)

Heart slowing somewhat, she looked at her child. Annie said, "Was that lady crazy?"

Mrs. Tyrell considered it with care. *Sick* was the gentler, more acceptable, clinical term, but measles and mumps and chicken pox still lay in wait for a five-year-old who might wake in the night and think—

"Yes," she said. Murder for gain might be almost as prevalent as the common cold—but a private christening party, so that names could be used openly and with wicked amusement?

She waited at the clearing, engine running no matter what it might cost in gasoline because she did not dare take the smallest chance. Was it eight minutes or twelve or fifteen before the gray Ford appeared, Nancy at the wheel, and angled south?

Mrs. Tyrell memorized the license plate, but she did not go immediately in search of a telephone. Instead, although she was now quite sure of what Nancy had been doing with the cane, she made a last visit to the deep grass behind the chain-link fence.

She got out of the car. She said flinchingly to the Dobermans, side by side ten feet away, at once alert and lazy on their forefeet, "Mr. Hopkins?" and then, "Mrs. Hopkins?"

And, eyes sharpening to a terrible expectancy, they came.

She was certain, now, how Mrs. Wadsworth had disposed of her husband's remains.

BRIAN GARFIELD

THE CHALK OUTLINE

Brian Garfield began his writing career in 1960 with a number of western novels, but switched quickly to crime and international intrigue. His best-known novels are Death Wish *(1972) and the MWA Edgar Award winner* Hopscotch *(1975), both of which have been made into successful films. A collection of his short spy stories,* Checkpoint Charlie, *was published during 1981, as was this powerful story of a tragic accident and its aftermath.*

S HE WASN'T EVEN HURRYING.

She turned the corner, driving sedately, and without warning the Murdochs' new puppy squirted into the lane like a seed popping from a squeezed lemon. Carolyn braked and turned, avoiding it, and that was when the little Murdoch girl, chasing the puppy, grenaded out from behind the hedge and it just wasn't possible to stop in time.

The lawyer's name was Charles Berlin. He had represented her in the divorce. He was the only attorney she'd ever dealt with. "This isn't my usual kind of case," he told her. "If you'd feel more comfortable with a criminal lawyer . . . ?"

"Criminal?" She hadn't thought of it like that.

"Manslaughter's a crime," he said gently.

It took her a moment to absorb what he was saying. Her mind hadn't been tracking very well since it happened. "I'm sorry," she said, and shook her head as if to clear it.

"Don't get into the habit of saying that all the time," he said.

"What?"

"That's about the tenth time you've said 'I'm sorry' since you walked in here."

"I'm sor—" Then she nearly laughed.

He smiled at her. "That's better."

He was a kind man; she'd appreciated that in him two years ago—he'd handled the divorce with grace and without abrasiveness. She tried to compose herself by sitting up straighter and tossing her hair back and glancing around the office as if to get her bearings. The room was like Charles's person—ordinary, matter-of-fact, quietly attractive. He was, she supposed, about five years older than she was—forty or so.

Carolyn said, "I just don't know what to do. What do you suggest?"

"I'll handle it if you like. I don't think it'll be difficult. Technically you've committed a crime but it obviously wasn't intentional. I hardly think they'll throw the book at you." And again the reassuring smile. It was the first time she'd ever noticed the dimple in his left cheek.

He was a comfortable and comforting sort of man: very low-key, but she supposed he'd cultivated that because a good many of his clients must be people who needed soothing.

He leaned back in his swivel chair with one leg crossed over the other knee, pivoting on the ankle, a yellow pad against the upraised knee and a pencil against his teeth. "Okay. Take it easy. I'm going to have to ask some direct questions. Ready?"

She dipped her head, assenting.

"Formally, then—you acknowledge that you ran down the child?"

She closed her eyes. She knew she'd have to force the words out sooner or later. It might as well be now.

"Yes. I killed the little girl."

It was all prearranged—an agreement between Charles and the State's Attorney. She was amazed how quickly it went, in the courtroom. She pleaded guilty to involuntary manslaughter. There were a few affidavits, and the judge—a surprisingly young but quite overweight woman—seemed less interested in the various depositions than in Charles's photographs of the scene of what Carolyn had finally been able to start calling The Accident (as opposed to The Day I killed Amy Murdoch).

Charles pointed out the overgrown hedge in the photos and showed how it would have been impossible for *anyone* to have seen the little girl in time. He also pointed to the brief black skid marks that showed up clearly against the pale gray pavement; according to the police analysis they showed she couldn't have been doing more than twenty-five miles an hour at the time she saw Amy emerge into the street.

(She'd been going faster than that but she'd already braked to avoid the dog.)

"In short," Charles summed up, "I think this incident represents a textbook example of an unavoidable accident. I would point out to your honor there wasn't any hit-and-run. Mrs. Benson stopped immediately and had the presence of mind to try and save the little girl's life. She called the police and the ambulance. She even went up to the Murdoch house and told Mr. Murdoch what had happened. I think this tragic incident must be chalked up as an act of God, your honor, and I think justice would be best served if Mrs. Benson were acquitted; but we recognize that a homicide *has* been committed and that may not be possible.

"My client is ready to accept whatever punishment this court decides to hand down, but I'd like to point out that in her own conscience she has already suffered far more than justice might demand of her. I suggest there were several victims of this horrible accident, your honor, and Mrs. Benson was one of them."

The judge lectured her a bit, had another brief look at the photos, agreed the accident had been clearly unavoidable, pointed out that under the laws of the state she had no choice but to find Carolyn guilty of involuntary manslaughter, and pronounced sentence: "Three hundred and sixty-four days. Sentence is suspended."

Charles had told her to expect just that. He'd explained what it meant, in practical terms: she'd have to report to a parole officer once a month—a formality—and she'd have to apply for the court's permission if she wanted to leave the state before the end of the year's period. She couldn't believe it was that simple. "You mean it's over? I can go?"

Getting up from the courtroom table he took her arm and gave her that smile. "All over. You've punished yourself enough."

It provoked a grunt from someone behind her. She didn't look back; she knew who it was. Stanley Murdoch. He'd been sitting at the prosecutor's table throughout the trial. He'd never said a word. He hadn't even looked at her very much. He didn't look enraged or even bitter; his face seemed rather slack, actually. But his presence in the room throughout the brief trial had disturbed her as if he were a ticking bomb.

Murdoch brushed past her without a word and strode out of the courtroom. Carolyn, feeling faint, reached for Charles's hand.

He took her to eat in one of those business-lunch places that was mostly bar, had no windows, and lulled you with Muzak. He bought her a drink and said, "I know a bit of how it feels. You feel as if you've been drugged. You're disoriented. Nothing's quite real. You don't know what's going to happen in your life tomorrow or next week or next year." Her hand was on the table and he touched it with his own. "I know it's hard to buy this idea at a time like this, but you will get over it. Life will resume."

She stared into the amber translucence of the drink. "I can't go on living three doors down from Stanley Murdoch. I couldn't stand him giving me those hurt accusing looks every time I passed by."

"The house is too big for you anyhow, by yourself. Why don't you move into an apartment? Buy one of those condominiums out by the lake shore."

"I'll think about it," she said listlessly.

She had an appointment that afternoon to help a fat woman in the Fairview tract choose carpeting and wallpaper. The fat woman's husband had got a raise and she wanted to do the house over and she'd gone through the Yellow Pages under "Interior Decorators and Designers"—Carolyn was the third decorator in the alphabetical listing and she had a suspicion that the fat woman probably had phoned the first two but got no answer.

She kept the appointment because she was still alert enough to realize she had to keep occupied. It was a tedious afternoon. The fat woman had poor taste and even so she couldn't make up her mind about anything. Carolyn tried to guide her into some sort of sensible combinations but her own aplomb was shattered and she didn't have her normal abilities to charm and persuade. Half of the time it was a chore merely to avoid screaming at the stupid cow.

Finally—line of least resistance—she let the fat woman have her way with some absurdly mismatched carpets that would clash dreadfully with the tweedy couch she had at home. Carolyn made a heroic effort, managed to summon one last feeble smile, said a hurried goodbye, and rushed away. Riding home in the back of the taxi—she still wasn't trusting herself to drive the car—she realized dismally that this wasn't going to work. Not right away. She didn't have the patience for it. One more appointment like this afternoon's and she'd start screaming her head off; she'd end up in a rubber room. There had to be some other focus for her attention, until these terrible anxieties and tensions began to settle down.

If they ever would . . .

She had the furtive impulse to hide her face when the taxi took her past the hedge—past Murdoch's house. Defiantly she lifted her head, put her face close to the window, and looked at the house.

She wished she hadn't. He was there. Murdoch. Standing on the porch of the old house watching her ride past. He was not reading or smoking or drinking; he was not doing anything. He was simply standing there—watching her, and it was as if he'd been standing on that spot all afternoon waiting for her.

His face didn't change. He only watched. But she could feel the burning impact of his eyes all the time while she paid off the cab driver and hiked her bag over her shoulder and walked—as slowly and proudly as she could, but it was an effort not to run—up to her door. Then, absurdly, she couldn't find the key and spent *ages* rummaging in the damned bag.

When she finally eeled inside and pushed the door shut, she peered out through the crack. He was still there, diagonally across the street on his porch, watching, watching.

She pushed the door shut and locked it. Then she sagged against it, both palms hard against her temples, trying to keep from screaming.

. . . Back in the worst Medusan entanglements of the divorce (and admittedly it hadn't been terribly messy but there was no such thing as a non-traumatic divorce), she had discovered the wonderful therapeutic value of showers: a scalding hot one followed by a needle-sharp cold one. In some way that she understood but couldn't explain, the hard and meticulous scrubbing was a process that cleansed more than just the epidermic surface. It seemed to work this time too.

She emerged from the steamy bathroom with her wet hair wrapped in a turban of towel and stood before the dressing-room's full-length mirror squinting at her flushed body, skin still taut from the shower. "Not bad for an old broad," she said aloud—she was thirty-six. She thrust out one hip and tried a lewd grin but it broke up in the mirror and she turned away.

Fido came in while she was sitting naked in the dressing room moving the hair dryer around her head. He miaowed and rubbed against her calf and tickled her knee with his upthrust tail. She reached down to pet him and she could feel, through the fur, that he was not purring. Fido *always* purred, but not today. So the edge of her own vibrations must be reaching out that far.

Fido, she thought. What an absurd suburbanite's name for a cat. At the time—when Richard had brought the kitten home and suggested the name—she'd thought it was cute. Fido was fuzzy, black and white, with a sort of negative Chaplin face—all black except for a white smudge of mustache. He was affectionate, lazy, reasonably bright—a thoroughly ordinary cat but since the divorce he was all the family she had.

A screeching squeal of tires on pavement almost lifted the top of her head off. She raced through the bedroom to the window.

She was in time to see the tailfins of Stanley Murdoch's twenty-odd-year-old station wagon slither away past the hedge;

then there was an angry flash of brake lights and another screech
of tires, after which the car was gone around the bend.
Murdoch didn't normally drive like that. *He did it to
frighten me.*

Rattled and distressed, she fixed something to eat—later she
couldn't remember what it had been—and fed the cat and sat
around in a housecoat, switching the TV on and off, picking up
magazines and putting them down, thinking vaguely about
getting dressed and walking the half mile down to the Mall to
buy a pack of cigarettes. She'd given up smoking three years
ago but at a time like this . . .

Don't be absurd.

A drink. That was it—that would calm her down. She went
into the cupboard and selected among the half-dozen bottles: a
Margarita, that would do the job. A good tall stiff one. She
tried to remember Richard's Margarita ritual: split the lime,
rub it around the rim of the glass, pour salt into the palm of the
hand, and twirl the glass in it until the entire rim was coated
with salt that adhered to the limejuice-wet surface. Then shove
the salt-encrusted glass into the freezer to harden. Then mix the
drink itself: tequila, triple sec, lime juice, ice cubes. Stir it for
quite a while, to get it thoroughly cold. Then bring the glass
out of the freezer.

Lick a bit of salt off the rim and drink . . .

The ritual was good because it occupied her. She was beginning to find some sort of equilibrium, beginning to feel even a
bit pleased with herself. Then the jangling phone nearly made
her drop the drink.

It was Charles Berlin. "I just wondered if you were getting
along all right."

"I think so. It's sweet of you to call."

"I happened to be talking to another client of mine today
and this is one of those wild coincidences but you remember we
were talking about those condominiums out by the lake shore?
Well, he's got one of them, and he's being transferred by his
company down to Atlanta or Birmingham or someplace like
that, and he asked me—the guy actually asked me this very afternoon—if I knew anybody who might be in the market to rent
the place from him on a sort of sublet. He doesn't want to put it
up for sale right away until he sees how he likes it down south,

but he'll be gone at least a year. It's a nice pad. I've been there for dinner a few times. You'd like it. Shall I give you his name and number?''

She thought of Stanley Murdoch standing on the porch staring at her, and the screech—filled with message—of Murdoch's tires on the very patch of pavement where the little girl had died; and Carolyn said, ''You bet.''

By the time she signed the lease that Charles had prepared for her, on the condominium, she had recovered enough self-confidence to drive there herself with the carload of fragile things she didn't trust to the movers. She emptied the car, left the cartons in the apartment, and drove back to her house to pick up a few more things, and Fido. She'd have taken the cat on the first trip but of course he'd been nowhere in sight. She remembered one of Richard's wry sayings: ''Cats are just like cops. Never around when you want 'em.''

When she drove into the lane, Fido was there. Squashed flat on the same spot of pavement where Amy Murdoch had died.

''I know he did it on purpose.''

''Murdoch?''

She gave Charles a look. ''Who else?''

''Well, you'll never prove that, will you?''

''I *know* he did it. He wants revenge for his little girl. He won't stop until—''

''Until what? Until you've been punished enough? God knows you've had enough punishment from this thing. I think I'd better have a talk with Murdoch.''

''If it'll do any good.'' She reached for the drink.

''I'll make the appropriate threats,'' Charles said drily. ''Take it easy on that stuff—that's your fourth one.''

''I didn't ask you to count my drinks.''

''Yeah, I know. How about having dinner with me? I know a quiet place out past the lake.''

''I don't go out with married men, Charles.''

''We're separated.''

It took her a moment to absorb that. Then she squinted at him. ''I'm in no shape to be made passes at.''

''Your shape is just fine, Carolyn, but right now I'm disin-

clined to take unfair advantage of you. I think you need company right now, that's all.''

''I don't want pity. I don't think I could deal with that.''

''A friend's concern isn't pity.''

''Oh, hell,'' she said, ''take me to dinner. I hope it's not
Chinese. Richard used to make awful little jokes about how
they run out of chickens in Chinese restaurants and they send
the cooks out into the alleys to round up cats.''

''Your husband always had a macabre sense of humor, didn't
he?''

''I'm sorry. I don't usually bring him into conversations like
that.''

''I understand. It's just that right now you haven't got any
anchor at all and you keep reaching for memories to prop you
up.'' Charles had very sincere warm eyes—brown eyes, nothing
startling—and his hairline was starting to go, and there was too
much flesh around too little chin, and he had a paunch and was
only about five-eight and generally speaking he wasn't the sort
of man she had fantasies about, but—

She said, ''Right now you're a rope and I'm drowning, and
I'm clutching at you like mad. Is that all right?''

''That's just fine. You see the secret truth is, I'm kind of
lonesome myself. I've only been separated a few months.''

''I always despised lawyers,'' she said. ''They feed on
people's misery. They stir up friction. It's their job to treat
everything as an adversary procedure—they're in the business of
creating enemies. I've hated lawyers ever since my father was
defrauded of his dry-cleaning business by some clever loophole-
bending gangster lawyer. So you will pardon me, I hope, if I
sometimes seem a bit distant with you. I'm not used to thinking of a lawyer as anything but loathsome.''

It only made him smile. ''Is that how you thought of me
when I was handling your divorce? Loathsome?''

''I regarded you as a necessary evil, I guess.''

''Most people think of lawyers like that.''

''Do they?''

''We are the lowest form of life, with the possible exception
of interior decorators.''

''Now you're making fun of me.''

"Yeah, I am. You need it."

"I do," she said. "Thank you."

"Do that again."

"What?"

"Dimple up. Smile."

But she didn't. She suddenly remembered the cat again.

She made herself go out into the world and behave as if there were a tomorrow and it mattered. She had to pick up several bolts of fabric for one client and work with the upholsterer on angling the pattern of the fabric properly for the furniture it was to cover; she had a doctor's waiting room to do in the new Medical Center court, and there were three messages left over from last week from the answering service. She returned all three calls, belatedly; two of the people had found other decorators. She made an appointment for Friday with the third.

But she kept thinking about Fido. It wasn't that she'd been inordinately fond of the cat; she hadn't—she wasn't that crazy about cats, really—but the cat had been the nearest thing to a child she'd had, and Murdoch had killed it deliberately.

Deliberately.

That was what frightened her.

She tried to get used to living in an apartment. Actually, since she was alone, it was quite roomy—two bedrooms (she set up her office in one) and a spacious terrace. It was on the second floor. It didn't exactly overlook the lake but if you leaned out over the railing of the terrace you could see a corner of the lake. The view mainly was of the country-club golf course, which was pleasant if over-groomed. Most of the golfers were overweight types who got their exercise in electric carts. She'd never had any interest in golf but being on the fifteenth hole was pleasant enough. She kept expecting a golf ball to come whizzing in through a windowpane, but nothing like that happened.

What did happen was that someone drew a chalk outline of a sprawled little girl's body on the floor of the hallway just outside her door.

It looked exactly like the outline of Amy Murdoch that the police had chalked on the asphalt lane.

•   •   •

"I talked to him again," Charles told her over the phone. "Of course he says he doesn't know anything about it. He'd say that whether it was true or not, but it makes it hard to pin anything down. You know it *could* just be some awful brat who read about the case in the newspaper." The photograph of the chalked outline on the lane had appeared on an inside page of the paper. Carolyn remembered it and made a face.

· She said into the phone, "I don't think it was just some little kid."

"Well, we can't prove it was Murdoch. I can't go around threatening him with legal action when we haven't got any evidence against him. We'd look pretty silly in court asking for a restraining order and watching his lawyer get up and say, 'Restrain from what?' "

"I know," she said wearily. "It's not your fault." But at least his voice had calmed her down enough so that she was able to go out into the hall with the mop and clean the chalk drawing off the floor.

Next day she received in the mail a copy of a children's magazine. It was the kind that was aimed at little girls the age Amy Murdoch had been—six, seven, eight. Full of cheery cartoons of fuzzy smiling animals. It had one of those addressograph-printed labels, with her name on it and the new address. Obviously a subscription had been taken out in her name.

In the next few days her mailbox began to fill up to the point of engorgement with magazines, newspapers, comic books, even cheap pornographic material—the kind that actually did come, she saw, in plain brown-paper wrappers.

Then the bills for all the subscriptions began to come in.

"Just write 'Please cancel subscription' on the forms and send them back," Charles told her. "Don't get rattled. He wants you to get rattled. Don't give him the satisfaction."

"For God's sake, Charles, I don't need avuncular advice. I need to have him *stopped*."

"I can't prove he's the one who's doing it. Neither can you."

"Talk to him anyway. Threaten him. Please?"

Finally a golf ball *did* come through the window. It was the bedroom window—which overlooked the parking lot, not the golf course—and it was in the middle of the night, when nobody could possibly have been playing golf. It made a hell of a noise; she thought she'd have a heart attack.

Wrapped around the golf ball and tied with a rubber band was a crumpled copy of that newspaper photo of the chalk outline on the pavement.

Trembling, she went into the kitchen, lit a gas ring on the stove, and set fire to the bit of newsprint. She watched it curl up and turn black, and wished it were Murdoch.

In the morning she called Charles at his office but the secretary told her Charles was out of town until Monday.

She went around the apartment half of the morning, pacing aimlessly, the hard leather heels of her shoes clicking angrily on the floor like dice. By noon she was distraught enough to think about having a drink, but she didn't. Instead she went down to the machine in the lobby and for the first time in three years bought a pack of cigarettes. A folder of matches came with it. The elevator had a big "No Smoking" sign, but she lit up anyway before she'd even got out of it.

She drew a deep chestful of smoke and it nauseated her and made her instantly, terrifyingly dizzy; she nearly fell to the floor, and had to lean with both hands on her doorknob until the wave of sick dizziness passed. She went inside, stumbled to the bathroom, threw the burning cigarette in the toilet, threw the pack of cigarettes in the wastebasket, leaned both arms against the sink, and stood there, head down, until she was sure she wasn't going to throw up. Then she looked up into the medicine-cabinet mirror.

Go ahead. Go to pieces. Fall apart.

"The hell," she said aloud. "It's just what he wants me to do. I'll be damned if I'll give him the satisfaction."

She found the golf ball where she'd thrown it into the bedroom wastebasket. Feeling cold and angry and determinedly calm now, she put the golf ball in her handbag and went downstairs to the parking lot. It was nearly one o'clock. Murdoch would be home for lunch, probably. He sold real estate in a crummy office out west of town but he usually came home for lunch every day. The housekeeper prepared it for him and always had it ready for him when he arrived, which usually was at about 1:15.

Murdoch was a widower, a very close-mouthed man although not normally a surly one—he had a salesman's hearty but insincere graces, although his gift of gab was one he saved up for customers and rarely displayed in his home neighborhood. Richard had invited him over once or twice in the old days but he'd been a singularly boring dinner guest and after a while their only contact with Murdoch was an occasional wave from the car as one or another of them went in or out—or a shared beer now and then on Sundays when both Richard and Murdoch would be out mowing the lawns. Murdoch's life had mostly been wrapped up in his little girl; his wife had died of leukemia quite young, when Amy was only two or so—several months before Richard and Carolyn had moved in.

Basically her relationship with Murdoch had always been distant—cordial enough, but indifferent. About three months after the divorce Murdoch had made a sort of half-hearted and apparently dutiful gesture of inviting her out to dinner, explaining in a toe-in-the-dust aw-shucks way that since the two of them were the only singles in the whole neighborhood it was almost incumbent on them to go out together. But she'd found some excuse to decline the invitation and he hadn't asked a second time.

He was physically unpleasant; she found him nearly repulsive, although she knew women who liked his type—he was muscular enough, a *macho* character with huge arms and a big chest and a military sort of crew-cut, flat on top. He had a beer-drinker's gut and the hands of a mountain gorilla; he looked more like a heavy-equipment mechanic than a realtor.

Mainly he sold small pre-war houses, in rundown areas, to blue-collar workers and their families. Presumably he looked to them like the kind of man they could trust. The word around the neighborhood was that his realty operation was a bit on the shady side—something to do with kickbacks to building inspectors and bribes to government mortgage people. Nobody had ever proved anything against Murdoch but he had just a slight unsavory aura. In any case, she had always thought him unattractive, to say the least. But up to the time of Amy's death she had not thought of him as *menacing*.

Now, however, there was clearly no question but that he was executing a deliberate and careful scheme of harassment against her. Revenge for Amy's death.

When she turned the car into the lane Murdoch's semi-antique Chevy station wagon was in the driveway. Good; it meant he'd come home for lunch. Carolyn got out of the car and walked halfway up the walk toward the Murdoch porch. It was one of those old clapboard places with the porch running around three sides of the house. Part of it, on the left side, was screened in as a sleeping porch. The rest had a little picket-fence type railing which was turning gray in patches and needed paint.

She fumbled in her handbag a moment and then looked up. Nobody was in sight. She gave the golf ball a good strong throw. It made a satisfying noise when it crashed through Murdoch's front window.

And it brought him boiling out of the place, as she'd thought it would. "Damn irresponsible kids—" he was roaring; then he recognized her and his face froze and he went absolutely still.

She spoke up in a clear strong voice. "I've had enough harassment from you. I'm sorry, very sorry, about what happened to Amy and I wish I could make it up to you. I know you don't understand this, or believe it, but I feel nearly as bad about it as you do. But I've had enough. Harassing me won't bring her back to you—you ought to know that. Now you've had your revenge and you've had your satisfaction and you've made me feel absolutely rotten all these weeks, and now I want you to stop it. Do you understand? Stop it!"

He hadn't said a word; he still didn't. His eyes narrowed down to slits and he merely watched her, unblinking. But she saw that one fist slowly clenched and unclenched. It kept doing that, with a terrible slow rhythm, closing and opening.

He didn't respond to her words at all. She looked at the massive strength of him and felt appalled by her own temerity but, just the same, she stepped forward—five paces, six, seven—until she was nearly nose-to-nose with him, and she shouted in his face with blind thundering rage: "Leave me alone, Murdoch! Do you hear me? *Leave me alone!*" And she slapped him, as hard as she could, across the face.

He didn't even move. He was like some sort of immutable granite rock.

She stood trembling, hyperventilating; she raised her arm again, to strike him, but he stirred then. It was as if he didn't even see her threatening rising arm. He merely turned slowly on one heel and walked back up the steps to the porch.

She screamed at his back: *"Did you hear me, Murdoch?"*

He didn't answer. He just disappeared inside; the screen door slapped shut behind him.

Lacking the courage to follow him into his house, she was forced to turn away and get in the car. She sat trembling for quite a while. She kept expecting to see his face at a window but he never appeared. Finally she drove off.

The phone: Charles. "Hi. I'm sorry I've been out of touch. I was out of town."

"That's what your secretary said."

"I, uh, hell, this is awkward. Look, my wife and I—we've, uh, well, we're going to give it another try. We're trying for a reconciliation. For the sake of the kids, you know, and—well, we've been together a long time, nearly twenty years now. A lot of shared experience there. A lot of understanding. I think we may make it. I know it doesn't usually work out, but we want to give it a try. I thought I'd better tell you . . ."

"I understand, Charles. Don't worry about me."

"Are you all right? No more trouble with Murdoch, I hope."

"He made a little trouble. I had it out with him today. I don't know if it will do any good, but at least it gave me the satisfaction of telling him off."

"That was a gutsy thing to do. What did he say?"

"Nothing. Maybe he's just chewing on what I said, thinking about it. Maybe something of what I said penetrated that little pea brain of his. I don't know. It's hard to tell. Anyhow he didn't do or say anything nasty."

"Well, maybe that's a good sign."

"Maybe. I hope so. Listen, Charles?"

"Yes?"

"I wish you good luck and every happiness. I mean that."

"I know you do. You're a damn good person, Carolyn."

"Goodbye."

She went to bed and hugged the pillow to her; she felt acutely alone tonight. *I have got to get out in the world*, she told herself with force, *and start making friends again.* This was ridiculous. She was a healthy thirty-six-year-old woman without any entangling attachments or encumbrances; she was no beauty but she was reasonably attractive in her chunky short-waisted way—after all, there were men who *liked* freckles and big chests on their women—and it was idiotic to confine herself in this kind of self-pitying isolation; there was no need for it.

Tomorrow, she resolved, she'd start making phone calls. Even if it made her look like some sort of shameless wanton.

She fell asleep filled with determination; she awoke filled with the harsh scent of smoke. She couldn't place it at first but then she coughed and tried to breathe and coughed again, choking.

The apartment was on fire.

The red glow flickered through the living-room doorway. She leaped out of the bed, flung the window open, and climbed out onto the narrow ledge. It was merely a decorative brick escarpment but it gave her purchase for her bare feet; she held onto the window sill and yelled for help.

It was only a one-story drop and finally, when the heat and smoke got too much for her, she jumped to the lawn below, managing to hit the grass without breaking anything. The fire engines were just arriving—she heard the sirens and saw the lights and then it was all a welter of men and machines and hoses and terrible smells.

By morning half of the building was gutted but the fire was out, and she was taken, along with a dozen other displaced tenants, to City Medical to make sure there were no serious injuries.

The fire apparently had started in the furnace room immediately below her apartment and had come up the air ducts, spreading through the building; the hottest part of it had attacked her apartment and it was there that the worst damage had been done, both by the fire and by the tons of water that had been used to extinguish it. The superintendent was a skinny little Italian man with sad compassionate eyes who kept shaking his head back and forth like a metronome. "I'm sorry but it's a total loss. You'll want to get in touch with the owner about the insurance, of course, but I doubt that will cover your own personal things. Were you insured?"

"No."

"Too bad, Miss. I am very sorry. If there's anything at all I can do—"

"You've been very kind. I think I want to sleep a while." He went, and she thought vaguely, in song-like rhythm, *Sorry-sorry-sorry-sorry* . . .

She took a room in a residential hotel. Furnished. With daily linen and maid service. She bought a few clothes, enough to get by. She thought of moving to some other city.

Charles seemed very distant. He lent her money but not a shoulder to cry on; she could understand that but she *needed* a shoulder and resented his not providing one. All he said was, "Try not to persuade yourself that Murdoch set the fire. If he didn't, you'd be making an unjust accusation. If he did, you'll never prove it. Either way it's no good torturing yourself."

She was walking home from a solitary supper trip to the delicatessen when a car came up on the curb behind her at high speed. She heard it—she'd always had acute hearing—and dived flat against the display window of a furniture store, and the car swished past her, inches away. It was a shadowed place in the middle of the block and the car wasn't running with any lights on, but she saw its silhouette vaguely in the darkness as it roared off and it looked like an old car. An old station wagon, with tailfins.

It had damn near killed her. She had that thought and then she crumpled and sat on the pavement for quite a while before she regained strength enough to walk.

Go to the police? And tell them what?

Call Charles? No, he's got other things on his mind now.

Move away. Nothing to hold her here any more. No real ties here. Go away. California maybe. Back to Illinois. New York. What difference did it make? Just get away from that madman.

That was it, then. Run. Run away.

And let him think he's won?

She watched him get out of the old station wagon, lock it, put a cigarette in his mouth, and light up. Then he turned and began to walk across the wide parking lot toward the low square stucco building that housed his realty office.

She let him get halfway across the parking lot. Right out in the open. Then she put her car in gear.

"Sorry, Murdoch," she muttered. "Sorry, sorry, sorry. It was an accident. I just couldn't help it. I'm sorry."

And she ran him down.

JONATHAN GASH

THE HOURS
OF ANGELUS

*Jonathan Gash is one of the new British writers of the
1970s, author of the award-winning novel* The Judas
Pair *(1977) and three others about an antique dealer
detective named Lovejoy. The novels manage to com-
bine Gash's obvious love of antiques with a rakish hero
and plots that effortlessly mix scenes of high hilarity
with formal detection. In this short story, the first of his
I've read, he uses many of the same elements to create a
uniquely new detective - private eye, Angelus Fluck,
who operates, quite incongruously, in a quiet English
village. The story itself is from a British anthology,* The
Fifth Bedside Book of Great Detective Stories, *one of a
fine series edited by Herbert van Thal. This marks its
first American publication.*

H E WAS EVERYTHING A DETECTIVE SHOULD BE,
because a private eye stops at nothing. Tall, lightning
speed in his sinewy walk. Eyes flashing fire, and a quirky smile
at once debonair and cynical. Good at languages, an M.A.
(Cantab) vaguely hinted at by his attention to quotations, but
astonishingly easy of manner with every social class. A miracle
with women—the ultimate phenomenal sexual athlete yet rid-
dled with tenderness. Incisive, even brutal. Some woman had
wounded him deeply which proved his depth of character. Sen-
sitive and aggressive. Introspective and the life and soul of every
party. A dynamo. Rich. He had a name, something aristocratic
like Kingsley Maltravers, easily abbreviated to the snappier
Kingy. He was crisp and cavalier, a bobby-dazzler, Kung Fu

and Kendo dan or whatever they were. He had investigated umpteen murder mysteries, all with complete success. He was a ball of fire. Cold but sexy. In short, *he* was everything Sherlock Holmes had just failed to be.

But one thing he wasn't. He was not Angelus Fluck, because Angelus Fluck was knackered after trying to jog half a mile. The only registered private eye in that part of East Anglia and not a single success in his entire life.

Angelus tottered into the Treble Tile gasping for a pint which his trembling hand failed to control. The beer slopped on the counter, over the carpet. You could hear his wheezes in Norfolk.

"Here he is, lads, Sherlock Holmes."

The few noon drinkers guffawed. Kingy Maltravers would fix these bastard jokers with gimlet eyes and laughter would die. In silence, Kingy would have splattered the lot of them against the fireplace, but Johnny Henson was a hard-as-nails farm labourer and big as a tram.

Angelus Fluck caught sight of himself in the bar mirror: a ton of bald flab, jowls running sweat in obscene rivulets staining his baggy track suit. Face puce, breath rasping. A picture of total collapse. Angelus averted his eyes from the obscene reflection and sank into a chair.

"Give it up, Fluckie." That from old Ben Arrowsmith, stonemason, and practically blind as a bat, drinking with his boss Mr. Curson. The master builder proved kindly as ever.

"Leave him alone," he said. "At least he's trying to keep fit. Not like you idle sods."

It was to no avail. They were still chuckling as Marge mopped up after Angelus. She was as bad as the rest, pulling his leg unmercifully and cackling out her abrasive laugh after every sally. Angelus said nothing. Kingy Maltravers would have teased the vindictive bitch to the brink of a panting orgasm then, smiling that cruel yet debonair smile, would withdraw his thick vibrant shaft, leaving her crawling after him, begging for that release only he could give as he drew on his immaculate gloves and departed for Monaco—

"You should be chasing the killer," Johnny said, only half joking now.

"Aye," agreed old Ben. Nobody agreed like Ben.

"Time somebody did!"

Marge flung into the taproom, leaving a momentary lull which Angelus did not want. For two years now he'd had to endure these reminders about Mary Cottesloe's disappearance. Beckholt was the only village in East Anglia with its own fully registered genuine private eye—and a genuine unsolved mystery disappearance. Everybody was sure it was murder, and blamed Angelus Fluck for not pulling his finger out and at least finding her body.

"What's the celebration?" he gasped, trying to sound all cruel and debonair. It came out a bleat. The builders were not usually in the pub until after one but here it was twelve o'clock and them swilling like troopers.

"Finished."

"Finished?" Angelus wheezed, in the dark.

"Hadn't you noticed?" Elsie Curson, all gold bangles and matching pastels, gave the innocent smile of a woman about to put the boot in. The others were already smiling in anticipation, even her husband.

"Noticed?" Angelus could not avoid sounding wary.

"There's an old church in the fields—"

"—St. Mary's," Johnny put in, as if Angelus hadn't lived in Beckholt all his life.

"My husband's been restoring it," Elsie crooned. "Surely you *must* have seen the scaffolding as you trotted past?"

"Happen he never got that far!"

Amid laughter old Ben added, "He don't even know it be Sunday, and him sidesman!"—which of course was further hilarity at Angelus's expense. The one weapon up his sleeve was his knowledge that, while Angelus Fluck was hauling his ponderous flab homewards, Kingy Maltravers would enter this very bar and have Elsie Curson drooling only to burst into tears of disappointment when, that cynical smile again playing about his lips, Kingy revealed that all the bastard lot of them were involved in the abduction of poor Mary Cottesloe. Backing nonchalantly to the bar, he'd say, "You're all under arrest," and then with one dynamic bound—

"Sidesman?" Angelus asked uncomprehendingly, and called for another pint.

Marge in the taproom clearly heard but ignored him. She was chatting to Pat from the shop. She, too, knew who had murdered poor Mary. She was in on it. Kingy would get her for complicity and she'd get life in Holloway, which would serve the bitch right.

"Your Sal put you down for sidesman," Mr. Curson explained.

"Who, me?"

"Service of dedication," Elsie said. "Now the restoration's done."

"He didn't *detect* that, either!" Johnny guffawed.

Angelus gave it up as a bad job, extracted his ungainly bulk from the clinging cane chair and lumbered towards the door. He knew without looking in the mirror there was that same old placatory grin on his stupid face. The Kingsley Maltravers quip failed yet again to come in time.

"So long," he bleated.

"Hey, Angelus!" Old Ben called. "When you takes the collection tonight, keep your hand on your ha'penny!"

To roars, even from the taproom mob, Angelus Fluck plodded out into the warm sunshine and turned down the lane. Angelo. It should have been Angelo. His stupid mother couldn't even get his name right. Women were always trouble. Look at Sal, putting his name (which, incidentally, was Angelus Fluck, not Kingsley Maltravers) down as sidesman for tonight's evensong in that crummy old barn of a church. Somebody was sure to trip him up, make him look a fool as usual. Whatever was Sal thinking of?

But Kingy was an Olympic walker. Wearily Angelus drew himself up on the balls of his toes, elbows to his sides, and wobbled erratically off between the hedgerows at the best speed he could manage. A passing car hooted in derision. Angelus was too engrossed to give it two fingers.

"Look at the *state* of you!" Sal hissed, smiling determinedly at the crowd around the church.

"We should have got a lift."

"Nobody will give us a lift. And stop panting."

The walk over the fields had been hell. Angelus was sure he

had broken his ankle in a rut. Village lads scagged the footpaths with their motorbikes. Angelus had complained to the village constable, but of course Jim Warboys took more notice of his homemade wine than of crime. He'd told Angelus to piss off out of it.

Sal tried a last few feeble pats at Angelus's collar, his tie, his jacket as they drifted into the summery crowd.

"How does anybody bald as you get covered in dandruff?" she fumed. Angelus gave no answer. He was wondering, Yes, how *does* anybody bald as me get—?

"Evening, Mrs. Fluck," from the vicar's wife. She knew Sal wasn't Mrs. Fluck at all, nor would be till the deed poll came through to change Angelus's name to something less shameful.

"Evening, Mrs. Williams."

"Isn't the church looking positively charming?"

"Charming."

"Such hard work Mr. Curson and Old Ben have put into this noble task."

Angelus simmered miserably, accepting her barbs like St. Sebastian took the arrows. Today's message: philanthropic Mr. Curson and poor old blind handicapped Ben slogged donkeys' years while useless private detectives like crummy Angelus Fluck littered East Anglia.

"And they did the Donaldsons' grave too!"

Sal pointed out for Angelus's benefit the grand, newly painted ironwork round the ornate vault. He pretended to be impressed. The Donaldsons had been Victorian brewers, drunkards to a man, who had exploited child labour and perpetuated tuberculosis and so were honoured by a reserved plot, all railings and phoney rococo. Some hypocrites—and we all know who—had tidied the grave and cleaned the lichen from the stonework. It looked brand new, though mercifully the Donaldsons were extinct, the lot of them.

"*And* kept the restoration costs down!"

"Marvellous!"

A chorus of approval rose from the flowered hats and portly waistcoats. Mr. Curson and his dressy wife moved smugly in with the rest. Sal smiled and nodded, caught between her approval of the successful master builder and her dislike of Elsie, for whom no glitter was too tawdry and no price too secretive to go unmentioned.

"Who's sidesman?" cooed Joan Haynes, a quiet venomous little piece who'd have given her eye teeth for an hour with Kingy Maltravers, but who knew bloody well it was Angelus Fluck.

"Angelus has offered," Sal said brightly. "Didn't you, love?"

"Erm, well, yes." Angelus tried to smile.

"Oh," said Joan Haynes, cold as only a twice-divorced potting maniac could be. "Good." But she meant her stockings were doomed because the entire congregation would have to scrabble under the pews for coppers when Angelus dropped the plate.

Reverend Williams was in the porch, shaking people by the hand and exuding the characteristically vigilant greed of any cleric blessing a construction job. "Glad you could come," he said disdainfully to Angelus, whose one coin always sounded more singular—despite its obvious lightness of weight—than everybody else's folding notes, which fell with hearty thuds on to the plate. He knew all about Angelus.

"Pleased to help," Angelus said.

"And Sal!" The smarmy creep wrung Sal's hand with unnecessary ecstasy, Angelus thought.

"Good evening, Reverend."

Sal nodded a temporary goodbye to Angelus and walked down the aisle, a glorious picture in her bright yellow frock and white accessories, with her edible little bum going hint, hint, hint at people's minds, and all those suddenly sinful villagers wondering how in the world a greasy cubic yard of unemployed lard like Angelus Fluck—Angelus Fluck for Christ's sake—ever met such a popsie in the first place, let alone got her to dwell with him in that ghastly thatched cottage so ludicrously labelled "The Fluck Detective Agency Inc.".

That left Angelus blocking the porch. He hastily stepped aside out of latecomers' way and knocked over a brass vase of tulips. The reverberations stunned the crowd. Heads turned. The organ faltered as Dolly Day, guessing Angelus had arrived, tried to spot which catastrophe he'd started with this time. Mrs.

Williams, smiling determinedly, yelped as Angelus dived after the vase and accidentally caught her ankle with his cufflink.

"What *are* you doing?"

"Sorry," he muttered, desperately trying to ram the flowers into the vase. Water rolled on the newly polished, reconstructed flooring.

"*Leave* it!" Mrs. Williams hissed down at him.

"Sorry."

Panting, he hauled himself upright. The pile of hymn books on the porch pew trembled. Some children tittered. Everybody was smiling or furious. Sal was in with them there somewhere, her ears bright pink.

"Leave them." Joan Haynes steaming to the rescue and Mrs. Williams approaching like a smiling panzer division.

"Sit down, Mr. Fluck."

"Erm . . ."

"Sit down this instant."

"Right, right." Angelus wedged himself in the sidesman's tiny pew, red-faced and ashamed. He tried clearing his throat the way they did in Chandler epics but only got himself glared at by the mafiose of the flower rota and shut up. He hardly fitted in the seat. The plaster bump where the holy-water font used to be knuckled his spine. He was practically hunched into a foetal position, his gross thighs squashed into obscene twin bulbs. His balls would be gangrenous before the *Nunc dimittis*.

Reverend Williams went to get robed up. A last-minuter arrived—earning fond smiles from one and all, Angelus observed bitterly. It was octagenarian Alice Cardice, never punctual in eighty years, to universal approbation, the old cow.

Miserably Angelus sat, wondering if he ought to close the church door now everybody was in. It was a serious problem. The evening sunshine still held warmth and the little rural church was cosily packed—so it would be more than Angelus's life was worth to shut all that lovely sun out. But if he didn't they'd all be tut-tutting at the draught as soon as the sun slanted below the treetops of Friday Wood. To tiptoe over and shut it then would cause Reverend Williams to pause, which would make Angelus anxious, which would ruin that tall flowerstand's chances of survival, which would—

The congregation rose. Angelus forced himself from the

sidesman's pew with a loud embarrassing rasping noise that caused nudges and heads to turn. He seriously wished the priest's first announcement would be to the effect that Angelus Fluck had definitely not broken wind, but prayer was unavailing because here came Reverend Williams to stand in an opportune shaft of sunlight, humble as any squeaky-voiced adenoidal Welshman who knew deep down he was God Almighty.

The congregation sat. Vibes of venom flowed back towards the sidesman's diminutive alcove, where on sitting Angelus managed to create an opposite noise to his original B flatus. But how the hell can you have a negative noise, for Christ's sake? Surely all noise is positive?

Sal's ears were now frankly white-hot. Never mind a mere evensong, there'd be Armageddon in the old town tonight. Angelus sighed wearily as Reverend Williams zoomed off on wings of balderdash.

"Friends," he squeaked. "This hour is one of the old Hours of Angelus, a remembering to pray." Angelus reddened at the titters. "Antecedent to commencing our dedicatory service, I am desirous of recapitulating . . ." The prattling parson embarked on a twenty-minute history of the old church which, founded in the fourteenth century "despite the vicissitudes of the Vikings," had nurtured the village's spiritual hopes until it had fallen into ruination for twenty long years. Then had come a "Solomon to judgement" (here Mr. Curson had the grace to blush).

"A mirrraculous mi-rrracle occurred," the rapturous goon intoned. "Expert at church restoration, he began the rescue . . ."

Angelus Fluck switched off and thought instantly of other things, because Kingy had this analytical knack. . . . At any rate, he would have thought of other things except his attention drifted outside into the sunshine.

The graveyard was pretty, weeds suppressed and paths tidy. A blackbird flew on to the railings of the Donaldsons' family vault—neatest of all, of course. The distant trees, the valley you could just about see . . . Oho. Here it came. Angelus had hated all Welshmen since a berserk goal-scorer had displaced him from a junior football team.

". . . especially auspicious, since we were still suffering from

the loss of our dear missing Mary Cottesloe, a young girl
who . . .''

All eyes turned balefully on Angelus who pretended to be
deep in prayer but whose suddenly red and sweaty face betrayed
him. God, didn't the fucking police have a share in all this
blame? And he'd honestly tried, going round for clues and
asking people who'd said piss off Angelus you duckegg, till he
was worn to the knees.

The priest whined on, inviting prayers for Mary's return. To
punish him, Angelus went back to wondering what that curious
blue sheen was; a minute but steady glim from among the
graves. Where had he seen that colour before? It was on the
edge of the Donaldson grave. Blue.

"Hymn number four-oh-two," the Celtic creep whimpered.

The congregation stood. Angelus struggled up to join them,
hoping in vain for a passing obstetrician to extract him silently
from this crummy little crevice. What had been wrong with the
old spacious uncomfortable sidesman's gargoyley pew? Once
these builders got going . . . Dolly Day blasted away on the
newly-restored grand old pump organ. Old Cartwright would
be on the handles, out of sight, infarcting away at the rattling
pace she always set.

"He-e who would valiant be . . ." everybody bawled.

Angelus knew something was wrong but thought it was just
his singing. He didn't know he was tone-deaf, merely realized
people moved off a little way when he started up.

The blue was the stained glass colour. Clear blue. In fact, the
identical blue of the robes in the newly-restored stained glass
east window. Angelus tilted his head. The sunlight sifted gently
through the Saviour's red robe, melted the brilliant blue of the
Virgin's dress. Clear. *Absolutely* clear? Angelus moved his head
again. The blue glass was lovely and even.

"To be a pilgrim," Angelus warbled.

A grey-haired man glanced despairingly across but Angelus
determined to ignore him. What did old Cartwright know
anyhow? He was only the organ pumper, out of a job anyway
since the new church over in the village went electric . . . .
Cartwright? Why wasn't he pumping the organ? On the rare
occasions this ancient church with its ancient old manual was

used, nobody but Eric Cartwright *ever* pumped the organ. Not for a zillion years. But maybe Mr. Curson had wired Dolly's old complexity into the jet age. But from the way Dolly Day's head was nodding she was pedalling or something. Foot bellows?

". . . This bright story . . ."

Angelus's attention drifted back to that blue. Wonderful what colours those medieval craftsmen achieved, with hardly any proper tools. Of course, colours tended to vary more than nowadays. . . . Angelus, crooning away, tilted his head again to catch the light of the leaded windows.

It was a problem, but of course quite easily explicable . . . surely? Yet the Virgin's dramatic blue robe was complete. Nothing missing. No space. And one plus nought equals one. Everybody knows that. So what was a piece doing jammed into the stone base of the Donaldsons' grave? It should be up there with the rest of its medieval mates. Unless . . . Angelus swallowed silently and missed a line, ruining the third verse for miles around. Everybody ground to a halt and sat, hating Angelus.

"Dearly beloved," John Knox squeaked, "the Scripture moveth us in sundry places. . . ."

There was a horrible pause. Angelus, in his anxiety to check that the collecting plate was under his mini-pew, had somehow nudged the church door. A work of counterpoise art, once it was bidden to close it gravitated into place with a thunderclap. The church quivered as the huge iron-studded oak boomed shut. Reverend Williams closed his eyes, waiting for the echoes to die. Eighty-nine pairs of eyes rivetted Angelus. He was unaccountably bent double, fingering the brand new collection plate he had at last found beneath his pew. Somebody whispered admonitions but that was par for the course. Angelus wheezed upright, clutching the plate.

"Dearly beloved," the priest icily resumed, "the Scripture . . ."

We're off, Angelus thought. An hour of spiritual mayhem. Once the nerk had got going Angelus rose with that awful farting noise and slid over to where Betty Dockett the people's churchwarden sat glowering near the baptismal font. Even on tiptoe he sounded like the Entebbe raid.

"Betty," Angelus whispered. "Will you tip me the wink when I have to take the collection? I've forgotten—"

"Get back to your place, Angelus!" Betty hissed feverishly, flapping her gloved hands.

"Will you—?"

"*Yes*! Shhh!"

A few people were surreptitiously looking round to see what was the matter. The rest whipped round as well when Angelus blundered into the tall wrought-iron candlestick and only just managed to stop it tumbling on to the ancient pewter font cover. It would have dented it for good. As it was, Angelus like a fool let his collection plate slam against the venerable metal. The Creed had had it for the moment while Angelus started to rearrange things as they were. Betty Dockett finally flustered him out of the way and took over to stop the crashes. She was a pleasant stoutish woman, a prolific breeder of daughters, and once the service resumed glided over to where Angelus was wedged into his alcove to press his arm compassionately.

She bent and whispered, "Don't take on so, dear. Not too many people noticed." There was no clap of thunder at this monstrous untruth, but Angelus could not answer. Tears rolled down his cheeks. Betty tiptoed back to her place thinking Angelus was not too bad after all to get so upset at a little mishap.

But Angelus was weeping for poor Mary Cottesloe, who would now never return home, seeing she had been murdered on the day she disappeared two years ago. And Angelus was weeping for her murderer, this very minute rising to read aloud the Testament from the restored lectern. And he wept for the existence of greed, that motive which makes prostitutes of all.

The service was a nightmare. Angelus pulled himself together during the sermon—a voracious appeal for money thinly veiled in misquotations from the *Nag Hammadi* Gospel of Judas Thomas, which went over big, judging from the loot in the collection plate when Angelus eventually fumbled it round the congregation. But he'd forgotten his entire *A Private Eye's Manual* (Cheap Edition, Revised) about a citizen's arrest which he could have sworn he knew by heart, and, if he couldn't remember the Magnificat after ten million goes, those legal cautionary phrases were on a loser.

As the sermon wound up Angelus thought frantically of rushing out to telephone the police but Constable Jim Warboys was right there in the same pew as the murderer and clearly praying for the unqualified success of his next batch of parsnip-and-elderberry hooch. And they knew Angelus Fluck down at the police station from a lifetime of false reports he'd put in. They'd only tell him to sod off again, because they always did.

Quick—what would Kingsley Maltravers do? Rise now, like this (Betty Dockett signalled to Angelus as he'd asked). Angelus's heart thumped. That's what he'd do—stroll casually forward, lean down over the murderer and say, daredevil smile playing on his lips, "You're under arrest—*murderer!*" Or, more casually, he would stroll in an appalled silence to the altar, lean elbows nonchalantly on its immaculate lace, and say loudly, "Two years ago, almost to the day, a young girl called Mary wandered past this old church on her way . . ." And the murderer would blanch, knowing that Kingy had triumphed over the forces of darkness yet again—

"Where are you going, Angelus?" tardy octagenarian Alice Cardice mumbled.

"Erm, sorry, Mrs. Cardice. I was just—"

"You start the collection from the front right side, stupid boy."

"Erm, sorry. But—"

"He always was a fool," the old psychopath quavered confidentially to the rest of the county.

The upshot was Angelus took the collection and painstakingly avoided everybody's eye, even the murderer's. Sal thought he looked pale and wondered if she'd done right volunteering him as sidesman. The murderer put a note into the collection with a bump like a Sunday newspaper. Angelus tried a knowing smirk, but two old ladies asked if he felt faint.

He was ready, though, when the church started to empty. He'd rehearsed all the arguments by then: an extra piece of medieval stained glass is an impossibility. So the entire valuable "medieval" stained glass window was missing, the high window a modern replacement. The spare bit wedged in the Donaldsons' vault was modern, too, having fallen when Mr. Curson buried Mary's body there. Naturally, concealment was cheap— a few quids' worth of restoration to a vault belonging to an extinct family, therefore by law nevermore to be opened. Where do you hide a tree but in a wood?

The ancient organ no longer reverberated when the church door slammed. It always had before. Angelus had had his ears boxed often enough as a lad. One visiting organist, a foreigner, had said that no other instrument except these rare North German baroque organs could be used for the playing of Buxtehude, whatever that was, and given Angelus a thrashing. So the "restored" organ was a sham.

And the ancient pewter font cover, when scratched by Angelus's collection plate, showed faint but clear circumferential machine grooves, the marks of modern ware. The original was gone.

And the pews were stained pine, imported. His falling vase had knocked a dent into the back pew, revealing the pale fawn of new wood. As a kid Angelus had laboured hours to put his initials in the rich, valuable, Cuban mahogany and matured walnut supports—wood now valuable beyond belief. The former was now simply unobtainable; and a good old English walnut tree could now cost more than the manor house in whose grounds it grew.

And the collection plate was new. The Chester hallmark of William III, which Angelus had traced and researched as a neophyte detective aged eleven, was missing. The silver-plated copy had no hallmark at all.

And the water he had spilled from the tulip vase did not soak into the ancient block flooring any more as it always had.

And the gargoyles which should be knuckling Angelus's spine now adorned some rich collector's attic on a varnished plaque.

And, and, and . . .

As people emerged Angelus was at last wearing his Kingy Maltravers expression. "Stick around," he said out of the corner of his mouth.

"Well, Angelus," people said, "you made a racket back there. . . ."

He weakened. "Wait here for the action," he gritted. "Cheerio, Angelus."

Johnny Henson and Vera his missus laughed openly. "The Good Lord heard us today, Angelus!" Johnny went past shaking his head.

"I got the murderer," Angelus finally said frankly to the people as they left. It sounded lame, some sort of mere excuse. Nobody took any notice. Jim Warboys told Angelus wearily, "Angelus, lad. Give it a rest."

"But, Jim. It's Mr. Curson—"

"Curson? He's just coming."

And people milled out into the evening air, trampling all over Angelus.

Sal marched out, blazing. "You come straight home, Angelus Fluck!"

"No, Sal. I've got Mary Cottesloe's murderer—"

"*Angelus!* Will you please stop all this? You've ruined the service—"

"Mr. Curson," Angelus bleated to the smiling man emerging from the porch behind Sal. "Excuse me, erm, please. You're under arrest, for—"

"Eh?" Mr. Curson grinned wider, handing his Elsie on to the path. "Arrest? Noticed a crack in the plaster, Angelus?"

There was a general laugh at that, and the crowd poured on over his protests.

"No. Wait. Erm—"

"Evening, Angelus. Calmed down, eh?"

"I know who killed—"

"Great, great. 'Night, Sal."

"Angelus! Come on this instant!"

"But, Sal—"

Cars started in the lane nearby. Reverend Williams and Betty Dockett started locking the postern and Dolly Day began hurrying home to her seventeen cats.

Angelus felt everything slipping out of his hands. It had to be done now, while people were still about.

In despair, he signalled to Sal that he needed a pee. Her lips went thin in fury but he grimaced and apologetically escaped towards the hedge. The old church had no amenities. Sal was left tapping her foot prettily by the old yew hedge while Jim Warboys and his missus chatted to her about the flower rota. Angelus hurried frantically from the churchyard. He vaguely supposed people didn't care in those days and simply used the hedgerows.

Jim's car was a new Ford, police property. It was parked on the old flint path which ran past the church, the path poor dead Mary had taken on that last fatal stroll when she had seen Mr. Curson replacing the stained glass window. Maybe she had even tried to steal a piece of the modern glass for evidence. It would all come out at Curson's trial.

Angelus paused beside the police car. Jim Warboys would do his nut. He picked up the largest flint cobble he could find. The one thing he could remember from *A Private Eye's Manual* was that you got nicked for damaging police property. That meant gaol. And that meant a statement, witnessed and authenticated, even if it was in a police cell. A trial even. And, oh Jesus, maybe even a sentence. But the dedicated private eye stops at nothing.

"God rest, Mary," Angelus said. He blinked away his tears and smashed the cobble against the police car windscreen. It crizzled at the first blow, producing such amazing patterns he almost forgot himself. Then he remembered his duty and did the rest, one after the other, regular as clockwork, with sounds like the crack of doom.

A smile played about his lips. It didn't feel debonair as all that, but it was the first of its kind and he kept it going as the shouts began and people came running.

MICHAEL GILBERT

CAMFORD COTTAGE

For more than thirty years Michael Gilbert has remained one of England's leading mystery writers, ever since his fourth novel, Smallbone Deceased *(1950), was hailed as a modern classic of the genre. He has written realistic police procedurals, romantic thrillers, pure detective stories, and highly acclaimed espionage tales. To my knowledge this is his first ghost story, but as one might expect from Gilbert, the ghost is secondary to a well-developed mystery plot.*

"THEN I KNOW IT," SAID MISS SYMONDSON, "I'M certain I know it. It's at the top of a cliff. Hardly a cliff, more a headland. It's in a little garden of its own, with fields all round it. And there's a long flight of steps leading down from it to a private landing stage."

"The same place, without doubt," said Miss Melchior. "It's some distance from any village. How did you come to be familiar with it?"

"I'd hardly call it familiar, since I had tea there, once only. But it was an exceptionally fine tea. That was thirty years ago. I cannot have been more than five or six at the time."

"It must have been in the days of 'Prince' Camford, the artist. He had no use for architects, you know. The house, we were told, was built by local builders from a sketch he made on the back of a drawing pad. And very well built, too, in local brick."

"I didn't realize, of course, that he was a famous artist. To me he was just a funny man with a beard. He'd come on my

older brother and sister and me, playing some game in the
bushes at the top of the headland, Pirates or Indians. We were
dressed in holiday rags and he got us to pose for nearly an hour
while he made sketches of us. Then he took us down to the
house for tea. Cornish butter and cream, on scones baked by his
wife, a dumpy little woman with grey hair.''

"Also an artist," said Miss Melchior. "A water-colourist.
You can still see her Cornish seascapes in the galleries." Miss
Melchior was a woman who knew things like that. "They are
both dead now. My brother bought the cottage—it had some
other name—I forget it—but he named it 'Camford Cottage'
after its famous builder and owner. He and Patricia spent their
honeymoon there. They were the only people who ever lived in
it.''

"What a tragedy," said Miss Symondson. She was not
thinking of the honeymoon, but of what had happened at
Camford Cottage some years later. A tragedy which had been
widely reported.

Frank Melchior and his wife were keen sailors; Frank possibly
a little keener than Patricia, who was apt to be sick if the sea was
rough. They had set out one evening intending to sail down to
the south-west, with a favouring wind, spend the night at sea,
round the point of Land's End, and finish up by beating up to
Fowey, where they had friends. It was a trip they had made
many times before. On this occasion they ran into rougher
weather than they had catered for. Their boat lost its mast, the
auxiliary engine failed, and they were driven on to the Pen-
Gallion Shoals. Fishermen, who had observed their plight in
the early dawn, picked up Frank; Patricia's body was never
recovered.

"He shut the cottage up for years after that. No one was
allowed into it. He wouldn't listen to any suggestion of selling
it. Not that he had to bother about the financial side of it.
Patricia was a Dupont, and her money went to him. Poor com-
pensation for a broken heart, but on top of what he was earning
already, it left him free to get on with his writing."

"I read his last one a few weeks ago, when I was in bed. The
nursing home got it for me out of the public library. I can't afford to pay nearly four pounds for a detective story."

"I don't believe anyone can," said Miss Melchior. "Have you met my brother?"

"Yes, once, when he came to give a talk at the school. We were all introduced. I thought him rather formidable."

"It changed him, of course."

"Has the cottage been closed ever since—ever since it happened?"

"No. In the end I persuaded him that he was being selfish." Miss Melchior spoke with the firmness of an elder sister. "We took some of his nephews and nieces, and I went down with him. I told him, 'You'll find no ghosts in Camford Cottage. It's a happy place.' The holiday was a great success. Pol-en-Perro is a wonderful place for children."

"I certainly remember it as such," said Miss Symondson wistfully. "I suppose that development has spoilt it now."

"Not a bit. The land round the cottage is farmland, and very good farmland too, I believe. No one can touch it. And, of course, when the weather was fine the children enjoyed the tiny private beach at the bottom of the steps, and the boating. Frank was nervous about letting them use the boat at all, but I told him, 'Forget the past, live in the present.' "

It had sometimes occurred to Miss Symondson that the reason Miss Melchior, who was handsome and well endowed, was not married might be on account of her firmness with everyone. She was one of the governors of the school where Miss Symondson taught, and ruled the Chairman and other governors with a rod of iron. Nevertheless, she could be kind. She had been very kind to her, when a bout of influenza, coming on top of an exceptionally hard term's work, had nearly carried her away. It was Miss Melchior who had whisked her out of her lodgings and into a private nursing home; and it was Miss Melchior who had dragooned the doctors into taking her case seriously. Now she was proposing a further kindness.

"A week will do you all the good in the world. It will quite set you up for the coming term. I'll order a stack of logs for the sitting-room fire. The cooking is all done by bottled gas. I'll have two cylinders delivered. They'll be outside the front door. I'm afraid you'll have to do your own cleaning. Local people won't go into the cottage—not since the tragedy."

"Oh, why?"

"They think it's haunted," said Miss Melchior, in the robust voice in which common-sense people speak of ghosts. "I'm sure you're not one of these people who believes in ghosts."

"If there was one, it should be haunting the Pen-Gallion Shoals, not Camford Cottage."

"*Exactly* what I told my brother. And I can assure you that when we all went down there, there were no psychic manifestations."

"But on previous occasions," said Miss Symondson, "it's only the family who have used the cottage? Are you sure your brother won't mind? Oughtn't we to ask him?"

"To the best of my knowledge, my brother is in Tangiers, gathering material for a new book. He was uncertain of his movements, and left no address. It could take weeks to get an answer."

"If you're sure he wouldn't mind."

"I am ab-so-lutely sure."

When Miss Melchior was ab-so-lutely sure, there was nothing more to be said.

For the first six days it was as agreeable as Miss Melchior had promised. Although it was still early April the summer, as sometimes happens in Cornwall, had seemed to come earlier than it did elsewhere. The days were warm enough for strolling over the headlands and through the deep lanes, already yellow with primrose and white with may-flower. The evenings were cool enough to enjoy the fire of logs which blazed in the wide brick fireplace, set squarely in the middle of the living-room wall.

The nights were a little troublesome at first. Miss Symondson put it down to sleeping in a strange bed, but she was honest enough to admit that it was more than this. She was a child of the city, born and brought up among streets of houses full of people. Holidays had been things you took, with others, in camps or hotels or hostels which were even fuller of people.

Here she was conscious of being surrounded by emptiness. On one side, the sea. On the other three sides, fields. The nearest human habitation was the farmhouse which she visited daily for milk and eggs, half a mile inland down a track which was easily negotiable at this time of year by the tradesmen's vans and by the old taxi which had brought her from Pol-en-Perro Station. It must have become difficult in winter. Her only direct connection with the world outside was a telephone line; a single umbilical cord joining her to the world of men and women.

In the times when she lay awake she comforted herself with what Miss Melchior had said. It was *not* an unhappy house. Why should it be? The tragedy had not happened here, in this snug and civilized cell, but out on the wild grey sea, in a driving wind, among mountainous waves. Sometimes she visualized the helpless boat, its mast gone, its engine useless, drifting on to the fangs of the Pen-Gallion rocks.

She had never herself been on the sea in anything smaller than a cross-Channel steamer, and it is possible that she exaggerated its perils. She looked down on it, timidly, from the edge of the cliffs, but had never even ventured to descend the steps down to the beach and the jetty. They seemed to her to be steep and dangerous. Adequate, no doubt, for nimble children in gym shoes, or for active men and women who took care to use the tarred-rope side rail.

It was on the evening of the sixth day, with the taxi ordered for nine o'clock the next morning, and she was standing at the top of these steps, when it happened.

The day had been the warmest so far, more of an autumn than a spring day, the heat no longer fresh, but turned damp and stale. As she looked out to sea, it was as though a veil, thin at first but thickening, was being drawn across her whole field of vision. The effect was so startling that she passed a hand across her eyes to wipe away what seemed to be a blurring of her sight. Then she realized what was happening. A white fog was rolling up towards the mouth of the Bristol Channel.

It came with astonishing speed. One moment she could see. The next she was blind. One moment she was warm. The next she was shivering with cold. Thank goodness, was her first thought, that I wasn't out on the cliffs, miles from home. I shouldn't have known what to do. She turned round, with great care, took six paces up the path which led from the stairhead, found the front gate, and was soon back inside the cottage.

She turned on the lights in the sitting room, and put a match to the fire, which was neatly laid. Warmth and light soon worked their magic. The fog was outside. She was inside, safe and sound. The next few hours were pleasantly occupied with cooking and eating supper. For this last meal of the holidays she had saved a half-bottle of red wine; and, greatly daring, she drank it all, finishing the last glass with her coffee.

As she sat, pleasantly drowsy, in front of the fire, she found her thoughts going back thirty years. How odd to think that she, the very same person that she was now, changed in body but the same in essence, had sat at almost exactly the same spot that she was sitting at now. Her brother had been on her right, at the top of the tea table, piling the delicious scones with butter and cream and honey, and stuffing them into his mouth one after another. She didn't want to think too much about him. His body was in Northern France, near the spot where his fighter plane had crashed.

Her sister had been sitting beyond him, half scandalized at the amount her brother was eating, half determined not to be left behind. Married now, with children of her own.

And what of herself? If she tried hard, could she summon back the six-year-old child, with pigtails, dressed in shorts, and a grubby aertex shirt, with sandals on the end of brown, scratched legs. She had always been the thoughtful one, the one who noticed things. What had she been thinking about, what had she been looking at, on that summer afternoon, thirty years ago?

There had been a tiny golden clock on the mantelshelf. That had gone, of course, and had been replaced by two vases. To the right of the fireplace, there had been bookshelves. This worried her. Because she was certain that the bookshelf had not been a detached piece of furniture. The shelves, five or six of them, had been fitted into the alcove on the right of the chimney breast. Yes. And in the corresponding alcove on the other side had stood the old grandfather clock. She could remember thinking, how unusual to have two clocks in one room. Big clock and little clock. Grandfather and grandchild.

Why in the world, she said to herself, should anyone have bricked up those two alcoves, so that the wall now stretched, level with the front of the fire, from side to side?

As she asked the question, the room seemed to change. She was looking at it as it had been. The books were back on their shelves on the right, the gold clock winked on the mantelshelf, and old grandfather swung his pendulum solemnly from the recess on the left. She knew that if she could turn her eyes she would see her brother and sister, and their kind host at the other end of the table, but her head was held, as in a vice.

Something was happening to the lights. They were dimming. And the room had grown deadly cold. But it was now, once again, the room of the present, not the past. She was looking at the blank stretch of bricks on the left of the fireplace and at the lady standing in front of them. She felt unsurprised, and unafraid. The lady was smiling. Clearly she meant her no harm. It was not Mrs. Camford. This lady was younger, slimmer, and more fashionably dressed than that grey-haired dumpy water-colourist. Surely she knew the face? She had seen it somewhere, in a fashion magazine. Of course, it was Frank Melchior's wife, Patricia.

Who was dead.

Drowned, battered to pieces, her bones washing about on the floor of the sea, under the Pen-Gallion rocks.

What was she doing here? Why was she standing, quietly, patiently. Standing like someone who had been waiting for help, and knew that help was at hand?

All at once Miss Symondson knew the terrible answer. Moreover, she knew what she had to do, and she was locked to the chair; her body shaken with uncontrollable spasms, the sweat cold on her face.

As she struggled to move, and realized that she was helpless, the spell was suddenly broken.

The telephone was ringing.

A male voice said, "Miss Symondson?"

Scarcely able to speak she gasped out something.

"I can't hear you."

"Yes. It's Miss Symondson."

"My sister told me you were using the cottage. Is something wrong?"

"No. Yes."

"What is it? You're very indistinct."

Miss Symondson said, in tones of one stating some unimportant but incontrovertible fact. "I have just seen your wife. She came out from the recess which used to be beside the fireplace in the sitting room."

During the long silence which followed, she began to realize what it was she had said. He must think her absolutely mad. Perhaps she was mad. People had sometimes told her she was psychic. Had she passed over the borderline between sanity and insanity?

"I'm sure you'll think I'm raving mad," she said, with a pathetic attempt at lightness, "perhaps it was the fog and the general atmosphere and knowing—knowing the story—"

When the man spoke again it was a surprise. Before, his voice, without being rude, had been cold and formal. Now it had reverted to a friendly, conversational level.

He said, "I was interested in something you said just now. You mentioned that this—this apparition—came from the recess which used to be beside the fireplace. How did you know that there was once a recess there?"

"I came to the cottage many years ago, when I was a child. I had tea here."

"That would have been in Prince Camford's time."

"Yes."

A further silence. Then, "I don't want to alarm you, Miss Symondson, but I think you may be in some danger. I don't think you ought to spend tonight alone in the cottage."

"But how—"

"I'm speaking from Plymouth, where I landed earlier today. Is the fog very thick?"

"Yes, very."

"It usually clears before midnight. It will only take me a couple of hours to get to you. I'll fix a room for you at Truro. Sit tight, and, Miss Symondson—"

"Yes?"

"My advice to you is, keep out of the sitting room. Light the stove in the kitchen. You should be safe there."

He rang off.

She had noticed the old black stove in the kitchen, but had not dared to tamper with it. Now she got sticks and paper, and a shovel full of coal, opened the front, and set it going. It showed a tendency to smoke, but this soon cleared, and she was able to put on a few small logs on top of the coal and closed the front. The stove gave out a companionable roar.

To be doing something was a comfort. It helped to keep her mind off the problems of what danger could possibly be lurking in that front room. It helped to pass the time. And that needed help. Only forty minutes since the telephone call. If the mist stayed thick it might take Melchior hours to reach her. He might not be there until morning.

There was a basket full of logs in the front room. They would keep the stove going for an hour or so. The alternative was to fetch a fresh supply from the woodshed, but this would involve making her way out into the fog and crossing the back yard. Surely it could not be dangerous, simply to go back into that room, just for a moment?

When she opened the door she remembered that she had turned out the light, and the switch was on the far side of the room.

She said, out loud, "Don't be such a goose. *There's nothing in the room that can hurt you.* Just walk across and turn on the light."

The fire in the grate had burned low, but it gave enough light for her to see, and avoid the furniture. Her hand was on the switch when she stopped.

The sound was definite and unmistakeable.

Someone was coming up the front path.

By the crunch of the footsteps on the gravel it was a man. He was coming cautiously, but was unable to avoid making some sound.

Miss Symondson was so paralysed with fear that she was unable even to raise her hand to the light switch. She stood in the darkness of the sitting room and watched the figure loom closer through the fog.

Now he was at the door. A hand came out to try the door. Very gently.

Thank God she had bolted it, top and bottom.

The man stood still for a moment, his head bowed as though he was listening. Then he turned and marched straight up to the window, and pressed his face against it.

Miss Symondson, cowering inside, recognized him at once. It was Frank Melchior.

She was filled with unimaginable terror. The first words which came into her head were, "He's come back for his wife."

Plymouth? That was nonsense. He must have lied about that, and lied quite deliberately.

Why had he told her to sit in the kitchen? Was it so that no light would shine out from the front room indicating to any chance passer-by that she was in the cottage?

The man was moving now, quietly, away from the window, on the path that would take him round the house and directly to the kitchen door.

Which, she realized with frozen horror, she had left unlocked.

She tiptoed across to the front door and, with fingers which seemed not to belong to her, slid back the top bolt, and stooped to open the bottom one.

At that moment she heard the sound of the kitchen door being opened, and a voice which said, "Hello, Miss Symondson. Where are you hiding?"

The second bolt slid back. She straightened up and eased the front door open. Gently, gently.

Footsteps crossing the kitchen floor, and the voice again, "Are you in there? I thought I told you not to go in there."

Then she was stumbling down the front path. The front door, as she let go of it, swung shut behind her. The noise must have warned the man that she was escaping. As she reached the front gate she heard heavy footsteps on the path. She stepped off the path, just inside the gate, and cowered down like a wild beast. Like a wild beast, she had the sense to realize that if she moved the man would hear her; and if he heard her, he would catch her.

The footsteps crunched past. The man outside the gate now. His steps were moving away, casting uncertainly, to right and left; lunging into the fog at some supposed shadow.

A sudden scratching of nails, on rock. A wild scream, and a series of horrible bumping noises. Then silence.

Miss Symondson got to her feet, and edged her way out of the gate until she felt the ruts of the track which led to the road.

Down it she stumbled for an eternity of time, blinded by fog, her heart hammering, choking, kept going only by fear of what might be behind her.

As she reached the main road a light showed through the mist; there was a squeal of brakes and a car slid to a halt almost on top of her. The Cornish voice of Police Constable Greig said, "Why the hell can't you look where you're going?" And then, "Why, Miss Symondson. What's to do here?"

"A killer," said Superintendent Assher to the Chief Constable of Cornwall. "A careful killer, and a killer for money."

They were standing in bright sunshine outside the door of the cottage, watching the workmen finish the demolition of the brick wall which concealed the recess behind the fireplace; a recess from which a skeleton, already identified as Patricia Melchior, had been removed and carried to the mortuary.

"You said, a careful killer?"

"Very careful. He must have been planning it for at least a year. He built that little summerhouse with his own hands." He pointed to a neat construction, in the same brick as the house, which stood at the end of the lawn. "He ordered a few hundred more bricks than he needed. And he taught himself, carefully and slowly, how to lay them. I expect his wife watched him, and admired his increasing skill. When the time was ripe, he strangled her, put her body inside, and bricked her up. To balance things, and make the wall look natural, he bricked up the other recess as well."

"Why not just bury her somewhere outside?"

"He was a writer of detective stories, sir. He knew that digging in farmland leaves traces. And if the body was recovered from the sea, the pathologist would know she'd been strangled. Safer to keep her in the house. No one had ever used it, except the two of them. No one ventured in afterwards. Maybe he spread the story of its being haunted. Later, of course, he didn't mind family parties as long as he was there to keep an eye on things. And then, by one chance in ten million, it was let, behind his back, to a woman who'd known the place as a child."

"What do you think he'd have done to her?"

"Thrown her down the steps, no doubt. Everyone would have assumed she was out in the fog, and had slipped, and killed herself. As he did."

The Chief Constable thought about it. He said, "Did you believe what she told us?"

"Most of it," said the Superintendent cautiously.

"About Mrs. Melchior appearing to her."

"I saw no reason to disbelieve that."

"Then you believe in ghosts."

"Certainly," said the Superintendent with a smile. "Good ones and bad ones. This was a good one. She'll sleep easy now, poor soul."

He was smiling because he knew that ghosts were hard things for a stolid Devonian like the Chief Constable to credit. He himself had been born and bred west of the Tamar, and like all Cornishmen knew everything there was to know about ghosts.

RON GOULART

SUSPENSE

*Much of Ron Goulart's best recent work has appeared
outside the mystery field, and at present he holds the
distinction of having had more stories published in* Fantasy & Science Fiction *than any other author. It's been
too many years since he's appeared in an annual best
mystery collection and it's a pleasure to welcome him
back with a story that lives up to its title in a unique
manner.*

WHEN HE HEARD THE HELICOPTER DIRECTLY
overhead, he stopped still beside the massive teakwood
desk. Then, pivoting, Kurt Timmons ran for the half-open
doorway of his spacious paneled den. From the threshold he
could see clean across the vast, stark living room and out the
high wideview window. A chopper, the familiar network logo
emblazoned on its tail, was chuffing down out of the crisp
autumn afternoon.

Before it settled on the slanting acre of lawn, Timmons
turned his back on the vista and grabbed the den door shut. After locking it, he returned the brass key to the pocket of his
khaki slacks. He took a deep breath, smoothed back his dark
curly hair, and strolled to the front door. There was an odd,
quirky smile on his tanned face.

A bulky man in sky-blue coveralls was already out of the cop-
ter, helping the slim raven-haired woman to disembark. She
came out handsome legs first, the brisk wind playing with her
short tweed skirt. Two shaggy-haired young men, one bearing a
portable video camera, the other decked with sound equipment, followed her. The four, with the dark pretty woman in

the lead, marched up across the estate grounds toward Timmons' mansion.

He opened the door before they reached it and looked out. "Was there something?"

The woman—she was thirty-seven and nearly as tan as he was—laughed. "I've heard about you," she said, holding out her hand. "You're a great kidder."

"You must be looking for Gurney Mott up the road. All of Westport, Connecticut, is in awe of his ready wit and—"

"I love banter, but I want to get this damn interview in the can." She circled him and stepped into the house.

"Ah, you must be Wendy Wales," he said. "I clean forgot you were due today."

"Sure—I'll bet." Wendy Wales, hands on her narrow hips, stood in the center of the white-and-black living room, scanning it. "Thirty-five million potential book buyers watch my show. Your publishers have tried cajolery, wheedling, near-seduction, and even out-and-out bribery to get some of their hopeless hacks on it."

"You can't be bought, huh?"

"I wouldn't be worth much if I could, Kurt. I'm doing you because you're hot. Your latest suspense novel—gee, I've got a blank on the damn title—"

"*The Dinglehoffer Gambit,*" he supplied.

"Right," said Wendy. "It's been on the *New York Times* bestseller list for nearly half a year. You just sold the paperback reprints for two and a half million bucks."

"An exaggeration," said Timmons, watching her technicians troop into his mansion. "These are hard times. I had to settle for one and three quarter million. Honest."

Wendy laughed, nodding her pretty head. "That's good— that's fine. Keep up that kind of wiseacre stuff when we're taping. Fifty percent of my audience will automatically hate you for your success—you might as well give 'em good reason."

"I was being truthful."

"Sure." She pointed at the cameraman and then the sound-man. "Both named Ed. Makes things easier."

"I would've thought it—"

"Is that the way he talks?" asked Ed the soundman.

"You'll have to compensate for it, Ed."

"My voice is pleasingly deep and mellow," Kurt said.

"You talk through your nose. Don't worry, we can fix it." She was moving around the big room in ever-widening circles. "What do you think, Ed?"

"Dull," said Ed the cameraman.

The third man said, "Gives us a sort of spartan mood though, Wendy."

"Where do you work?" she asked Timmons.

"In the den, over there." He absently patted the pocket that held the key.

"Maybe we ought to use that."

"I'd prefer to tape the interview out here."

"Why?"

"I'm superstitious about where I work—about having outsiders seeing where I do my stuff."

"You're letting forty million people into your damn house."

"But not into my den." Timmons crossed to a low white sofa and sat on it. "We'll do it here."

The cameraman was looking at Timmons and the sofa through his camera. "Dull."

Wendy went and sat close to Timmons. "Do I brighten it up?"

"Some."

"How about sound, Ed?"

The soundman was on his hands and knees, returning from a wall plug. Now he hooked a tiny mike to the collar of Timmons' checkered shirt. "Know in a second."

"I think the overall look, Wendy—the white walls and drab furniture—is a neat contrast with his colorful books," said the third man as he settled into a black wing-chair.

Wendy sighed. "O.K., we don't have time to futz. We'll do it here. Where's the damn book?"

"*The Dinglehoffer Gambit?*"

"I sure don't mean the Gideon Bible, Kurt."

"Over on the end table there." He started to get up.

"Sit," Wendy ordered. "Ed'll get it."

The soundman deserted his gear to fetch the fat hardcover suspense novel. "I just about finished this," he said, handing it to Timmons. "The scenes in Budapest in 1944 are very convincing."

"They are, yes," agreed Timmons, resting the novel on his knee.

Wendy gently slapped it off. "Sit it on the coffee table when we start," she said. "Then I'll pick it up and hand it to you. At least it's get red on the cover."

"Swastika's going to play nice too," commented Ed the cameraman.

Wendy leaned back and shut her eyes for a few seconds. "O.K., let's do one," she said, coming alive and smiling into the camera. "In this final portion of tonight's show we'll be talking with the most successful suspense writer in America. From his first novel—Cut! I can't remember the damn title of that one either."

Timmons said, "*The Bildocker Strategy* was my first. Then came *The Hermansdorfer Defense*. *The Dinglehoffer Gambit* is my third."

She nodded. "Check—O.K. I've got it." She smiled and the camera resumed running. "For this segment of tonight's show I'm at home with the most successful suspense writer in the world. His first novel, *The Bildocker Strategy*, was an international bestseller, earning him over $24,000,000 to—"

"Twenty-two, actually," put in Timmons.

"He's very truthful and honest is Mr. Kurt Timmons. His second novel, *The Hermansdorfer Defense*, did even better, and his latest, *The Dinglehoffer Gambit*, bids fair to being one of the most successful suspense novels of all time."

She leaned toward Timmons and smiled at him. "How does it feel to be so fantastically successful at such an early age?"

"Actually, Wendy, I'm thirty-seven, and I worked a lot of years before I had my first big one."

She said, "I think our viewers would like to see just exactly how you work, Kurt. Could we get a glimpse of your studio?"

"Perhaps later," he said, grinning and not moving.

She tapped her fingers on the copy of the novel. "I'm pretty well known for not pulling my punches," she said. "So let's try for some controversial stuff. I'd like to talk about your relationship with Leon Saxon."

"You make it sound like an illicit love affair."

Wendy frowned off camera at the man in the wing-chair. "What I meant was, until you came along Saxon was the acknowledged master of the international suspense field you now dominate," she said. "His novel, *The Eisengruber Ploy*, was the bestselling thriller of all time—until your book."

"True."

"Some critics have noted similarities between your work and Saxon's. Coincidence?"

Timmons rubbed his hand on his knee. "I thought perhaps you'd bring up the matter of Leon Saxon," he said slowly and carefully. "As we've been sitting here getting to know each other, Wendy, I've come to a decision."

She studied his tanned face. "Are you kidding me? I know you're noted for your deadpan humor."

"No, no, this is sincere," he assured her. "You really are good with people and, well, listen—I'm going to have to tell this all sooner or later. I might as well unburden with you."

"This has to do with Leon Saxon?"

"With him, with me, with why our novels are so similar," he replied. "It's a somewhat complicated story, Wendy, but I can fit it into the time we have. It'll make a first, an exclusive for you."

"Go ahead," she urged. The camera came in closer to Timmons.

I was married a good deal in my twenties (Timmons began). When I realized the names of all my wives had rhymed—Lilly, Millie, Billie—I decided to call a moratorium on marriage. Quitting my job with the Greater Manhattan Credit Agency, I moved into a seedy apartment on the fringes of Greenwich Village and devoted myself to freelance writing. The first six months I managed to sell an article on self-flagellation to a girlie magazine called *Buttocks*, a crossword puzzle about American Indians to *Jack & Jill*, and a suspense paperback to Bathtub Books. What with rent, household expenses, and alimony to Lilly, Millie, and Billie, my savings account was swiftly dwindling.

It was about this time I first noticed the suspense novels of

Leon Saxon. Every damn bookstore I passed had mounds of his fat bestselling hardcovers in their display windows. And there were all those images of Saxon himself, smirking and leering from the backs of the jackets. He was always bedecked with cameras, claiming he'd visited all the fabulous foreign cities he wrote about in his novels of World War II intrigue.

I hated him.

Once I went inside one of the bookstores, an enormous palace on Fifth Avenue, and pretended I was someone else. I demanded a copy of my paperback and the clerk told me the book didn't exist. He even opened up the latest *Books In Print* to prove it. On my way out I managed to swipe a copy of Saxon's current one, *The Kockenlocker Syndrome*. That evening, huddled in front of the oven in my freezing shabby apartment, I began reading the thing.

It didn't seem fair. Saxon wrote no better than I did. Sure, he seemed to know his 1940s Europe, but his prose was flat. Still, the guy was earning millions while I owed Lily more than four hundred dollars and Millie over six hundred. I made up my mind I was going to topple Saxon. Kurt Timmons was going to have heaps of *his* books in every damn bookshop in the damn country.

"So you set out to ape Saxon's style and format?" asked Wendy.

"Well, I had meant to, but then I encountered Corliss Knapp," he said. "That's K-n-a-p-p. She pronounced it Kuhnap."

"I don't think I know who she—"

"Few people do."

I met Corliss three years ago (Timmons continued). No —four, almost. In Manhattan. It was the annual awards banquet for the Committed Writers of America at the Taft Hotel. I'd never been to a macrobiotic banquet before and I was sort of dawdling over my meal. I wasn't actually much of a committed writer either, but an editor friend who couldn't buy anything from me had sent me a free ticket. I never turned down a meal in those days.

A very pretty young woman took the seat next to mine. She was slim and auburn-haired, and she'd commenced chattering while still lowering herself into the chair. "I'm always late. It's odd too, because I got up earlier than I usually do. People tell me I'm just destined to be late all the time. Not that I know all that many people, being shy most of the time and a recluse sort of except I seem to be always going out to parties and dinners and such. What I'm really more like is a hermit, I guess. You know, who lives in a cave. Except my flat in Soho isn't a cave, though you could sure grow mushrooms there without any help. Hi."

"Hello," I responded. "I'm—"

"My name is Corliss Knapp. That's K-n-a-p-p, pronounced Kuh-napp. Although why am I telling you how to pronounce it when you just heard me say it? I do all sorts of odd things like that. Partly, I believe, because I was an only child. 'One like you is enough,' my late father told me. Did you ever know of anyone who was killed by a falling gargoyle? He was. On Lex and Forty-ninth when they were remodeling a bank. The bank was very considerate—paid for his funeral, gave me a digital clock and a toaster.

"Living with my uncle, Balzac Knapp, didn't help my character much either. I had to move in with him after my father was felled. He was a very eccentric man, Uncle Balzac, and then his car blew up. With him in it. He was a retired spy."

Thus began my relationship with Corliss. It wasn't exactly a romance, although we were fond of each other and spent a good deal of time together. She really was an attractive girl and her name didn't rhyme with Lilly. She had a tendency to prattle, but I'm a good listener. It was during one of her monologues that I came upon the knowledge that would catapult me to the position of America's top suspense writer.

"I actually know him," she told me. "It was the strangest sensation, watching Wendy Wales interview him on television. Not that I much like Wendy Wales, she's so superficial and mock-sincere. And that hair. If I had a wig like hers I'd return it and tell them to give it back to the cat. But, since I'm trying to break into the pages of the *National Lampoon* with my cartoons, I have to be up on what all the fools in the country are into, right? That was what Uncle Balzac always said. Get to know the locals. He was with the OSS, you know, which was something we had before the CIA, and he was in that too, and some other government organizations that were so secret they didn't even have initials.''

"Who was it you saw on the show?" I managed to ask.

This was late on a winter Friday in a booth of a Mexican restaurant on Bleecker. Soft snow was drifting down outside.

"Leon Saxon, who else? I know you loathe him, professional jealousy and all. But you should've watched—you can never get to know your opponent too well. Uncle Balzac always said that. He was a tricky man, and smart. Which is the point.''

"Point of what, Corliss?''

"Leon Saxon. I know him. He's the man who pretended to be a CIA agent after Uncle Balzac blew up in the garage and nearly half the house burned down. I was perplexed and distracted those next few days, arranging for the funeral, wiping soot off what was left, and he claimed he was the CIA and flashed some sort of ID. The more I think of it, the more certain I am it was fake.''

"I've read up on Saxon," I said. "He was never with any government agency. If he had been, he'd be crowing about it.''

"Not necessarily. You aren't supposed to write books if you've been a spy. They're afraid you'll give away all sorts of secrets, which is why Uncle Balzac wrote only for his own fun.''

"This uncle of yours wrote suspense novels?''

She nodded. "Didn't I mention that? It's almost certainly one of the reasons I like you. I just naturally seem to enjoy people who write about international intrigue so—''

"Wait now," I cut in. "Are you saying your late uncle wrote some novels? And Leon Saxon took them?''

"He certainly looks exactly like the man who did. He flashed this fake ID and told me he was with the CIA and they had to take away all Uncle Balzac's papers, because it was SOP. Which means Standard—''

"I know. This guy took how many book manuscripts?''

"Sixteen.''

"Sixteen! Sixteen complete novels?''

"When he retired from the CIA he had more than enough money to live on, so he amused himself by writing these terrific novels. As he finished each one he'd put it in a cardboard carton in his den. Writing was for him what knitting is for some people. He never even bothered to have them typed or anything. He wrote them all in longhand on yellow legal tablets in his very neat handwriting. I have a scratchy penmanship, even when I draw, and I really envied Uncle Balzac his handwriting. When I lived with him he let me read several of the novels and they were really good and I told him he ought to see if there was some way he could have them published. But he said he didn't want the CIA poking around and he didn't want to be a professional writer anyway.''

''Have you read Saxon's new one?''

She said, ''The first chapter. I stopped in a bookshop on the way over here, which is why I was a few minutes late. Well, that and I misplaced one of my mittens. I had to look all through the—''

''Did you recognize the chapter?''

''Yes,'' she said. ''Almost word for word, as I remember.''

I sat back, smiling broadly. ''Corliss, Leon Saxon is a plagiarist.''

''He certainly is,'' she agreed. ''Except I've been pondering it, Kurt, and I don't see, since he took all the manuscripts and notes, how we can ever prove it.''

''I'll prove it,'' I assured her.

Getting the goods on Leon Saxon wasn't all that difficult. It didn't require even the ingenuity of a secret agent in one of his novels—in one of Uncle Balzac's novels, that is.

Through a friend of mine left behind at the credit outfit I did some digging into Saxon's background and learned he never was with Central Intelligence. He'd been living in South Norwalk, Connecticut, when he'd met Corliss's uncle a few years before. Like me, he'd been making a second-rate living grinding out romance paperbacks, usually $2,000 per book and no royalties. He augmented his writing income by teaching creative writing at various Adult Ed night classes in Fairfield County.

The six-week course he taught at the Westport YMCA attracted a male high school English teacher, two housewives, a teenage boy who weighed just under three hundred pounds and wanted to follow in the footsteps of Ray Bradbury, and Uncle Balzac. Uncle Balzac sat in on the course mostly to amuse himself. He never submitted any of his work for criticism and analysis. One evening, however, he and Saxon had a couple of drinks together down at the Arrow and Corliss's ex-spy uncle talked about his novels. After a few rounds he invited Saxon over to his house—this was before Corliss's father had been felled by the gargoyle and she wasn't in residence with her uncle.

When Saxon read the first chapter of the first novel in the pile, even numbed by a few drinks he realized Uncle Balzac was an infinitely better writer than he was. The book was packed with suspense, rich in first-hand local color about Europe, and deft in its handling of the political intrigues of the Nineteen Forties and early Fifties. Always eager to turn an extra buck, Saxon offered to act as his literary agent. There were sixteen novels in all and he was betting they were all equally good and all saleable.

But it could only be a hobby for Corliss's uncle. He just wanted to write for his own amusement. That was it.

To a confirmed scuffler like Leon Saxon, who'd never been able to write just for the fun of it, Balzac Knapp's attitude seemed idiotic.

Five months later Uncle Balzac suffered his fatal accident.

Wendy made a nervous gasping sound. "Are you hinting that Leon Saxon murdered the man? Killed him so he could get his hands on these potentially valuable manuscripts?"

"Oh, no," said Timmons, grinning. "I'm only accusing Saxon of fraud, theft, and plagiarism."

Saxon posed as a CIA agent come to clamp down a lid of security (Timmons went on). He got the whole lot of sixteen handwritten novels plus all the notes and related papers.

He spent the next week in his apartment and read every word of all the novels. He was stunned—awed. This crusty fifty-six-year-old ex-spy had been able to turn out a string of books better than anything Saxon could ever produce. But he had them now.

He was cautious. He waited anxiously for two full months, to be absolutely certain Corliss had truly been conned, then he proceeded. Saxon was an excellent typist and he turned out a nice clean copy of the first book in under two weeks. That was *The Hickenlooper Bypass.*

The second publisher he showed it to offered him $25,000—the price of twelve and a half paperbacks. Scared inside, he held out for $40,000. They upped the offer to $30,000 and he took it.

Well, as you know, that book took off fantastically. It was on the *New York Times* list from the day it appeared, stayed there a full year, and was still on the hardcover list when the paperback edition took the number-one spot on the softcover list.

He realized that by husbanding his store of stolen manuscripts he'd be able to go on for maybe twenty to twenty-five years, getting bigger and bigger advances and more and more peripheral benefits.

The first few months after that first one took off were anxious ones. He was worried about what would happen if Corliss happened to read it. But she apparently didn't, and gradually he came to think of the books as his.

He'd still be thinking that if I hadn't swiped the remaining dozen from him.

Saxon was living well by then—damned well. He had an enormous beachfront mansion in Southport on the Sound. One evening while Saxon was out on the Coast talking over his latest movie deal I broke into the mansion.

There was an alarm system, but it was quite primitive. I'd done enough crime research to be able to outfox it with no real trouble. I was fairly certain he wouldn't store the unused original manuscripts in an obvious place like the big safe in his redwood-paneled study—a room, by the way, larger than my entire apartment and full of books, phonograph records, and expensive cameras. I was right. They were stashed, each wrapped in brown paper, in a cabinet in his game room, mixed with other similar-looking parcels, all marked "Tax Records." Stuffing them in a laundry sack I borrowed from his sparkling laundry room, I departed.

At home in my tacky apartment I read one of the novels. The

manuscript was in Balzac Knapp's handwriting, each page dated. There was absolutely no way Leon Saxon could ever dare claim them—any of them—as his.

This was absolute proof that he had indeed stolen his whole career from Corliss's uncle. With a good attorney she ought to be able to collect plenty from Saxon.

But suppose I typed up this book myself? I might be able to get twenty or thirty thousand for it—more than I could earn in a year of hustling paperback assignments. Hell—more than I could earn in *two* scrabbling years.

The trouble was Corliss. She had a strong sense of justice, of what's right and what's wrong. If any more of these books were to be published I knew she's insist Balzac Knapp's name appear as the author. And if the CIA ever got wind of that they might *really* swoop down and grab the manuscripts.

So I lied to Corliss.

I told her I hadn't been able to find a thing.

That first appropriated novel was *The Bildocker Strategy* and it was more successful than anything Saxon had ever put out under his name. Incredible amounts of money started coming my way. I gave up my apartment on the fringes of the Village and bought this place. Everything went beautifully. I even believed Corliss wasn't going to have time—being so busy pursuing her cartooning—to read it.

She came out to see me often. One lovely autumn afternoon we went for a hike in a nature preserve over in Weston called Devil's Den.

"It's so idyllic and primeval, just the two of us, climbing this rocky hillside hand-in-hand," Corliss said. "No one around, no problems. It's like life must've been in the Garden of Eden, although I wonder if they had maple trees and those little prickly weeds there. But they had two of everything, didn't they? Or was that on the Ark? Why'd you do it?"

"Do what?" I asked her. I glanced down into the rocky ravine on our right.

"Steal Uncle Balzac's books."

"I didn't. You've got me mixed up with—"

"C'mon, don't con me, Kurt. We're old pals and we shouldn't lie to each other. You *did* find the manuscripts that night, and you took them. Maybe, since I'm sure there's a scrap of decency in you, you really and truly intended to return them to me and help me expose Saxon, but the temptation was too great. You'd been envying Saxon for so long and now you had a way to imitate his success and catch up with him. It was borrowed plumage, but you'd look good in it, you decided."

"You're uncle's dead. The money from the books won't help him," I told her. "Look, I'm sorry I lied to you. We can split all the profits fifty-fifty. Although, since I did sell the book, maybe I ought to get a slightly larger—"

"No, I couldn't do that." She shook her head. "It simply isn't honest. I'm nothing without my integrity. If it was money I wanted I'd simply have blackmailed Leon Saxon. What I'm seeking is justice. We have to bring this sorry mess out into the open, alert the media, make the truth known."

"I can't do that, Corliss. For one thing, it would stop my income."

"You have to have faith in youself. I'm sure a book you write yourself could be nearly as good as—"

"No!" I shouted.

She lost her balance then and went falling down into the rockstrewn ravine.

I scrambled down after her and—made sure she was dead.

While I was bending over her I thought I heard something from above—a faint scraping and then a click. I straightened up, looked around, saw nothing.

The day was fading when I left Corliss. I went running back toward the entryway to the preserve, shouting and sobbing. "Help! Help! There's been a terrible accident!"

Where I made my mistake was in underestimating Leon Saxon. He'd been doing some investigative work himself and, by various means, had found out a good deal about me. After he read *The Bildocker Strategy* he knew I was the one Corliss had told about the manuscripts. He began patiently tracking us and was in Devil's Den, moving quietly in our wake, on the afternoon she fell to her death.

Of course the camera-laden bastard had taken pictures. He didn't intend to turn me in, only to use the photos of me using a stone on Corliss's skull to get what he wanted.

When he came to call on me he had the photographs and the negatives on him. "There are still nine manuscripts left," he said in that smirky voice of his. He was gloating as he sat facing me across my teakwood desk. "That's the price of these photos and negatives."

"All nine, huh?" I said.

"You dumped me from the bestseller list." He tapped the incriminating photos on the edge of the desk. "I need to get back. But I'm realistic enough to know I can't do it without the Balzac Knapp manuscripts. I tried a novel on my own and—" He shuddered.

"Nope," I told him, "those books are going to appear as Kurt Timmons novels."

"Royalties won't do you any good in prison, my boy," Saxon countered, "and that's exactly where you'll be, doing life for murder. Maybe, considering your literary reputation, you'll only have to serve twenty or thir—ooof!"

I'd stood up and smashed a heavy stone paperweight down on his skull.

His pudgy chin whacked the desk top and his eyes fluttered. I hit him again. Twice more. Then again.

His skull made crackling, crunching noises and he slumped to the floor, the pictures falling free from his dead fingers.

I gathered them up, frisked him, and took the negatives.

Stepping around his body, I threw them all into the study fireplace and burned them up.

There were several seconds of dead air. Finally Wendy asked, "Why are you confiding all this to me?"

"Because Leon Saxon called on me this very afternoon." Timmons stood up. "Just as I was watching the photos and negatives turn to ashes I heard your helicopter arriving. I locked the den and put on a smiling face to greet you and your crew, but I realize there's no way I can keep what I've done hidden—not with all of you here."

Wendy took a deep breath, then laughed tentatively. "I get it—this is one of your pranks," she said. "The whole yarn is a put-on, isn't it?"

Timmons crossed to the door of the den and unlocked it. He beckoned to her and the cameraman. "Come on," he invited. "Take a look."

JOYCE HARRINGTON
SWEET BABY JENNY

Joyce Harrington is one of those few writers who won the Mystery Writers of America Edgar Award with her first published short story and then went on to top it with a series of fine stories and two recently published novels, No One Knows My Name *(1980) and* Family Reunion *(1982). If you're not a Harrington fan already, this story should make you one.*

I NEVER HAD A MOTHER, LEASTWAYS NOT ONE that I can remember. I must have had one sometime, 'cause as far as I can tell I didn't hatch out from no egg. And even chicks get to snuggle up under the hen for a little space before she kicks them out of the nest. But I didn't have no hen to snuggle up to, or to peck me upside the head if I did something wrong.

Not that I would ever do anything wrong. Leastways not if I knowed it was wrong. There are lots of things that go on that are pure puzzlement to me, and I can't tell the right from the wrong of it. For instance, I recollect when Ace—that's my biggest big brother and the one who taken care of us all after Pop went away—I recollect when he used to work driving a beer truck round to all the stores in town and the root cellar used to be full of six-packs all the time. I said to him one day, "Ace, how come if you got the cellar full of beer, I can't have the cellar full of Coke-Cola? I don't like beer." Guess I was about nine or ten years old at the time and never could get my fill of Coke-Cola.

Well, Ace, he just laughed and said, "Sweet Baby Jenny" —that's what they all called me even after I was well growed up—"Sweet Baby Jenny, if I drove a Coke-Cola truck you could float away to heaven on an ocean of it. Now, just drink your beer and learn to like it.''

I wasn't ever dumb, even though I didn't do so good in school, so it didn't take much figuring to catch onto the fact that Ace was delivering almost as much beer to the root cellar as he was to Big Jumbo's Superette down on Main Street. So it didn't seem fair when I got caught in the five-and-dime with a lipstick in my pocket for him to come barreling down and given me hellfire and damnation in front of that suet-faced manager. I just stood there looking at him with pig-stickers in my eyes until we got out to the truck and I said to him, "What's the difference between one teensy-weensy lipstick and a cellar full of beer?''

He says to me, grinning, "Is that a riddle?''

And I says, "No, I would surely like to know.''

And he says, "The difference, Sweet Baby Jenny, is that you got caught.''

Now I ask you.

It was different, though, when he got caught. Then he cussed and swore and kicked the porch till it like to fallen off the house all the while the boys from the beer company was hauling that beer up from the root cellar and stowing it back on the truck. When they drove away, I says to him, sweet as molasses, "Ace, honey, why you carrying on so?''

And he says, "Dammit, Jenny, they taken away my beer. I don't give a hoot about the job, it was a jackass job anyway, but I worked hard for that beer and they didn't ought to taken it away.''

"But, Ace," I says, hanging onto his hand and swinging it like a jumping rope, "ain't it true you stolen that beer and you got caught and you had to give it back just like I did with that lipstick?''

Well, he flung me away from him till I fetched up against the old washing machine that was resting in the yard waiting for somebody to fix it, and he yelled, "I ain't stolen anything and don't you ever say I did! That beer was what they call a fringe benefit, only they didn't know they was givin' it. They don't even pay me enough to keep you in pigtail ribbons and have beer money besides. I only taken what I deserve.''

Well, he was right on one score. I didn't have anything you could rightfully call a hair ribbon, and I kept my braids tied up with the strings off of Deucy's old Bull Durham pouches.

Deucy, you maybe guessed, is my second biggest big brother and a shiftless lazy skunk even though some people think he's handsome and should be a movie star. Ace's name in the family Bible is Arthur, and Deucy is written down as Dennis. Then there's Earl, Wesley, and Pembrook. And then there's me, Jennet Maybelle. That's the last name on the birth page. Over on the death side the last name written in is Flora Janine Taggert. It's written in black spiky letters like the pen was stabbing at the page, and the date is just about a month or so after my name was written on the birth page. I know that's my mother, although no one ever told me. And no one ever told me how she died. As for Pop, there ain't no page in the Bible for people who just up and go away.

Deucy plays guitar and sings and thinks he's Conway Twitty. Says he's gonna go to Nashville and come back driving a leopardskin Cadillac. I'd surely like to see that, though I don't guess I ever will. That Deucy's too lazy to get up off the porch swing to fetch himself a drink of water. It's always, "Sweet Baby Jenny, get me this and get me that." Only thing he's not too lazy for is to boost himself up to the supper table.

That don't keep the girls from flocking round, bringing him presents and smirking like the pig that et the baby's diaper. They all hope and pray that they're gonna be the one to go to Nashville with him and ride back in that Cadillac. And he don't trouble to relieve their minds on the subject. You ought to hear that porch swing creak in the dark of night. They are just so dumb.

Now, Earl and Wesley, they try. They ain't too good-looking, though they do have the Taggert black hair and the Taggert nose. I remember Pop saying he was part Cherokee and all his sons showed it. But while Ace and Deucy came out looking like Indian chiefs, Earl is crosseyed and Wesley broke his nose falling out of a buckeye tree and lost most of his hair to the scarlet fever. So they try. They are always going into business together.

Once they went into the egg business and we had the whole place full of chickens running around. They said they would sell

their eggs cheaper than anyone around and make a fortune and
we'd all go off to California and live in a big hotel with a swimming pool and waiters bringing hamburgers every time we
snapped our fingers. Well, people bought the eggs all right,
but what Earl and Wesley kind of forgot about was that 200
chickens eat up a lot of chicken feed and they never could figure
out how to get ahead of the bill at the feed store. I could have
told them how to do it was raise the price of the eggs and make
them out to be something special so everyone would feel they
had to have Taggert's Country-Fresh eggs no matter what they
cost. But Earl and Wesley just shoved me aside and said,
"Sweet Baby Jenny, you are just a girl and don't understand
bidness. Now go on out and feed them chickens and gather up
them eggs and let's have some of your good old peach cobbler
for supper. Being in bidness sure does make a man hungry."

Well, pretty soon the feed store cut off their credit and there
wasn't nothing left to feed the chickens, so we had to eat as
many of them as we could before they all starved to death and
that was the end of the egg business. Earl and Wesley, being
both tender-hearted and brought down by gloom, couldn't
bring themselves to kill a single chicken. I like to wrung my arm
off wringing those chicken necks. I used to like fried chicken,
but I don't any more.

Pembrook, he's the smart one. He don't steal, sing, or go
into business. He's off at the state college studying how to be a
lawyer. He's the only one used to talk to me and I miss him. I
was always planning to ask him what happened to our mother,
how she died, and why Pop ran off like he did. But I just never
got up the nerve.

Pembrook writes me letters a couple times a month, telling
what it's like up there at the college. It sure sounds fine. He's
always going on at me how I should go back to school and finish
up and come to the college and learn how to *be* somebody.
Well, I'd kind of like that, but who'd look after the boys?
Reason why I didn't do so good in school was I never had no
time for studying, what with looking after the boys like I was
their mother instead of Sweet Baby Jenny like they call me.
Only Pembrook never called me that.

Another thing I always meant to ask Pembrook and never did

is how come I come out looking like a canary in a cuckoo-bird's nest. Pembrook looks more or less just like the other boys, though he keeps his black hair real clean and he wears big eyeglasses on top of his sharp Taggert nose. His eyes are dark brown like theirs, and he weathers up nice and tan in the summer sun. But in summer my freckles just get more so while the part in between the freckles gets red. And my hair, which is mud-yellow most of the time, gets brighter and brighter and kinks up in tight little curls unless I keep it braided up. And never mind my eyes. They're not a bit like the boys'. Greeney-blue or bluey-green depending on the weather. As for my nose, it couldn't be less Taggert if it was a pump handle. Small and turned up and ugly.

Could be I taken after my mother, though I don't know that for a fact 'cause I never set eyes on her nor saw any picture of her.

Pembrook says I'm pretty but that's just because he likes me. Pembrook says I look a lot like Miss Claudia Carpenter who is regarded as the prettiest girl in two counties, but I never saw her to make the comparison. She's the daughter of the town's one and only bank president. She's a year or so older than me, and she don't stick around much. Got sent away to school and always taking trips here and there. Can't be much fun, never being home in your own home place. Pembrook told me our mother used to help out at the Carpenter household, at parties and such or when their regular maid got sick. Maybe I could get such a job and put aside a little money, just in case I ever decide to do what Pembrook says.

One thing I do remember about Pop before he went away. He used to tell me stories. He used to sit himself down in his big maroon armchair and he would sit me down on his lap and he would say, "Now, listen. This here's a story about a bad little girl." The stories were always different but they were all about a girl named Bad Penny. She was ugly and mean and spiteful and nobody liked her. She was always making trouble and in the end she always got punished. Sometimes she got et up by the pigs and sometimes she got drowned in the creek. Once she got cut up in little bits by the disc harrow. And another time she fell into the granary and suffocated in the wheat. But she always came back, as mean and nasty as ever, and that's why she was called Bad Penny. After the story Pop would take me up to my room and put me to bed.

I liked the stories, even though they scared me some. I knew pigs didn't eat little girls, but I was always pretty careful around the pigpen. We don't keep pigs any more, but we had a few then and I used to carry the slops out to them.

Well, things got so bad after Ace robbed the gas station down at the crossroads and got recognized by Junior Mulligan who just happened to be having his pickup truck filled up with gas at the time and never did like Ace since the time they two went hunting together and Ace claimed it was *his* deer and knocked Junior into Dead Man's Gully and broken his leg. So off Junior went to the police and they come and drug Ace out of the Red Rooster Café where he was treating everyone to beer and hard-boiled eggs.

It was sad and lonesome around the place without Ace to stir things up, and quiet with Deucy's guitar in hock and him not able to sing a blessed note through mourning for it. Earl and Wesley tried selling insurance round about, but nobody we knew could buy any and the folks we didn't know wouldn't. So it was up to me.

I harked back to my idea of going as a maid like Pembrook had told me our mother had done. I didn't mind working in someone else's house, though Deucy said it was undignified and not befitting a Taggert. Far as I could see, Deucy thought any kind of work was undignified except maybe wearing out the porch swing. So one morning I washed my whole body including my hair, and cut my toenails so I could put shoes on, and got out one of our mother's dresses from the wardrobe in the attic, and made ready to go see Mrs. Carpenter. The dress fit me right well, though it was a little long and looked a bit peculiar with my high-top lace-up sneakers but that was all I had, so it would have to do.

I walked into town, fanning the skirt of the dress around me and blowing down the front of it from time to time so the sweat would not make stains on the green-and-white polkadots. I got to the Carpenter house before the sun got halfway up the sky, about the time Deucy would be rolling out of bed and yelling his head off for coffee. This was one morning he'd just have to find his own breakfast. I stood for a while with my hand on the iron gate looking up at the house. It was a big one, shining white like a wedding cake, and there must have been about two dozen windows on the front of it alone. It set back from the street on what looked like an acre of the greenest grass I ever saw sloping up to a row of prickly bushes that trimmed the porch.

I'd seen it before, times Ace used to take me riding in the beer truck and tell me how all he needed was to rob the bank and then we'd be living in this part of town alongside the rich folks. But I never really took a good close look, 'cause I thought he was joking. Now I looked until I got to shaking and wondering if I ought to march right up to the front door or sneak around to the back. I stood there so long I felt like my feet had taken root to the pavement, and if I could only get loose I'd run home and stay there forever.

But then I thought about how there was less than a half a pound of coffee left and just enough flour for one more batch of biscuits, and I pulled open that iron gate and set my face toward the big front door. It felt like an hour that I was walking up that path with my feet feeling like big old river rafts and my hair jumping out of the braids that I'd combed and plaited so neat. But I got up on the porch and put my finger on the doorbell and heard it ding-donging away inside. I waited. But the door stayed closed.

It was a pretty door, painted white like the rest of the house, and I studied every panel of it and the big brass doorknob and the letter box beside it while I waited. I wondered if I should ring the bell again. Maybe no one was home. Maybe I'd come all this way for nothing. They probably wouldn't want me to be their maid even if they were home. The green-and-white dress was sagging down around my shinbones and my sneakers were covered with road dust. Maybe I'd just go home and wait until I got a better idea.

I turned away and started down the porch steps, and then I heard the door open behind me and a sharp voice like a bluejay's said, "Yes?"

I looked back and saw a tall skinny woman staring at me with a frown betwixt her eyes that made me shiver in spite of the heat. "Miz Carpenter?" I said.

"Yes, I'm Mrs. Carpenter," she said. "Who are you? What do you want? I'm very busy."

My throat got choked and I couldn't swallow, so when I said, "I come to be your maid," I thought maybe she couldn't hear me, 'cause I couldn't hear me myself.

"What?" she said. "Speak up. What's this about a maid?"

"I come to be it," I said. "If you'll have me."

"Well, sakes alive!" she said, showing all her yellow teeth. "If you aren't the answer to a prayer! Where did you spring from, and who told you to come here? Well, never mind all that. Come in the house and let's get started. You look strong. I just hope you're willing."

"Yes, ma'am," I said, and quick as a wink she drug me through the house and into the kitchen and right up to the sink where there was more dishes than I'd ever seen in my life and all of them dirty.

"Just start right in," she said. "The dishwasher's right there. I'll be back in a few minutes."

Now I'd seen dishwashing machines in the Sears Roebuck wish book, but I'd never been right up close to one. I knew what *it* was supposed to do. I just wasn't too sure what *I* was supposed to do. And I didn't trust anything very much except my own two hands. So I started getting those dishes as clean as I could before I put them in the machine, just in case we had a misunderstanding. They were the prettiest dishes I ever did see, even when they was all crusted with dried-up gravy.

Mrs. Carpenter came back in a few minutes carrying a pair of black shoes and a white dress. She plopped herself down on a kitchen chair and smiled at me. "What's your name, child?"

"Jennet Maybelle."

She didn't let me get the Taggert part in, but went right on talking.

"Well, I'll call you Jenny. That Marcelline quit on me last night right in the middle of a dinner party, and I was just about to start calling around when you walked in the door. I'll pay you five dollars a day plus meals and uniform, but you have to pay for anything you break, so be careful with those dishes. Each plate cost twenty dollars."

I put down the plate I was holding and tried to think what it could be made of. It didn't look to be solid gold. Our plates at home were old and cracked and been around as long as I could remember. I didn't know what they cost. When one got broke we just threw it down in the creek bed behind the house along with all the other trash.

Mrs. Carpenter was still talking. "Now you can't be wearing those sneakers around the house, so I brought you an old pair of Claudia's shoes. Maybe they'll fit. And this uniform might be a little big for you, you're a skinny little thing, but we can cinch it in with a belt."

I didn't think much of her calling me skinny when she so closely resembled a beanpole herself. But I didn't say anything. The shoes looked nice with just a little bit of a high heel and shiny black, and the uniform dress was starched and clean.

She stopped talking for a minute and started looking me over real close. Then, "Haven't I seen you somewhere before? I could swear your face is familiar. Where do you come from?"

I pointed in the direction of home and said, "Out Clinch Valley Road." I was going to tell her how my mother had once worked as a maid for her, but she didn't give me a chance. She jumped up, left the shoes on the floor and the dress on the chair, and shook her head.

"I don't know anyone out that way. You can change your clothes in the maid's room back there." She waved her hand at a door on the other side of the kitchen. "And when you finish the dishes you'll find me upstairs. I'll show you how to do the bedrooms."

The day wore on. I didn't break any dishes and figured out on my own which button to push to start the machine. It sure gave me a start when it began churning and spattering behind its closed door, and I prayed it wouldn't go breaking any of those twenty-dollar plates and blaming it on me. Mrs. Carpenter showed me all over that house and told me what I was to do. At noon, she showed me what to make for lunch. We both ate the same thing, cold roast beef left over from the night before and some potato salad, but she ate hers in the dining room and I ate mine in the kitchen.

I drank two glasses of ice-cold milk and could have drunk some more, but I didn't want to seem greedy. In the afternoon she set me to washing windows. It wasn't hard work, I worked harder at home, and it was a treat to be looking out at the roses in the back and all that green grass in the front while I polished those windows till they looked like they weren't there at all.

Along about four o'clock she hauled me back to the kitchen and told me what Mr. Carpenter wanted for his dinner. "He's very partial to fried chicken, but nobody seems able to make it to his satisfaction. I know I can't. And he has the most outrageous sweet tooth. I don't eat dessert myself, but he won't leave the table without it."

Well. I set to work cooking up my specialties. I'd had lots of experience with chicken, and my peach cobbler was just about perfect, if I say so myself. Mrs. Carpenter left the kitchen to take a nap after telling me that Mr. Carpenter expected to sit down to his meal at 6:30 sharp.

At 6:30 sharp I brought in a platter of fried chicken and Mr. Carpenter whipped his napkin into his lap and dug in. He didn't even look at me, but I looked at him. He was a freckly sandy man with gold-rimmed glasses and a tight collar. He still had all his hair, but it was fading out to a kind of pinkish yellowish fuzz. His eyes were blue, or maybe green, it was hard to tell behind his glasses, and his nose turned up at the end like a hoe blade.

I'd fixed up a mess of greens to go with the chicken and he dug into those, too, dribbling the pot liquor down his chin and swabbing it away with his fine napkin. Mrs. Carpenter pecked at her food and watched to see how he was liking his.

When I brought in the peach cobbler he leaned back in his chair and sighed. "That's the best meal I've had in years, Marcelline."

"This isn't Marcelline," said Mrs. Carpenter. "Marcelline quit last night. This is Jenny."

He looked at me then. First through his glasses and then without his glasses. And then he polished his glasses on his napkin and put them back on and tried again. "Ah, ha!" he said. "Jenny. Well. Very nice." And he got up from the table and left the room without even tasting my peach cobbler.

Mrs. Carpenter was after him like a shot. "Paul! Paul!" she hollered. "What about your dessert?"

It didn't matter to me. Peach cobbler is best while it's hot, but it's just as good the next day. I carried it back out to the kitchen, finished cleaning up, and got back into my going-home clothes. I did hope that Mrs. Carpenter would pay me my five dollars so I would have something to show to Deucy and Earl and Wesley, so I hung around for a bit.

But it wasn't Mrs. Carpenter who came into the kitchen. It was him. He stood in the doorway, pulling at his ear and looking at me as if he wished me off the face of the earth. Then he sloped into the kitchen and came right up to me where I was standing with my back against the refrigerator and took my chin in his hand. He held my face up so I had to look at him unless I closed my eyes, which I did for half a minute, but I opened them again because I was beginning to get scared. Then he put his hand on my shoulder and took the collar of my dress between his fingers and felt of it softly. At last he spoke.

"You're a Taggert, aren't you, girl?"

"Yes, I am. I'm Jennet Maybelle Taggert." I spoke up proudly because I'd learned in the little bit of time I'd spent in school that lots of folks thought Taggerts was trash and the only way to deal with that was not to be ashamed.

Then he said something I didn't understand. "Am I never to be rid of Taggerts? Will Taggerts hound me to my grave?"

"You look pretty healthy to me," I said, adding "sir" so he wouldn't think I was being pert.

He didn't say anything to that, but took his wallet out of his pocket and opened it up. I thought he was going to pay me my five dollars, so I got ready to say thank you and good night, but he pulled out a photograph and handed it to me.

"Who do you think that is?" he asked me.

Well, I looked but I didn't know who it was. The photograph was in color and it showed a girl about my age with yellow curling hair and a big smile. She was wearing a real pretty dress, all blue and ruffly, like she was going to a party or a dance. I handed the picture back to him.

"She's real pretty, but I don't know who she is."

"She's my daughter, Claudia."

I didn't know what else to say, so I said again, "She's real pretty."

"No, she's not," he said. "She's a spoiled brat. She thinks she's the most beautiful female creature that ever trod the earth. But she's useless, vain, and unlovable. And it's all my fault."

I didn't know why he was telling me all this, but it was making me fidgety and anyway I had to get home to get supper for the boys. They'd be pretty upset that I was so late. "Well," I said, "I guess I'll be getting along."

"Don't go." He grabbed my arm and hauled me over to where there was a mirror hanging on the wall and made me stand in front of it. "Look there," he said. "Who do you see?"

"Well, that's just me." I tried to pull away from him, but he held on tight.

"That's a pretty young woman," he said. "That's what a young woman is supposed to be, decent and clean and modest. I wish you were my daughter, Jenny Taggert, instead of that hellion who won't stay home where she belongs and behaves so no man in his right mind would marry her. How would you like that? Would you like to live here and be my girl?"

Well, I felt my neck getting hot, 'cause Ace had told me that when a man starts paying compliments there's only one thing he's after, and I'd sure heard enough of Deucy speaking sugar words to his ladies on the porch swing.

"Excuse me, Mr. Carpenter," I said, "but I got to be gettin' home and would you please pay me my five dollars so I can carry home some supper to those boys?" I know that was bold, but he was making me nervous and it just came out that way.

He let go of me and pulled out his wallet again. "Is that what Clemmie's paying you? Five dollars? Well, it's not enough. Here and here and here."

The bills came leaping out of his wallet and he stuffed them into my hands. When I looked, I saw I had three ten-dollar bills. Not only that, he started hauling out the leftover chicken that I had put away and shoving it into a paper sack.

"Take the peach cobbler, too," he said, "and anything else you'd like. Take it all."

"Now I can't do that. What would Miz Carpenter say?"

"I'll tell her I ate it for a midnight snack." He laughed then, but it wasn't a happy-sounding laugh. It sounded like something was breaking inside him.

"Thank you, sir," I said, and skedaddled out the back door before he could think up some new craziness that would get me into trouble.

His voice came after me. "You'll come back tomorrow, won't you?"

"Sure thing," I called back. But I wasn't so sure I would. All the way home I pondered on Mr. Carpenter and his strange ways. But I just plain couldn't figure it out. All I could think was that having so much money had addled his mind and I thanked God that we was poor and couldn't afford to be crazy.

I put it all out of my mind, though, when I reached the dirt road that led up to our place. The moon was just clearing the top of the big old lilac bush at the edge of the property, and its kindly light smoothened away some of the ugliness you could see in daylight. The house looked welcoming with lights shining from its windows, and there in the dooryard was Pembrook's dinky little car. I ran up the porch and busted into the house, shouting his name.

They was all gathered in the kitchen and I could see from their dark Taggert faces that I had interrupted an argument. But I didn't care. I set the Carpenter food down on the table and said, "Here's supper, boys. Dig in." Deucy and Earl and Wesley did just that, not even bothering with plates but snatching up that chicken in their fingers.

Then I sat down and took off my left sneaker and pulled out the money. "There and there and there," I said, as I counted the bills out on the table. Deucy's eyes bugged out, and Earl and Wesley shouted, "Whoopee!" as best they could with their mouths full of drumstick meat.

Pembrook looked miserable.

"Where'd you get all that, Jenny?" he asked.

"I went as a maid," I told him.

"Where did you go as a maid?"

"To Miz Carpenter."

"And she gave you all that?"

I was about to lie and say she did, but I was never very good at lying. It makes my nose run. "No. He did."

"You're not to go there any more," said Pembrook.

Well, I'd just about decided that for myself, but I wasn't about to have Pembrook, much as I dearly love him, telling me what not to do. "I will if I want to," I said. "And when did you get home, and how long you staying for?"

"Forever, if I have to, to keep you out of trouble."

"That's pretty nice trouble," piped up Deucy. "Thirty dollars for a day's work and all this food. You ought to have some, Pem."

"Shut up, you idiot!"

I had never seen Pembrook so angry. Taggert blood boils easy, but until this minute Pembrook had always managed to keep his temper under control. He turned back to me, his eyes glittering and mean, like a chicken hawk about to pounce.

"You are not to go back to the Carpenter house, not ever again. You are to put it right out of your mind. And tomorrow I am going to mail that money back. And that's the end of it."

I only said one thing. "Why?"

"Never mind why."

Well, that did it. I had worked hard for that money. Whether it was five dollars or thirty dollars, it was mine. The first money I had ever earned. And Pembrook had no right to take it away from me. I had done nothing wrong, as far as I could see, and it wasn't fair for him to punish me. I reared back in my chair, looked him square in the eye, and opened my mouth.

"Pembrook Taggert, in case you hadn't noticed, I am no longer Sweet Baby Jenny. I am a woman growed and able to make up my own mind about things. You can't stand there and give me orders and tell me to never mind why. I took it from Pop and I took it from Ace and I been taking it from these three, while you've been off at your college learning your way out of this mess. I ain't gonna take it no more."

The hard bitterness faded from his eyes and he took my two hands in his.

"You're right, Jenny," he said. "There are things you ought to know. Come out to the porch swing and I'll tell you."

"Don't make it a long story," Deucy called after us. "Ardith Porter's comin' over tonight and we got things to discuss."

But it was a long story that Pembrook told me. One that went back through the years to the time before I was born. All the boys knew it, but Pop had sworn them on the Bible never to tell me. It accounted for all the things I'd wondered about and never had the gumption to ask. If I had asked, they wouldn't have told me, although Pembrook said he was mighty tempted from time to time because it was my life and I had a right to know.

He told me that Pop wasn't my true father, that Mr. Carpenter was. He told me that about a month after I was born, our mother had told Pop the truth and packed her bag and said she was running off with Mr. Carpenter to have a better life than scratching around on a poor old dirt farm. He told me that Pop had choked the life out of her right there in the bedroom with me looking on with my blind baby eyes from the cradle beside the bed. And then Pop had gone to Mr. Carpenter and told him the whole thing and got him to hush it up because the scandal wouldn't have done anybody any good. They gave out that our mother had died of childbirth fever.

The tears were rolling down my face, but I managed to ask, "How could you keep on living here, after he did that?"

"Well," said Pembrook, "Ace was the oldest and he wasn't but twelve. We had nowhere else to go. And he was our father."

"What happened then?" I asked. "Why did Pop run off?"

"He didn't," said Pembrook. "He lies buried under Mr. Carpenter's rose garden."

He went on to tell me how the years went by and Pop took up drinking and the farm went even further downhill until it was just a wasteland. Then one day Pop got it into his head that Mr. Carpenter ought to be paying money to take care of his child, meaning me. He went up to the Carpenter house, full of liquor and hate, and demanded a thousand dollars. Pembrook and Ace tagged along behind and listened outside the window of a room that was full of books and a big desk and a hunting rifle on the wall over the fireplace.

"I seen that room," I told him. "Miz Carpenter calls it his study."

Pembrook nodded. "That's where Pop got it."

He said how he and Ace heard them arguing in the room, and Mr. Carpenter shouted that it was blackmail and he wouldn't stand for it, and then there was a lot of scuffling around, with Pop shouting that he would kill Mr. Carpenter for ruining his life. And finally there was a shot. Just the one shot, but it was enough. They peeked over the window sill and saw Pop lying on the rug bleeding his life out, and Mr. Carpenter standing there like a statue with the rifle in his hands.

They were about to run away home, but Mr. Carpenter saw them and made them come into the house and help him carry Pop out to the rose garden. The three of them dug up the roses and put Pop in the ground and planted the roses back on top of him. Then Mr. Carpenter told them to get on home and keep their mouths shut or he'd have the marshal come and chuck us all off the farm and into reform school.

And they did, until this minute.

"I guess," said Pembrook, "I guess that's why Ace is so wild, but that's not the way to fix it up. That's why I'm studying to be a lawyer. One of these days I'll know how to take care of Mr. Carpenter legally and make it stick. So that's why I don't want you going back there, Jenny. You're likely to spoil my plan, and it isn't good for him to be reminded that you exist. I need to get him off guard when I'm ready."

I wiped my eyes and blew my nose and said, "Thank you, Pembrook, for telling me. Now I understand."

"And you won't go back."

"I'm going to bed."

And I did. But I didn't sleep. I lay there pondering over the things that Pembrook had told me, trying to find the right and the wrong of it. Our mother was maybe wrong for pleasuring herself with Mr. Carpenter, but if she hadn't I wouldn't be here. Pop was wrong for taking life away from our mother, but she gave him cause in his eyes. Mr. Carpenter was wrong for shooting Pop, but the Taggert blood was up and Pop probably attacked him first. Hardest of all to think about was me being Mr. Carpenter's daughter. If it was true and he knew it, how could he have let me live all these hard years as Sweet Baby Jenny Taggert while that other girl, that Claudia, had everything her heart desired and then some?

Just before dawn I decided what to do. The boys, even Pembrook, were all sound asleep. I got up quiet as a mouse and dressed in our mother's green-and-white polkadot dress and my high-top sneakers and snuck out to the barn. The barn used to be a busy place, but it was still and empty that morning. No more cows to bellow for me to come and milk them, no horses to gaze sad-eyed after an apple or a carrot. Way in the back, behind the piles of rotten harness, in a dark corner draped over with cobwebs, I found what I was looking for.

It was a can of stuff that Pop used to put down to kill the rats that infested the barn and ate their way through the winter fodder. There wasn't much left in the can, and what there was looked dry and caked. Maybe it was so old it wouldn't even work any more. But I scooped some out with a teaspoon and put it into one of Deucy's Bull Durham pouches and set off down the road.

I kept up a good pace because I wanted to get there before Mr. Carpenter went off to the bank, and before the boys woke up and came after me in Pembrook's car. The morning was fresh and cool, and I didn't sweat one bit.

When I got to the Carpenter house, the milkman was just driving away. I went around to the back, picked up the two quarts of milk, and knocked at the back door. Mrs. Carpenter opened up. She looked sleepy-eyed but pleased to see me.

"Why, Jenny," she said, "you're here bright and early. Come in. Come in."

"Yes, ma'am," I said. "I came to make breakfast."

"Well, that's wonderful. Mr. Carpenter is shaving. He'll be down in a few minutes. He likes two four-minute eggs, I never can get them right, two slices of toast, and lots of strong black coffee. And now that you're here, I think I'll go back to bed and get a little more beauty sleep." She giggled like a silly girl, waved at me, and pranced out.

I put the milk away and started in making the coffee. There was an electric coffee pot, but my coffee is good because I make it the old-fashioned way. I boiled up some water and when it was bubbling away, I threw in the ground coffee, lots of it, to make it nice and strong. Then I turned the fire down to keep it hot while it brewed, and I cracked an egg so I could have an eggshell to throw in to make it clear. And I emptied out the stuff that was in the tobacco pouch right into the pot.

When I heard his footsteps on the stairs I put on another pot to boil up water for his eggs. He came into the kitchen smiling and smelling sweet.

"Well, Jenny," he said. "You came back. I'm glad, because you and I are going to get along just fine. You'll be happy here. I'll see to that."

I got out a cup and saucer.

"I been hearing things, Mr. Carpenter," I said. "Things I never dreamed of."

He frowned. "What things have you been hearing, Jenny?"

I poured coffee into the cup.

"I hear that you're my daddy."

He sank down into a kitchen chair. "Yes," he said, "that's true enough."

I put the cup and saucer on the counter to let it cool off a bit so it wouldn't be too hot for him to take a nice big swallow.

"I hear that you shot our Pop and buried him in your rose garden. They're mighty pretty roses you got out there."

He held his head in his two hands. "They swore never to tell you. Those boys swore."

"Pembrook told me because he's afraid I'll come to some harm in your house." I set the cup and saucer on the table in front of him.

"Oh, Jenny, sweet baby Jenny, I would never harm you. If anything, I'd like to make up for all those years I tried to put you out of my mind. I'd like you to come and live here and be my daughter and let me give you all the things you should have had."

"Don't call me that. I'm not a baby any more."

"No, you're not. You're a fine lovely woman, just like your mother was. God, how I loved that woman! She was the only wonderful thing that ever happened in my whole life. I wanted to take her away with me. We were all set to go. We could have gone to some other town or to a big city where no one knew us. We'd have taken you along. And we'd have been happy. Instead, she died."

"Pop killed her. Because of you."

"You know that, too." He sighed. "Yes. He killed her and I killed him, and I've been living out my days in an agony of remorse. There's no one I can talk to. Clemmie doesn't know any of this. Sometimes I wish I were dead."

"Drink your coffee."

The water for his eggs was boiling. Gently I rolled the two eggs into the pot and stuck two slices of bread into the toaster. He left the table and came to where I was working.

"Jenny." He put his hands on my shoulders and turned me around to face him. "What can I do to make it up to you? I'll do anything in my power, and believe me that's a lot. You name it. It's yours."

I thought a minute. Would it be right or wrong to take from this man? I was having my usual trouble figuring out the difference between the two. Would it be right or wrong to let him drink the coffee?

Then I said, "Could you put Pembrook through law school?"

"Consider it done."

"And Earl and Wesley, can you find jobs for them? They're good workers, only down on their luck."

"Tell them to come to the bank."

"And what about Deucy? Would you get him a new guitar and a ticket to Nashville? He sings real fine."

"Not only that. I know Johnny Cash personally. We'll work something out."

"Now this one's hard. Can you get Ace out of jail and set him on a straight path?"

"The warden is Clemmie's cousin. And I own a ranch in Wyoming. He can go there and work off his wildness. But what about you, Jenny. What can I do for you?"

I shrugged. "Oh, I guess I'll just live here for a while. I can help Mrs. Carpenter and sort of keep an eye on things."

He hugged me and planted a big kiss on my cheek. "That's my girl," he said. "That's what I was hoping you'd say. You'll never regret it. Mmm, that coffee smells good."

He was heading back to the table and his coffee cup. But I got there first and swiped it out from under his nose.

"That's coffee's cold," I said. "Come to think of it, the whole batch is bitter. I tasted it before you came down. I'll make some fresh."

I poured all the coffee down the drain and dished him up his eggs and toast. We drank the fresh coffee together, and he went off to his bank.

And that's the way it is now. Pembrook's way *is* better, and he's studying real hard. He'll graduate sooner now that he doesn't have to work his way through. Earl and Wesley really like being bank tellers, and Deucy has his leopard-skin Cadillac and all the girls he can handle, although he says he misses the porch swing. Ace sent a photograph of himself on a horse wearing a big old cowboy hat. He looks funny but he says he's doing fine.

And me? Every day while the roses are blooming I cut some and put them in the house. Mrs. Carpenter just loves them. I'm waiting. Someday us Taggerts are gonna dig up that rose garden.

EDWARD D. HOCH

THE PROBLEM OF THE OCTAGON ROOM

This story of mine, in which country doctor Sam Hawthorne solves a locked room murder on the day of the sheriff's wedding, was a favorite of several readers.

OLD DR. SAM HAWTHORNE ANSWERED THE DOOR on the second ring, and stood blinking into the harsh afternoon sun. He recognized at once the person who stood there, even though they hadn't seen each other in fifty years. "Come in, come in!" he urged. "It's been a long time, hasn't it? A long time since that day in Northmont. No, no, you're not disturbing me. I was expecting someone else, though—a friend who often drops by to hear my stories of the old days. Funny thing, I was going to tell him about you, and about all the others and what happened on the day Sheriff Lens was married. I often think about it, you know. Of all those old mysteries I helped solve back then, the business with the octagon room was unique. Would you like to hear about how it seemed from my viewpoint? Fine, fine! Settle down there and let me pour you—ah—a small libation. We're both old now and a little sherry is good for the circulation. Or would you like something stronger? No? Very well. As you know . . ."

It was December of 1929 (Dr. Sam Hawthorne began), and a mild December it was in Northmont. By Saturday the 14th, the day of the wedding, we'd had no snow at all. In fact, it was a sunny day as I remember it, with the temperature hovering around sixty. I was up early, because Sheriff Lens had asked me to be his best man. We'd grown to be close friends during my years in Northmont, and even though he was nearly twenty years older than me he still liked the idea of me being at his side during the wedding service.

"Sam," he'd told me earlier, "it was back in October, that day at the post office, when I realized how much I really loved Vera Brock." Vera was our postmistress, a spunky, solid woman in her forties who'd run the post office in the general store and now had a building of her own. Vera had never been married, and Sheriff Lens was a widower without any children. They'd drifted together out of companionship more than anything else, and now it had blossomed into love. I couldn't have been happier for them both.

Vera Brock, it turned out, had a hidden streak of sentimentality. She told Sheriff Lens that more than anything else she wanted to be married in the famous octagon room at Eden House, because her mother and father had been married at an octagon house on Cape Cod forty-five years earlier. Now the sheriff was a religious man, even if it didn't show too often, and he wanted to be married at the Baptist church just as he'd been the first time. They had a little disagreement about that until I solved the problem by talking to the minister, Dr. Tompkins, who reluctantly agreed to perform the ceremony in the octagon room.

Eden House was a fine old place on the edge of town. It had been built by Joshua Eden in the mid-1800's, during the so-called "octagon craze" that swept the nation and was especially prevalent in upstate New York and New England. His fascination with octagon houses caused him to install a mirrored octagon room on the main floor of his new home. Its construction had been quite simple. He'd taken a large square room, originally designed as a study, and cut off each of the four corners with a mirrored cabinet that reached from floor to ceiling. The width of the mirrored doors was the same as the sections of wall between them, so the shape of the room was a true octagon. When you entered through the room's only outer door you faced the large sunny window on the south side of the house. The walls to the left and right, between the mirrored segments, were hung with 19th Century sporting prints. It was an odd but cheerful room, if you didn't mind the mirrors.

Behind each of those mirrored doors was a cabinet with shelves reaching from floor to ceiling. There were books and vases and tablecloths and silverware and china and every sort of knickknack crowded onto the shelves. The room itself was almost bare, with only a small table by the window holding a vase of fresh flowers.

At least that's how it looked when I came to inspect it a few days before the ceremony. My guide was young Josh Eden, grandson of the builder, a handsome young man well aware of the family's tradition in Northmont. He unlocked the thick oak door of the room and pulled it open. "As you know, Dr. Sam, we occasionally rent out the octagon room for weddings and private parties. A lovely place like this should be shared by the community, and the sheriff's marriage is an event that deserves the best setting."

"I'm too young to know much about octagon houses," I admitted.

He grinned at that. "I'm younger than you by a year or two, but I'll try to enlighten you. The eight-sided shape was both functional and efficient, but superstition had something to do with it too. Evil spirits were believed to lurk in right-angled corners, and an octagon house without right-angled corners was believed to be free of them. For this reason the houses were popular with spiritualists. In fact, it's said that seances were held in this very room by friends of my grandfather. Seems to me the spirits they conjured up might have been just as bad as the ones they were avoiding."

I glanced at him. "The room is haunted?"

"Some old ghostly stories," he said with a chuckle. He showed me the crowded cabinets and the view from the window as we discussed the wedding. Before we left I noticed him check the window to make sure it was latched on the inside. The heavy wooden door had a key lock and an inside bolt. He couldn't work the bolt from outside, but he did turn the lock with a long slender key.

"Keeping the ghosts locked in?" I asked with a smile.

"There are some valuable antiques in those cabinets," he explained. "I keep the room locked when it's not in use."

Josh's wife Ellen met us at the front stairs, coming down with a load of laundry to be washed. Her blue eyes sparkled as she greeted me. "Hello there, Dr. Sam. I was wondering when you'd come by. Good to see you again!"

She was flushed with the health and beauty of youth, and a bright cheerfulness that always made me envious of Josh Eden. They'd met at college and married soon after, and though they were both a few years younger than me they seemed somehow to be in full charge of their lives. Josh's father Thomas deserted the family after the war, preferring to remain in Paris with a dancer he'd met there. The shock had been too much for Josh's poor mother, who'd died from it, and from the influenza outbreak of 1919.

Josh went on to college and in time the courts ruled his father was dead too, though there was no evidence of it except his continued silence. Eden House had passed to Josh, along with a small inheritance. He'd wisely invested in land rather than stocks, and the recent Wall Street crash had left him virtually unscathed. Still, there was money to be made from renting out the octagon room on occasion. Ellen even talked of converting the entire house to a restaurant if an amendment to repeal Prohibition was ever passed. There was already talk that mounting unemployment might be countered by the jobs created through the rebirth of the liquor industry.

"We're getting ready for the big day on Saturday," I told Ellen. "I just came over to look at the room."

"I'll bet Sheriff Lens is nervous," she said with a grin.

"Not so's you could notice. After all, he's been through it before. It's the first time for Vera."

"I know they'll be very happy," Ellen said.

She seemed quite pleased by the prospect of the wedding, and when we trooped over for the rehearsal on Friday evening she surprised Vera and the sheriff with a hand-made quilt as a wedding present.

"That's so nice!" Vera exclaimed. "We'll have it on our bed!"

"It's just a little something from Josh and me," Ellen murmured. She seemed more subdued than on my previous visit, possibly because of the intimidating presence of Dr. Tompkins.

The minister arrived dressed in a gray suit, greeted Sheriff Lens and Vera with somber good wishes, and then turned to me. "You understand, Dr. Hawthorne, that the service tomorrow morning must be at ten o'clock sharp. I have another wedding over in Shinn Corners at noon. In a church.''

"Don't worry," I assured him, beginning to feel a bit sorry I'd ever become involved with such a pompous man.

We ran quickly through the rehearsal in the octagon room, with Josh and Ellen Eden watching from the doorway. The sheriff and Vera had wanted only two attendants. I was the best man and Vera's close friend Lucy Cole was the maid of honor. Lucy was a charming Southern girl in her late twenties who'd moved to Northmont a year earlier. She helped out sometimes at the post office and had become a close friend of Vera's in the past year.

"You know, Sam," Vera had told me earlier, "if it wasn't for Lucy's encouragement I never could have agreed to marry the sheriff. Once you pass forty, gettin' married for the first time is an awesome decision.''

"But she's never been married, has she?''

"No, not unless she's got a husband down south she's not talkin' about.''

Lucy was an open, attractive young woman—not unlike Ellen Eden in some ways. I couldn't help feeling they were the vanguard of a new age. The books and magazines might be filled with stories of big-city flappers, but I preferred women more like Lucy Cole and Ellen Eden.

After the rehearsal Josh carefully locked the door of the octagon room and walked out with us to my car. "We'll see you all in the morning," he said. A wedding breakfast for a few close friends would be held nearby, followed by a reception later.

I drove the wedding party back to my apartment and opened a bottle of genuine Canadian whiskey. Sheriff Lens sputtered some about breaking the law, but after all it was the night before his wedding. We toasted the bride, and we toasted the groom, and then we toasted Lucy and me for good measure.

I was up early in the morning because I'd promised my nurse April that I'd drive her to the wedding in my car. She was chatty and excited, as she always was at the prospect of weddings and parties. We picked up Sheriff Lens on the way, and I had to admit I'd never seen him dressed so handsomely. I adjusted his formal morning coat and straightened his tie.

"Keep your stomach in and you'll be fine," I said as we walked to the car. "You look great."

"You got the ring, Doc?"

"Don't worry." I patted the pocket of my own coat.

"You both look handsome enough to be on the wedding cake!" April exclaimed as we climbed in the car. "Can I marry the one that's left over?"

"Being a doctor's wife is even worse than being a doctor's nurse," I told her with a chuckle and started the car.

As we pulled up to Eden House, Vera was just getting out of Lucy Cole's little sedan. "Oh, look!" April pointed. "There's the bride!" Then, remembering our passenger, she quickly added, "Don't you look, Sheriff Lens. You're not supposed to see her till the ceremony."

Vera Brock was all in white, with a fancy lace wedding gown that trailed to the ground. She held it up with both hands as she ran to the door of Eden House. In that moment she was a girl again, half her age, and I could see why Sheriff Lens loved her. I parked the car and walked over to meet Lucy.

"Beautiful day for it," I remarked, looking at the cloudless sky. "Maybe this'll be the year without a winter."

Vera had reappeared at the front door, looking slightly exasperated. "They can't get the door of the octagon room open. It's stuck or something."

This seemed to be yet another job for the best man. "I'll go see about it," I said.

Inside I found Ellen Eden and her husband standing together at the thick oak door of the octagon room, looks of bafflement on their faces. "The door won't open," Josh said. "This has never happened before."

I took the key from him and tried it in the lock. It turned, and I could tell the lock was working properly, but still the door would not open. "There's a bolt inside, isn't there?"

"Yes," Josh replied, "but it could only be worked by someone inside the room. And there's no one inside."

"Are you sure about that?"

Josh and his wife exchanged glances. "I'll go around and look in the window," she said.

At this point Dr. Tompkins walked in, already glancing at the large gold pocket watch in his hand. "I hope we're on schedule. As you know, I have a noon wedding in—"

"Just a short delay," I told him. "The door seems to be stuck."

"That doesn't happen in churches."

"I'm sure not."

Ellen hurried in through the back door, out of breath. "The shade is drawn, Josh! You didn't leave it like that, did you?"

"Certainly not! Someone's in there."

"But how could they get in?" I asked reasonably. "I saw you lock up and latch the window."

"The window's still latched," Ellen confirmed.

The minister began to sputter and Josh said, "Please bear with us. We'll break down the door if necessary."

I tapped it with my fist. "That's pretty thick oak."

Josh joined me and pounded on the door. "Open up in there, whoever you are!" he shouted. "We know you're there!"

But there was only silence from behind the door.

"A burglar, probably," Sheriff Lens reasoned. "Trapped and afraid to come out."

"We can break in the window," I suggested.

"No!" Ellen said. "Not unless we have to. We couldn't replace it before Monday and it's December, after all. A sudden storm could damage the room. Look, can't you all pull on the knob? That bolt on the other side of the door isn't very strong."

We followed her advice, turning the knob and yanking. The door seemed to move a fraction of an inch. "April," I called over my shoulder, "bring the tow rope from the trunk of my car."

She returned with it in a few moments, grumbling about getting her hands dirty. We attached the stout rope to the doorknob, made sure again it was unlocked, and Josh and I tugged.

"It's giving!" he said.

"Sheriff," I called out. "I know it's your wedding day, but could you lend us a hand?"

The three of us gave a mighty pull on the rope. It was like the games of tug-of-war I'd played as a child, and we were rewarded by the screeching of screws being pried from wood. The door sprang open, sending us backward, off balance for an instant. Then Josh and I ran into the octagon room together, with Ellen close behind.

Even in the dim light from the shaded window we could make out the man in the center of the floor, arms and legs thrown wide. His clothes were the shabby costume of a tramp, and I'd never seen him before. But with a slim silver dagger in his chest, I had no doubt that he was dead.

Behind me, Lucy Cole screamed.

I stepped around the dead man and crossed the dim room to raise the shade. The single window was indeed latched, and though it was only turned halfway that was enough to lock it firmly. The latch turned easily and I tried to see if it could have been operated somehow from outside, but the window frames fit together snugly, leaving no gap. The panes themselves were unbroken.

I turned back to the room. The door had opened outward, so there was no hiding place behind it. The mirrored cabinets—

"Aren't you going to examine the body?" Josh asked.

"I can see he's dead. Right now it's more important to examine the room."

I was especially interested in the inside bolt which had been pried from its wooden moorings by our tugging. It hung now from the door jamb, the twin screws having been pulled from the door itself. But examining the holes and the traces of wood shavings on the screw threads, I was convinced the bolt had been firmly screwed into the wood of the door.

I noticed a piece of string knotted around the doorknob and tried to remember if it had been there the previous evening. I didn't think so, but I couldn't be sure.

"He's dead, all right," Dr. Tompkins was saying.

I turned from the door. "Dead several hours, judging by the color of his skin. I didn't mean to seem heartless but sometimes you can tell by looking. Does anyone know him?"

Ellen and Josh shook their heads and the minister grumbled, "A tramp passing through town. Sheriff, you shouldn't allow—"

"I recognize him," Lucy Cole said quietly from the doorway.

"Who is he?" I asked her.

"I didn't mean I knew him, just that I recognized him. There were two of them yesterday, walking near the railroad tracks. Both hobos, I suppose. I remember that long stringy hair and the dirty red vest, and those little scars on his face."

Josh Eden came forward to kneel beside the body. "That dagger looks like a silver letter opener from one of our cabinets. Ellen, see if it's missing."

She walked carefully around the body and opened the mirrored door to the left of the window. After rummaging for a moment she said, "It's not here. There may be other things missing too. I can't be sure."

"While we're at it," I suggested, "we'd better check all four of these cabinets."

"What for?" Josh asked.

I was staring down at the body. "Well, unless the killer is hidden inside, on one of those big shelves, it looks like we've got ourselves a murder committed in a particularly impenetrable locked room."

So many things happened in those next few hours that it's hard now to remember them all. But we searched each of the four mirrored cabinets with care and found no one hidden there. I also took measurements to make sure no cabinet had a false back. When we finished I was convinced the killer was not hiding in the room—nor was there any secret passage or trap door out of the room. There was only the single door, bolted from inside, and the single window, latched from inside.

I'd already studied the window latch. Now I went and knelt on the floor by the door, examining the piece of string I'd found knotted around the knob. "Is this string usually here?" I asked Ellen Eden.

She stared at it. "No, it's not ours—unless Josh tied it there for some reason."

But he hadn't. That left the killer or the victim as the likely possibilities. A year or two earlier I'd read S.S. Van Dine's mystery novel, *The Canary Murder Case*, which included a diagram of how a pair of tweezers and a piece of string could be used to turn a door handle from outside a room. It was a clever idea, but it didn't apply to this situation.

I tried to imagine a way in which the string could have been looped around the bolt and pulled to close it, but for one thing the string wasn't long enough. And for another, the door fit so snugly to the jamb that there was not even room for a string to pass through. Even on the bottom, a small strip of wood was nailed to the floor inside the door, apparently to cut down on drafts. I found a longer piece of string and tried shutting the door on it. The fit was so tight the string could not be pulled.

My preoccupation with the locked room had made me forget everything else. Sheriff Lens came to me presently and said, "Doc, it's almost eleven o'clock. The minister's about to leave for Shinn Corners."

"My God! The wedding!"

For all Vera's enchantment with the octagon room, she refused to be married in a room where the blood was not yet dry on the floor. The wedding guests, kept waiting in the cool outside air, were told of the change in plans. We all piled into cars and drove to the nearby church. Though he was miffed by the delay, Dr. Tompkins felt some sort of triumph in getting the ceremony moved to the church. He hurried through the ceremony, paused long enough to shake the groom's hand and peck at the bride's cheek, then vanished toward his noon appointment in a cloud of dust.

"How's it feel to be married again?" I asked the sheriff.

"Wonderful!" he said, hugging his bride with an uncharacteristic display of emotion. "But it looks like we'll have to delay the honeymoon."

"How come?"

"Well, I'm still the sheriff here, Doc, and I got a murder on my hands."

For the moment I'd forgotten about that. "You go ahead on your honeymoon, Sheriff. Your deputies can handle things."

"Them two?" he snorted. "They couldn't find a skunk in a suitcase!"

I took a deep breath. "Don't worry, I've got it under control."

"You mean you know who killed that guy? And how it was done in a locked room?"

"Sure. Don't you worry about it. We'll have the killer in a cell by nightfall."

His eyes widened in admiration. "If that's true we can leave on our honeymoon right after the reception."

"By all means. Don't give the murder another thought."

I turned away, wondering how I'd go about fulfilling that promise.

I started out by taking the maid of honor for a ride in my car. "This isn't the way to the reception," Lucy said after a few minutes. "You're heading back toward town."

"Right now this is more important than the reception," I told her. "You said you saw the dead man walking with someone else."

"Another hobo, that's all."

"Would you recognize the other man if you saw him again?"

"I don't know. I might. He had a bald spot on the back of his head. I remember that much. And a plaid scarf wrapped around his neck."

"Let's go looking."

"But the reception—"

"We'll get there."

I drove down by the railroad station and then followed the street that ran parallel to the tracks. Chances were the dead man's friend was miles away by now, riding some fast freight, especially if he'd been involved in the killing. Still, it was worth the time to try to find him.

A few miles the other side of Northmont we came upon a hobo camp in among the trees. "Wait here," I told Lucy. "I won't be long."

I made my way down the worn path, moving openly through the trees in hopes that the men around the campfire wouldn't panic and flee. One of them, warming his hands near the flames, turned as I approached. "What you want?" he asked.

"I'm a doctor."

"Nobody sick here."

"I'm looking for a man who passed this way yesterday. Wearing a plaid scarf, with a bald spot on his head." I added, "No hat," since that seemed obvious.

"Nobody like that," the man by the fire said. Then he asked, "What you want with him? He ain't got a disease, has he?"

"We don't know what he's got. That's why we're trying to find him."

One of the other men came over to the fire. He was small and nervous and spoke with a southern accent. "It sounds like Mercy, don't it?"

"Shut up!" the first man growled. "This might be a railroad dick for all we know."

"I'm not any sort of dick," I insisted. "Look here." From my pocket I produced a pad of blank prescriptions with my name and address printed across the top. "Does this convince you I'm a doctor?"

The first man looked suddenly sly. "If you're a doctor you could write us a prescription for some whiskey. They sell it in drug stores."

"For medicinal purposes," I said, beginning to feel a bit uneasy. A third man had appeared and was moving around behind me.

Then suddenly Lucy began blowing the horn on my car. The three men, realizing I wasn't alone, backed away. One of them broke into a run toward the tracks. I grabbed the little one, nearest to me, and asked, "Where's Mercy?"

"Let go!"

"Tell me and you're free. Where is he?"

"Down the tracks by the water tower. He's waiting for his friend."

"You know who the friend is?"

"No. They're just travelin' together."

I let go of his collar. "You'd better clear out of here," I warned. "The local sheriff's a mean one."

I ran back to the car and climbed in. "Thanks for blowing the horn," I told Lucy.

"I got scared when they started circling you."

"So did I." We drove down the road along the tracks. "The man we want may be at the water tower."

The tower came into view, outlined against the sky, and suddenly we saw a man in a long shabby coat break from cover and run toward the woods. "I think that's him!" Lucy exclaimed.

I followed after him as far as I could in the car, keeping the bald spot and the flapping plaid scarf in sight. Then I was out of the car and chasing him on foot. I was a good twenty years younger than he was, and I ran him down quickly.

He squirmed in my grip and whined, "I didn't do anything wrong!"

"Are you the one they call Mercy?"

"Yes, I guess so."

"I'm not going to hurt you. I just want to ask some questions."

"What about?"

"You were seen with another man yesterday. He had long stringy hair, turning gray, and was wearing a dirty red vest. Man in his fifties, about your age, with some scars on his face."

"Yeah, we rode up from Florida together."

"Who is he? Tell me about him."

"Name's Tommy, that's all I know. We shared a boxcar from Orlando to just outside New York, then we hopped another train up here."

"Why'd you want to come here?" I asked. "Why travel from Florida to New England in December? Do you like snow?"

"He wanted to come here, an' I didn't have anything better to do."

"Why was he coming here?"

"Said he could get a lot of money up here. Money that belonged to him."

"And he told you to wait here?"

"Yeah. He left me last night. Said he should be back by noon, but I haven't seen him."

"You won't be seeing him," I said. "Someone murdered him during the night."

"God!"

"What else did he say about the money that belonged to him? Where was it?"

"He didn't tell me."

"He must have said something. You were with him all the way from Florida."

The man called Mercy looked away nervously. "All he said was that he was coming home. Coming home to Eden."

I dropped Lucy Cole at the restaurant where the reception was being held and then drove back to Eden House. It was almost dark when I pulled up in front, the brief December sun already vanished beyond the line of trees to the west. Josh Eden came to the door, looking tired and troubled.

"How did the wedding go?" he asked.

"Very well, all things considered. They'll be leaving on their honeymoon soon."

"I'm glad this terrible event didn't ruin the day for them."

"I was wondering if I could see the octagon room again. Sheriff Lens asked me to assist his deputies in the investigation."

"Certainly." He led the way into the house. The door stood open and I could see he'd been working on repairing the damaged woodwork where the bolt had been torn loose. The room itself was in semi-darkness, with the drawn shade admitting only a single spot of fading light through a pinhole in its middle.

"I had to draw the shade," Josh Eden explained. "The neighborhood kids were all coming to look in at the murder scene."

"Kids will do that," I agreed. "But the shade was usually left up at night, wasn't it?"

"Oh, yes—you saw me lock up yesterday. The shade was up."

"Then either the victim or his killer had to lower it."

"Seems so. If they had a light on they might not have wanted outsiders to see what they were doing."

"Which was—?"

"Why, robbing me, of course! It seemed obvious enough. Lucy Cole said she saw the dead man with another tramp yesterday. The two of them got in here to rob me, had an argument, and the other one stabbed him with that dagger letter opener."

"How'd they get in without forcing a door or window? More important, how'd the killer get out?"

"I don't know," he admitted.

"The dead man's name was Tommy."

Josh raised his eyes to meet mine. "How'd you find that out?"

"He traveled north from Florida to come here, to Eden House, to regain his fortune."

"What are you saying, Sam?"

"I think the dead man was your father. The father who never came back from the war."

It had grown so dark in the octagon room that we could barely see each other. Josh reached for the wall switch and snapped on the overhead light. Instantly our mirror images were reflected in the cabinet doors. "That's insane!" he said. "Don't you think I'd know my own father?"

"Yes, I do. You might have known him enough to kill him when he returned after twelve years to take back your house and inheritance. He wasn't your father any more. He was merely the man who'd deserted you and your mother all those years ago."

"I didn't kill him," Josh insisted. "I didn't even know him!"

I heard a movement behind me in the hall. "I know you didn't," I said with a sigh. "Come in, Ellen, and tell us why you murdered your father-in-law."

She stood there, pale and trembling, in the doorway of the octagon room. I had seen her reflection in the glass, knew she'd been listening to every word. "I—I didn't mean to—"she gasped, and Josh ran to her side.

"Ellen, what's he saying? This can't be true!"

"Oh, it's true enough," I told him. "And she'd have had a much better chance convincing a jury it was an accident if she hadn't gone to such lengths to cover her traces with this locked-room business. Your father, Tommy, came here last night to take back what was his. You slept through it all, but Ellen heard him at the door and let him in. I suppose she took him into this room so their voices wouldn't awaken you. And there he was, this tramp insisting he was your father, saying he wasn't dead at all and he'd come to take back Eden House. She saw her plans for the place—the restaurant and all the rest of it—going up in smoke. She went to the cabinet, seized that silver letter opener shaped like a dagger, and plunged it into his chest in a moment of insane fury."

Josh was still shaking his head in disbelief. "How could you know that? How could she have killed him and left the room locked from the inside?"

"I didn't know how it was done until I came back here just

now, until we walked in here and I saw that pinhole of light in the center of the shade."

"There is a hole in the shade! Funny I never noticed it before."

"I'm sure it wasn't there until last night. You see, this octagon room is different from many rooms in two respects—the door and the window are exactly opposite each other, and the door opens outward."

"I don't see—"

"Ellen tied a string to the doorknob and attached the other end to the window latch. Then she went out the window. When we yanked open the door this morning, the string turned the latch and locked the window. It's as simple as that."

Josh's mouth fell open. "Wait a minute—"

"I examined the latch as soon as we entered the room. It worked very easily and it was only turned halfway—just enough to lock the window. She'd put a loose loop of string around it, and when the latch reached the halfway mark, pointing into the room, the string slid off just as she'd planned. Of course I never thought of anything like that because the shade was drawn. That's why she made the tiny hole in the shade—for the string to pass through. After she climbed out the window she had to lower the window and the shade together to keep the string in position, but that wasn't difficult. The slight slack in the string was taken up quickly enough when we opened the door."

"If this is true what happened to the string?"

"The loop was yanked off the latch and through the hole in the shade. It probably trailed along the floor somewhere. We didn't notice it in the dim light when we burst into the room. I went immediately to the window to examine it, and you two were right behind me. Ellen simply grabbed the string and snapped it off the doorknob. She'd have liked to get it all, but it broke and she had to leave the piece around the knob."

"Even if I believe that, why does it have to be Ellen? There were several of us present. Myself, Lucy Cole—"

He wanted so much to believe in her innocence. I hated to shatter his last hope. "It had to be Ellen, Josh—don't you see that? It was Ellen who went around the back of the house and told us the window was latched. It was Ellen who persuaded us not to break in through the window but to pull on the door—that was the only way her scheme would work. It had to be Ellen and no one else.''

"But why make it a locked room in the first place? Why go to the trouble and risk?''

"He was too big for her to carry the body off somewhere. Ideally she should have left the window open so he would look like a burglar killed by his partner. But you see Ellen didn't know about any partner until Lucy mentioned seeing two hobos together. That convinced me Lucy wasn't involved—because she surely would have left the window open to implicate the other hobo. No, Ellen had to leave the body where it was, so she wanted it locked away from the rest of the house, cut off from you and her. She bolted the door and set the string to latch the window, perhaps imagining the death would be blamed on the old ghostly stories about the room.''

Finally he removed his protective arms from his wife and stepped back to ask, "Is this true, Ellen?''

Old Dr. Sam Hawthorne leaned back in his chair and reached for his glass. "And of course it was true, wasn't it, Ellen?''

The woman across from him was almost as old as he, but she held herself erect and proud. Her face was lined and her hair was white, but it was still Ellen Eden, not that much different, considering the passage of fifty years. "Of course it was true, Sam. I killed the old man then and I would do it again. I don't blame you for helping send me to prison. They were long years but I never blamed you for that. What I blame you for is my loss of Josh.''

"I had nothing to do with—''

"I went to prison and after a time he divorced me. That was the blow—to know that I'd never be going back to Eden House. And then I heard he married Lucy Cole.''

"Those things happen. The two of you were very much alike. I'm not surprised he turned to her after you were gone.''

"But you see I killed the old man to save Eden House, to preserve my dream of its future. And that was what you took away from me—Eden House and Josh.''

"I'm sorry.''

"After I was released from prison I moved across the country. But I never forgot you, Sam. Sometimes I thought I wanted to kill you for ruining my life."

"You ruined your own life, Ellen."

She sighed and seemed to slump in her chair. The life, the fight, had almost gone out of her. But not quite. "I killed a man who deserted his family for another woman, who came back a bum to steal from his own son. Was that such a bad thing for me to do?"

Sam Hawthorne studied her face for a long time before replying. Then he said, very quietly, "Tommy Eden never left his family for another woman, Ellen. He stayed in France after the war because his face was terribly disfigured by a wound. To me as a doctor those little scars meant plastic surgery, and that explained why Josh didn't recognize his own father's body. I never mentioned it at the trial because Josh had enough grief already. But the man you killed didn't deserve to die. And the sentence you served in prison was a just one."

She took a deep breath. "Ten years ago I might have killed you too, Sam. Now I'm too tired."

"We're all tired, Ellen. Here, let me call you a taxi."

"Well," Dr. Sam Hawthorne said, "come right in! I was expecting you earlier. That old woman getting into the taxi? Funny thing, I'd planned to tell you about her this very day. Settle down while I pour us a little refreshment. If you've got the time, after I tell about the octagon room, I'll give you another story that happened soon afterward—a baffling medical mystery at Pilgrim Memorial Hospital, about a man who died with a bullet in his heart but not a wound on his body!"

CLARK HOWARD

MEXICAN TRIANGLE

Clark Howard, MWA Edgar winner for his 1980 story of New Orleans jazz, returns with an equally powerful story in an entirely different setting—the Mexican oil fields where convicts worked as laborers. Howard has written both fiction and nonfiction about American prisons, and his latest book is American Saturday, *an account of George Jackson's life and death in San Quentin Prison.*

T HE MEN ARRIVED AT VILLAHERMOSA ABOARD A faded yellow bus that had once transported school children before it was phased out as being too antiquated and unsafe. The prison department took it over then, had some bars welded on the windows, and used it for a while to haul convicted men from the Mexico City courts out to Lecumberri Prison. But now that Pemex, the national petroleum company, had begun a pipeline operation in the state of Tabasco, the bus was used to transport *contratistas*—contract prison laborers—from Lecumberri down to the oil fields.

There were fourteen men in this latest shipment—twelve Mexican nationals and two *Norteamericanos*. When they got off the bus, they were lined up in front of a prefab field office. A Mexican police captain addressed them from the porch.

"You men have all volunteered to work in the government oil fields to earn a sentence reduction. All of you are serving two years or less for crimes of a non-violent nature. If you perform well in the fields, your respective sentences will be reduced by one half. In addition, you will receive sixty pesos a week for canteen supplies." Sixty pesos was about five dollars. It was better than nothing.

As the captain was speaking, two Anglos in work clothes came out onto the porch. They were sunburned, weathered men; thickarmed and thick-wristed; narrow-eyed from years of squinting; oil-field men. As the captain spoke, they studied the prisoners.

"Some of you might have volunteered for this job in order to escape," the captain continued. "If so, you will find it relatively easy to do. But when you are captured—as you probably will be—your original sentence will be doubled, and you will be required to serve it at Santa Marta Acatitla."

There was a wave of low muttering at the mention of Santa Marta. The federal prison just outside Mexico City was considered the country's worst hellhole. "I leave you now to Señor Waters, the field foreman, who will give you your labor assignments."

The captain retired to the shade of the field office and one of the Anglos stepped down off the porch. "My name's Glenn Waters," he said in Spanish. "I'm the field foreman. That gentleman there"—he nodded at the older, heavier Anglo—"is Mr. Clyde Madden, the field supervisor. First off, do either of you *Norteamericano* prisoners speak Spanish?"

A young man named Tommy Kerry raised his hand. Waters walked over to him. "What are you in for?"

"Smuggling."

"Smuggling what? Dope? Guns? Young girls? What?"

"Dope. Marijuana. I was down here on vacation and decided to take a kilo back with me. They caught me at the airport."

"What'd you get?"

"Two years."

"Any criminal record in the States?"

"No." Kerry shrugged as if embarrassed. "This was the first time I ever tried anything like, you know, criminal."

"Well, it only takes once, kid," Waters said tonelessly. "Step out of line and wait for me by the porch. The rest of you men turn left and follow me in single file."

Tommy Kerry waited by the porch. Clyde Madden, after

staring at him for a minute, went back into the little field office with the captain. Kerry, hot and tired from the long bus ride, looked around, saw no one who could object, and sat down on the steps. He was twenty-six but had a baby face that made him look younger. Large dark eyes and soft, almost feminine lips made most women want to mother him. He had a reputation for being charming.

Waters returned in a little while and said, "Okay, kid, come with me." He led Tommy to a supply shack. "Give this man three sets of new khakis," he ordered the supply man. While the order was being filled, he said, "Kid, this must be your lucky day. You're going to work in Mr. Madden's house as a helper for his wife. The guy she had run off the other day. Got caught and shipped up to Santa Marta. Mrs. Madden don't speak Mex, so she needs somebody to talk to the help for her. You're it."

Kerry studied Glenn Waters as he talked. Waters was about forty, Kerry figured. A younger version of Clyde Madden: no belly yet, no red veins in his nose from too much tequila, no persistent rivulets of sweat down his neck. Not yet.

"Where you from, Mr. Waters?" Kerry asked as he was handed his khakis.

"Waco, Texas. Why?"

"I thought I recognized your drawl. I'm from Lubbock."

"Lubbock, huh? Good place to be *from*. What are you doing down here—besides smuggling pot, I mean."

Kerry shrugged. "I just got out of the army. Met this girl at a party and she invited me to come to Mexico with her and some of her friends. It sounded better than going back to Lubbock, so—"

"So you came along," Waters finished the story for him. "And when you got ready to go back, somebody suggested taking enough pot along to pay for the trip. You drew straws or rolled dice or something to see who'd carry it—"

"Cut cards."

"—and you were the lucky winner. But the marijuana dog was on duty at the airport that day and sniffed you out of line, right? So you got busted and your friends flew back home to the good old U.S. of A., leaving you holding the bag—or in your case, the kilo."

"Sounds like you've heard the story before."

"That one and a dozen others, kid." They left the supply shack and walked down the rutted dirt road. "I been working the fields for twenty years, kid, since I was younger than you. I've worked 'em in Texas, Oklahoma, Alaska, Iran, Kuwait, just about any place you can name that's got oil underneath it. And one thing I learned a long time ago: if a man's smart, he don't break no laws in no foreign country. Doing time is bad enough—but doing time in a foreign slammer is the pits. You're lucky you got this labor deal, otherwise you'd have to do your whole two years at Lecumberri. Things can get pretty rough on a *gringo* at *el Palacio Negro*."

"At what?"

"*El Palacio Negro*. That's what they call Lecumberri—the Black Palace. Except for Santa Marta, it's the worst prison in Mexico. Nearly a hundred years old. Rat-infested. Built to hold 800 men—and it's got more than *two thousand* crammed into it. *Frijoles* and rice at every meal, every day. And if you get out of line they turn you over to a gun called *El Turko*, who used to work in one of them Istanbul prisons. They say *El Turko* is an expert at teaching prisoners how to behave properly."

"I guess I'm lucky to be out of there," Kerry said.

"Double lucky," said Waters. "Lucky not to be in Lecumberri, and lucky to get the job in Mr. Madden's house."

After Kerry cleaned up and dressed in a new set of khakis, Waters took him over to the Madden house. They went in through the back door and waited in the kitchen where two *campesinos*—local people—were cooking and cleaning. Presently Clyde Madden and his wife Lorna came in. Lorna was younger than Kerry expected, probably a couple of years under forty. Plain, angular, bony-hipped, she also had perfect calves and wide attractive shoulders.

Madden sat down at the table and hollered for two cold beers to be brought over for him and Waters. "All right, boy," he said to Kerry, "lemme tell you 'bout the kind of work them other cons on the bus with you's gonna be doing. They gonna be tarring our drilling pipe. For twelve hours a day they'll be working with boiling tar. So hot it'll burn your skin right off, so shiny black that it half blinds you, so stinking the smell of it stays in your nose permanent. We give 'em a ghost cream, a kind of white paste, to put on their faces to protect 'em from splatters, and we give 'em 'spestos gloves for their hands. That makes the job a little easier, but not much. The only thing that'll keep our drilling pipe from corroding is that hot tar when it dries. Putting it on is the worst job in the fields—that's why we give it to the cons. I want you to 'member all that when you're doing this nice clean work up here for my wife. Understan' me?''

"Yes, sir, I do," Kerry said. "I appreciate the job, sir." He glanced over at Lorna Madden. "I'll do everything I can to help Mrs. Madden." Their eyes met, held for an instant, parted.

"There's three domestics," Madden said. "A cook, a cleaning woman, and a handyman. Miz Madden will give them their daily orders through you, an' you'll be responsible for seeing that ever'thing gets done. Keep your nose clean and stay in line, understan'?" Madden studied Kerry for a moment. "You ain't got no sex offenses on your record, have you?"

"No, sir," Kerry replied emphatically. "Not me, sir. Just dope smuggling, is all."

Madden got up and walked over to Lorna. "All yours, sweetie," he said, patting her on the rear. Kerry heard her say, "Clyde, please," and push his hand away.

"Let's go, Glenn. See you later, sweetie."

Madden and Waters left. Tommy Kerry remained standing next to the back door until finally Lorna looked over at him and said, "Well, come on over here and get yourself some coffee if you want to."

"Yes, ma'am. Thank you, ma'am."

Kerry came over to the stove. While the cook poured his coffee, he held out his hand to Lorna Madden. "It's nice to meet you, Mrs. Madden."

Lorna shook hands with him. Kerry held onto her hand for just a second longer than necessary. And they both knew it.

Kerry's work around the Madden household was easy

enough. He translated to the three domestics whatever instructions Lorna Madden had for them; checked periodically throughout the day to make sure they were doing their jobs properly; and the rest of the time he just made himself generally useful. For a while he kept busy painting the outside trim around the windows, and the railing around the front porch. He stripped and stained a couple of old straightback chairs, making them look like new; and sanded the runners of two dresser drawers that stuck. He even put new shelves in the pantry and built vegetable and fruit bins under the bottom one.

"My, you *are* handy," Lorna praised. "Where in the world did you learn to do all those things?"

"My granddad, mostly," Kerry told her. "He raised me on his farm out in west Texas. When you grow up on a farm you pick up a lot about mending and building and fixing. Seemed like there was always something that needed repair."

Sometimes Lorna asked him to help with her flowers. She had a planter box outside every window and experimented with anything she thought might grow. "I'm always surprised when a new variety blooms," she admitted. "Sometimes I wonder how anything beautiful can flourish in this awful place."

"You don't like it here very much, do you?" Kerry asked.

"No, I'm afraid I don't. Not any more. I used to. When Mr. Madden first brought me here, why, this valley was one of the loveliest places you can imagine. It was a lush tropical landscape where all sorts of wildflowers and fern and ivy grew. And the little village was quiet and sleepy, just like on a picture post-card."

Lorna paused and looked past her front yard, at the sprawling oil field beyond. Her expression tightened. "Then the chainsaw operators came in—an army of them. They cut down everything in sight, everything that grew. After them came the bulldozers to shave off the stumps and leave the land flat. Then the diggers, the drillers, the pipelayers. They turned the village into a shantytown filled with cheap little cantinas and sleazy street-walkers. They made the town square a little dump of paper and plastic and aluminum cans. They brought in a caravan of peddlers selling digital watches, transistor radios, imitation Swiss Army knives, and a lot of other junk to keep the workers from getting home with their wages.'' She shook her head wryly. ''All for the oil. The petroleum. The black gold. The Mexican crude.''

''If you hate it so much, why do you stay?'' Kerry asked.

Lorna answered softly, almost as if she were speaking to a slow child, ''I'm thirty-eight years old, Tommy. I have been married to Mr. Madden since I was sixteen. For twenty-two years I've never been anything but his wife. I'm completely dependent on him for everything—the food I eat, the clothes on my back, the roof over my head. To answer your question, I stay because I have no choice. It's not easy. I have a bottle of sleeping pills in my bathroom. When I can't stand it any longer, I take two or three of them and go to sleep. It's not much of an escape, but it's the only one I've got.''

Before Kerry could say anything further, they both noticed Clyde Madden's pickup coming down the road in front of a funnel of dust. They looked at each other for a moment, then Lorna sighed.

''You'd better get on around back. Mr. Madden wouldn't like us working together like this.''

That night in the barracks Kerry asked his friend Paco, who bunked next to him, how far it was to the nearest U.S. border station. Paco laughed. ''Oh, not so far, *amigo*. Only about eleven or twelve hundred kilometers.''

''How far is that in miles?''

Paco shrugged. ''I'm not sure. I think about seven hundred.'' His expression turned serious. ''*Too* far, *amigo*,'' he said quietly.

Kerry was lying on his bunk. As usual he tried not to breathe too deeply because of the pervading smell of petroleum in the air. It was a constant thing, that smell; it got into a man's nostrils and mouth, throat and lungs; you could taste it with every word spoken or every bite taken. The only time Kerry ever got away from it was in the air-conditioned cleanness of the Madden house.

Getting up, Kerry stuck his head out the glassless window to see if there was any breeze outside. There was not. All he got was a breath of night air thick with the fumes of natural gas burnoff from the wellheads. In the distance the otherwise dark sky had an orange glow from the burning. As Kerry stared at the glow, he saw above it in the black upper sky a minute light moving slowly from south to north. A plane. Turning, he sat on the edge of Paco's bunk.

"How far to the nearest commercial airport?"

Paco thought for a moment. "I think that would be Gutierrez. It's about a two-hour drive south."

"Good road?"

"Narrow," said Paco, "but paved all the way."

"Do you know where they have air service to?"

"Mexico City. Maybe Vera Cruz and Campeche, I don't know."

"But Mexico City for sure?"

"*Sí*. That's the one place you can always get to. But listen, *amigo*, you'd be a fool to try it. A *gringo* like you, all alone—"

"Maybe I won't be alone," Kerry murmured.

The next time Kerry was helping Lorna Madden with her flowers, he said matter-of-factly, "I've decided to escape, Lorna."

She stared at him incredulously; he was not sure whether it was because he had told her he intended to run, or because he had called her by her given name.

"You're crazy," she said after a few moments.

"Maybe I am. But I'm going to try anyway. I've made up my mind."

"If they catch you, you'll get put back in prison with a double sentence."

"*If* they catch me."

"They catch nearly everybody that runs. The few who do make it are Mexes. No white man has ever escaped from these fields."

Kerry shrugged. "Maybe I'll be the first. Anyway, if I do get caught, it'll still be better than being here." Seeing a frown come to Lorna's face, Kerry quickly took her hand. "I didn't mean that the way it sounded. It's wonderful being here with you. You're the only good thing that's happened to me since I got out of the army and came down to this damned country. But I've begun to feel about these oil fields as you do; I've begun to hate them as you do. The smell of petroleum, the dust, the ugliness. Then there's—well, never mind, that's no concern of yours—"

"What?" she asked, squeezing his hand. "I want to know."

Kerry looked away, refusing to meet her eyes. "The Mexes in the barracks are jealous because I've got such an easy job. They—they've been talking about ganging up some night and dragging me into the shower room. I don't know how much of it is just talk—" He shrugged and still did not look at her.

"My God," Lorna said softly.

They stood in silence for a little while, their hands still together; it was her holding his hand now—the older woman comforting the younger man. He seemed so vulnerable with his large dark eyes and soft, almost feminine lips. Lorna thought about the shower room and shuddered.

"Come on in the kitchen," she said. "Let's have some coffee and think this out."

The cook had gone to the market and the cleaning woman was upstairs, so they had the kitchen to themselves. Lorna brought in a bottle of Clyde Madden's brandy and laced their coffee.

"I want you to help me, Lorna," Kerry said. "I won't ask you to do anything that would involve you directly, that would get you into any kind of trouble, but I'd like to be able to count on you for a little information."

"What kind of information, Tommy?"

Their eyes held for a moment. There was something about the way she said his name.

"It would be a big help if I knew when Madden was going to be away for the day—so I could get a good headstart before I was missed. And I'd appreciate knowing the shortest way across the fields to the road to Gutierrez."

"Gutierrez? You're making for the airport then?"

"Yes. I'm going to try and stow away on a cargo plane. I found out that the drums of barite drilling mud are flown in from south Texas and then trucked up here. The empty barrels are flown back to Texas. I figure if I can slip onto one of those return planes—''

"How do you plan to get to the airport? It's a hundred miles.''

"I'll hitchhike.''

"That's crazy—a white man hitchhiking on a Mexican highway. How far do you think you'd get?''

"I'm going to steal some wet coffee grounds from your kitchen and darken my face. I think I'll have a good chance.''

Lorna shook her head. "You won't get twenty miles.''

Kerry shrugged. "Maybe not. But I'm going to try. I've *got* to try.''

From outside came the sound of Clyde Madden's pickup again. Lorna quickly took their cups to the sink and rinsed them. Kerry started out the back way. When he got to the door, Lorna's voice stopped him.

"Tommy?''

Kerry looked back at her.

"I'll help you,'' she said. "We'll do it together.''

Kerry nodded. As he went out the back door, he smiled a knowing smile.

That evening, as Kerry was walking down the road that led to his barracks, Glenn Waters pulled up alongside him in a company Jeep. "Hop in,'' he said. Kerry climbed into the passenger seat. Waters threw him an unsmiling look. "You sure put one over on me, didn't you, kid?''

"I don't know what you mean.''

"Like hell you don't. Lecumberri Prison sent me a copy of your record today. The Texas authorities tracked you down here and put an extradition hold on you. You're an escapee from Huntsville and you've got a record as long as my arm.''

Kerry fished a cigarette out of his shirt pocket and lighted it. "What do you figure to do about it?''

"I haven't decided yet,'' Waters replied.

Kerry smiled the same kind of knowing smile again. "While you're making up your mind, you'd better be thinking about how Mr. Madden's going to feel when *he* finds out about my record. We both know how particular he is about who you pick to work in his house. I don't imagine that he's going to be too pleased that you let me work around his wife for two months—especially with that rape conviction I've got. Could cost you your job.''

Waters pulled over to the side of the road and parked. "Pretty smart, aren't you, kid? I didn't know they grew 'em that smart in Lubbock.''

"Just a shade smarter than they grow 'em in Waco,'' Kerry said. He locked eyes with Waters. "Do we make a deal or do we butt heads?''

"What kind of deal did you have in mind?''

"I want out of here.''

Waters shook his head emphatically. "If I got caught helping you escape, *I'd* end up in Santa Marta prison. No, thanks. I'd rather lose my job.''

"You don't have to get directly involved,'' Kerry assured him. "I already have a plan. All I need from you is capital. If you could arrange to leave some money where I'd find it—''

"How much money?''

"A thousand dollars.''

Again the emphatic shake of the head. "I don't have that much—and you don't *need* that much. I'll give you five hundred. Take it or leave it.''

Kerry quickly nodded. "It's a deal. But I'll need one other thing—a company ID badge to get out the gate. An old one will do—one turned in by an ex-employee.''

"Okay. But that's all. And I don't want to know any of the details—not how or when or anything. Understood.''

They worked out a plan. On the next payday Waters would get three hundred in U.S. dollars and two hundred in Mexican pesos, and leave the money and the ID badge in a manila envelope under a drainage pipe at the side of the road. Kerry would pick it up on his way to work.

Kerry told Lorna he would be ready to go anytime after payday. "A couple of guys owe me a few dollars. I want to collect before I go.''

"That'll be perfect,'' said Lorna. "The day after payday Clyde will be gone all day. He has to drive over to the west field and inspect the new rigs that just went up. It's a three-hour drive each way. If we leave thrity minutes after he does, we can get to the airport in Gutierrez and be on a plane for Mexico City before—''

"We?" Kerry interrupted.

"Yes," Lorna said firmly. "I'm going with you." She took hold of his arm with both hands. "Look, I know I'm twelve years older than you, and not very pretty either, so I don't expect you to stay with me. But if we could just help each other get out of here, and maybe stay together until I can find some kind of work—''

"I'll stay with you," Kerry promised. "And I'll take care of you."

"Tommy, don't say that if you don't mean it. I'm so scared of being alone—''

"You won't be alone," he told her. "Stop worrying. Tell me how you want to do it."

Lorna composed herself. "Clyde will be taking Glenn Waters, his field foreman, with him. They usually take Glenn's Jeep because it does better on the field roads. Clyde's pickup will be left here. As soon as they leave, I'll pack my clothes, take all the household money, and be ready to go. You can come in and put on some of Clyde's clothes—they'll be a little big but you can get by. Then you can hide under a tarp in the back of the truck until we get past the gate and out to the Gutierrez highway. It should work all right." She looked quizzically at him. "Shouldn't it?"

"Yeah," Kerry said. "It should work just fine."

On the day after payday Kerry was washing windows at the back of the house when Glenn Waters drove up and parked his Jeep next to Clyde Madden's pickup. On his way into the house Waters paused and looked inquiringly at Kerry. The young convict nodded almost imperceptibly, just enough to let Waters know that he had picked up the manila envelope with the money and the ID badge. The envelope was tucked neatly under his khaki shirt.

Waters knocked and went into the kitchen. A few minutes later he came back out, accompanied by Clyde Madden. The two of them got into the Jeep. Neither man even glanced at Kerry as they drove away.

Kerry continued to wash the windows for several minutes, and then the cook and the cleaning woman emerged from the house and started toward the company store on errands. The handyman was already gone—Kerry had sent him over to the carpenter shop to get a chair leg repaired.

When he was certain no one was around, Kerry went into the house. Lorna was at the breakfast corner, nervously sipping coffee. "Everyone's gone," Kerry said. "Let's get moving."

Lorna put down her cup and swallowed hard. "Upstairs," she said. "Everything's ready."

As they left the kitchen, Kerry slipped a carving knife from the wall holder and held it concealed at his side.

Lorna led the way to the master bedroom. From the closet she handed Kerry some clothes. "These are some things Clyde wore a few years ago when he wasn't so heavy. They'll probably fit you better." Then she saw the knife in his hand. "Why do you have that?" she asked.

Kerry didn't answer. Instead he asked, "Where's the household money"

"It's in the bureau."

"Get it." Kerry put down the knife and undressed to change clothes. He watched Lorna closely as she got a roll of bills from the bureau.

"You're not taking me, are you?" Lorna asked quietly.

"You guessed it, lady."

"I thought we were going to help each other."

"You were only half right." He took the money from her hand and began counting it.

"You need me to get out the gate," she said.

"I don't need you for anything. All I need is that pickup out there." He put the money on a chair with the manila envelope and the knife. Then he had a sudden thought. His eyes swept down to Lorna's perfect calves. Wetting his lips, he glanced at the clock. "On second thought, maybe I do need you for something—"

Stepping over to Lorna, Kerry put both hands on the front of her dress and ripped it open.

"Just hold it right there, punk," said Glenn Waters from the bedroom door. Kerry whirled around and froze. Waters had a pistol leveled at his chest. "Back up against the wall," he ordered.

Lorna hurried over to Waters. "I was afraid you weren't going to make it in time."

"Everything's right on schedule, honey," he said, kissing her briefly on the cheek. "But this next part is going to be hard."

Lorna took a step away from him. "Do it, Glenn," she said determinedly.

Waters hesitated.

"Do it!" Lorna ordered.

Waters shifted the gun to his left hand, closed his right fist, and punched her solidly in the jaw. Lorna dropped to the floor in a heap.

Kerry stared incredulously at Glenn Waters. "What the hell's going on, man?"

Waters gave him a slight smile. "Seems there was an escape attempt this morning," he said matter-of-factly. "The convict assigned to Supervisor Madden's house. The supervisor and I had started out for the west field when he noticed he'd forgotten his inspection log. We drove back to get it. Madden came inside and caught you attacking his wife. There was a struggle and you stuck that kitchen knife in him. His wife ran upstairs. You caught her in the bedroom. I was waiting in the Jeep outside and heard her yell just before you slugged her. I got my pistol out of the utility chest and came inside. You rushed me with the knife and—" Waters shrugged.

Kerry's eyes narrowed. "So it's been you and her all along."

"You got that right, kid. Me and her and old Clyde's company insurance policy. You know that Pemex insures its field supervisors for two hundred thousand?"

"Where's Madden now?"

"Lying on the kitchen floor where I left him, dead to the world. Lorna put six of her sleeping pills in his coffee this morning." He smiled. "It won't matter though, because there won't be an autopsy; not in a stabbing death, not out here. I'll finish him off later."

On the floor, Lorna rolled over and groaned. Glenn Waters

looked down at her, taking his eyes off Kerry for a split-second. But that split-second was long enough. Kerry snatched a lamp from the bedtable and hurled it in Glenn's face, knocking him backward. Then he leaped across the bed for the knife on the chair. Desperately his fingers closed on the handle. Turning, he saw Waters on the floor, groping for his fallen gun. Kerry dove on him with the knife just as Waters rolled over and pulled the trigger.

Glenn Waters' bullet drilled Tommy Kerry in the center of the forehead, and Tommy Kerry's knife plunged directly into Glenn Waters' heart.

When Lorna woke up, it was not difficult for her to figure out what had happened.

Men, she thought. They couldn't be depended on to do anything right.

Quickly she revised her story. Clyde came back for his inspection log and caught Kerry attacking her. There was a struggle in the kitchen and Kerry stabbed Clyde. She ran upstairs. Kerry followed her, ripped her dress, punched her in the face—

Gently she touched her swelling jaw. At least you did that right, Glenn.

—anyway, Glenn came running into the bedroom with the gun. Kerry stabbed Glenn, and Glenn shot Kerry.

Lorna pursed her lips. Yes, that sounded fine. She looked around the room. Everything was perfect—except for one last little detail. She wet her lips. This was something she had not counted on. She wondered if she could do it.

Glancing out the window, she saw the barren, brown oil field in all its ugliness. She thought of the twenty-two years she had spent with Clyde. And she thought of freedom. Freedom and two hundred thousand dollars.

Lorna smiled. She could do it, all right.

Wrapping the knife handle with a handkerchief, she pulled it out of Glenn's chest and went down to the kitchen.

CLEMENTS JORDAN

WON'T DADDY BE SURPRISED?

Clements Jordan is a new writer whose work has been appearing with increasing frequency in Ellery Queen's Mystery Magazine. *She resides in Virginia, where one can only hope she's hard at work on more stories as good as this one—my choice for the best short-short of the year.*

S HE LEFT HIM ON THE BED, WENT INTO THE bathroom, and applied a heavy coat of grease paint to the rapidly blackening bruise under her eye. She brushed her hair smooth. She must appear neat and calm. She removed her gown, and taking the car keys from the dresser went swiftly and quietly into the children's room, turning on only the night light. She dressed in jeans and a long-sleeved T-shirt that hid the bruises on her arms. Dragging the already packed suitcase from the closet, she wrapped her gown in cleaner's plastic and squeezed that carefully into it. In the far corner was a pocket-book filled thoughtfully with hoarded money, driver's license, important papers, and odds and ends to amuse the children.

She went first to the boy's bed and roused him gently. "Come along, Dicky, let's play our game." Pleased and instantly awake, he put on his sneakers while she lifted the baby wrapped in her blanket. They left by the back door making no noise except the faint click as they closed the door behind them.

They went out to the street where the car was parked. First they laid the baby on the floor in the back, Dicky getting in beside her and holding the door nearly shut. She got in under the wheel and started the car, blessing the quiet motor, carefully holding the door open. She drove two blocks, turned the corner, and finally closed the door. Dicky closed his door and climbed over beside her.

"We're off!" she said gaily, switching on the lights.

Dicky laughed softly. "Won't Daddy be surprised if he wakes up?"

"He sure will," she answered, and added to herself, "So will I."

In her mind's eye she pictured having hit Ted with the plated candlestick just above the ear as he lay in drunken slumber. He hardly bled at all and only on the gown she had with her which she could dispose of easily miles away, maybe in pieces.

Peacefully they drove through the deserted streets. The baby slept in the back as though in her bed. Dicky amused himself counting stars, not minding that it was impossible to keep track. His head began to nod. She had to check to be sure he remembered. "Let me hear what you are going to say at the service station," she said.

"Mama, how much longer before we get to Ohio to Aunt Molly's house?"

"That's exactly right," she praised him, and allowed him to sag against her in sleep. Anyone looking for her would be seeking a woman with two children, not a woman with one child heading for Ohio which she was going nowhere near. She would drive to the airport where she would leave the car. In the bustling crowd she would dress the children in a restroom, then ride the airport bus to some bus station. She would somehow get the children to her folks in Oregon, hopefully before the body was found. She herself would depart for a place as yet unknown to herself. Maybe in a couple of years she could reclaim her children. Surely an experienced typist could find some job. She would take *anything!*

Tears blurred her vision as she thought how wonderful a friendly divorce would be, but the worst beating she had received was the time she had suggested that. "You just try to get me in court! Just *try!* I'll tell you-know-what."

She slowed up at one of the service stations she had found

that stayed open day and night. She nudged Dicky to say his lines. As she handed the money through the window to the attendant, Dicky said, "Mama, how much longer before we get to Ohio to Aunt Molly's house?"

"A long time, darling," she answered for the attendant's benefit.

At the airport she lifted out the bag and the baby. She glanced at her watch, then hurried into the restroom. While Dicky brushed his teeth and washed his face, she did the same. She renewed her makeup, getting no notice at all. Last of all, she changed the baby and gave Dicky clean shorts and a clean T-shirt.

She found by checking her watch that they were ready to travel in less than half an hour. The angel baby still slept. They went out and she asked the departure time for the next airport bus. Due in thirty-five minutes. At the cafeteria she bought orange juice and hamburgers for herself and Dicky. They ate them in twenty minutes, taking their time, and reached the airport bus before it pulled away.

"Isn't this fun?" she demanded a little desperately.

Dicky, tired but cheerful, said it sure was.

They went back to the car and got in as before and started back home. Dicky cuddled up to her and went back to sleep. The baby had never actually awakened. She drove along, thinking and rethinking. She had been so trusting, so in love when she married Ted, and hadn't known how badly he drank and how mean he became while drinking. Her greatest mistake, however, had been confiding to him that she had taken money during a bookkeeping job. She had never been discovered. He was the only one who knew.

Hitting Ted with the candlestick would probably not work. She must think of something else. She knew she would, and soon. She had learned a lot. After she got rid of him, she was going to buckle down, work hard, be a good person.

Before she got too close to the house, she stopped at another service station and filled the tank to its original level, this time at a self-service station. She got back in and awoke Dicky, cautioning him to be very quiet and warning him to secrecy, for if he told, they could never play the game again. Dicky was hurt. Had he *ever* told? His mother's eyes were pleading, so thinking of the cool starry ride, the airport full of swooping planes, the delicious night feast, Dicky promised cross-his-heart.

They coasted the last half block, left the car silently, and closed the car doors quietly. They entered the back door, groped into the children's room where she took her gown and Dickie's pajamas out of the suitcase. They put them back on, repacking Dicky's outfit. She pushed the suitcase and pocket-book to the back of the closet, placing all the empty luggage in front of them. Dicky and the baby were now deeply asleep.

She washed her face again, her lips tightening and sparks of anger snapping in her eyes at the sight of her bruised face. She would pay him back! She glanced at her watch. The whole rehearsal had taken under four hours. It was still dark outside.

She eased into bed where Ted snored unaware. In a few hours he would wake, gather her into his arms, kiss her bruises, and apologize glibly. "I'm so sorry, honey. You know I'd never hurt you if I was myself. I'm really going to stop drinking. Honest, I am. Say you forgive your old monster."

She would swallow the bitterness in her throat and answer, "Sure, Teddie, I know you're sorry. It's okay, lover. Everything will be better, you'll see."

DONALD OLSON

A TOKEN
OF APPRECIATION

*Donald Olson's stories have been entertaining
readers for some fifteen years with their distinctive plot
twists and unexpected endings. This is one of his best,
and was nominated by the Mystery Writers of America
for its annual Edgar Award.*

"I'M A COWARD, DARLING," CHERYL ADMITTED,
"but can you really blame me?"

Reed Terner gave his pretty young wife an apologetic peck on
the cheek. "There's a kiss for courage." And then, wishing he
could believe what he said, "A year may have made all the difference in the world in how he feels. Going off to college. Being
away from home. A lot of it could have been Joyce's fault, you
know."

"Oh, Reed, I don't think it's fair to blame his mother. She's
never acted like a vindictive ex-wife. I honestly can't see her
poisoning Ricky's mind against me."

He had to agree. "But Joyce was the innocent party, and
Ricky knows it. Joyce and I were probably wrong in keeping our
differences from him. The divorce hit him like a freight train.
But now that he's had time to come to terms with the situation . . ."

Cheryl responded with a bleak smile. "I still dread having to
pick him up by myself, the drive back from the village with not
a word out of him, just stony silence. The same old simmering
resentment."

"Honey, you know I'd go myself if I could. But I've got to be here for the tournament committee meeting. You know how important it is."

Limberlost Lodge had started out as a ski resort in the Allegheny Mountains until Reed had bought it with a view to realizing its year-round potential. Now it had a golf course, riding trails, tennis courts, and an Olympic-sized swimming pool. The lodge itself, a sprawling stone and half-timbered Tudor structure, had been extensively restored and refurbished. The views from its site halfway up the mountain were spectacular. And luring one of the big annual golf tournaments to Limberlost would be of immense publicity value.

Cheryl checked the time as if wishing the dreaded confrontation were still weeks away. Ricky was coming to spend two weeks with them and if events repeated themselves it would seem like a lifetime. The memory of last year's visit foreshadowed endless days of nerve-grinding tension.

"Reed, promise me you'll go easy on him. Don't let him get you stirred up. I couldn't face another two weeks like last year."

He tried to make light of it. "It wasn't all *that* bad."

"It wasn't? Are you forgetting that he tried to kill you? Your own son tried to kill you!"

"That's ridiculous. We both lost our temper, that's all."

"But you're the one who almost drowned. And that frightful scene in the dining room. A dozen people heard him threaten to kill you."

"Honey, he's just a kid. He was going through a very difficult time. Come on—his bus arrives in forty-five minutes and I want you to take your time driving down the mountain."

He kissed her again and walked her to the jeep. But for all his attempts to reassure her, he was just as edgy as she was. He loved Ricky and he loved Cheryl. He could only hope that the very excessiveness of Ricky's resentment at least proved how much he cared for his father and that that very caring—and time—would heal the breach.

The bus was twenty minutes late and by then Cheryl's nerves were very badly strung out. She knew that everything depended on this visit. When the bus finally pulled in, she fixed a brave smile on her face and started waving even before Ricky came into sight.

Her first impression was that he looked even more formidably young and attractive. He was a truly handsome boy, tall and brown and broad-shouldered, his face leaner yet noticeably more mature. But, oh dear, how solemn he looked!

"Ricky!" she greeted him. "How wonderful to see you again! Good heavens, you're an absolute giant!" She might have kept up a line of nervous chatter had he not shocked her into silence by dropping his bag, throwing his arms around her, and planting a kiss on her cheek. Cold acknowledgment of her presence being the most she had hoped for, she found this even more unsettling.

"Hey, you're a pleasant surprise," he told her. "I expected Dad."

"He wanted to come but he's tied up in an important committee meeting."

With a rueful glance he said, "You deserve a medal."

"I do?"

He faced her squarely. "Look. We might as well get this over with right now. All the way here I've been rehearsing my apologies to both of you. Man, what a spoiled brat you must think I am."

"You had every right to react as you did. There's nothing to apologize for."

With a sigh of relief he stretched and took a hearty breath of the meadow-fresh summer air. Then he loaded his bags in the jeep and jumped in beside her. "You've got to say this for getting away from home for a year—it sure does make a guy think."

"Oh, Ricky, you can't imagine how glad I am to hear you say that. And your father will be ecstatic." Then, after a moment's deliberation, she asked, "How's your mom?"

"Great. She sends her regards."

"That's nice of her."

"She's a nice lady."

Although Cheryl had been Reed's secretary before he sold

Terner Enterprises she had never met his first wife. Joyce had never come to the office.

Cheryl had not exaggerated when she said Reed would be ecstatic. He was. Once he realized Ricky's change of attitude, tears came into his eyes. He couldn't stop hugging his son. Dinner that evening in the richly appointed lodge dining room was a festive celebration, and Ricky kept them both amused with accounts of his freshman-year tribulations. "Pre-med's no snap," he concluded, "but even in high school I was a minor whiz in chemistry and biology. I think I can hack it."

Reed talked about his plans for improvements at Limberlost while Cheryl listened, her eyes moving from father to son, noticing how much alike they were, two big, good-looking men with minds of their own.

Later she checked the dinner receipts and performed a few more of her nightly chores before crossing the thick-carpeted lobby to the long shallow stairs that led to the top-level gym and swimming pool, stopping along the way at the first level of out-branching corridors of guest rooms. When she reached the last room on "A" level she made sure the corridor was clear before tapping softly on the door.

Clay Winslow—ski instructor, tennis pro, and general factotum—grabbed her in his arms the moment she stepped inside the room. He was a lithely built, powerful man with smoldering eyes.

"I thought I'd see you in the dining room," Cheryl said.

"I ate early. Pleasant reunion, I hope not."

She gave him a dismal look. "Wrong. You should have been there. Clay, I couldn't believe it. Ricky's an entirely different boy. He wallowed in apologies for last year. We're all buddies now."

His face darkened. "So where does that leave us?"

Her answering shrug infuriated him.

"You had it all figured out," he said. "The kid had threatened to kill his old man. Everyone heard him. All we had to do was set it up—knock your beloved hubby off and frame the kid. Simple, you said."

"How did I know he'd change? He acted like a psycho last

year. You'd know that if you'd been here then. He was one hard case.''

''So?''

She plucked thoughtfully at her full lower lip. ''We have to stick with our plan. Reed has to die, and Ricky has to be convicted of his murder. It's the only way I can get the money. A murderer can't inherit.''

''But who'll believe the kid snuffed him now?''

''Let me work on it. I've got an idea, but you may not like it. I told you how the kid constantly lied to Reed last winter—even told him I'd tried to seduce him. He did everything he could to turn Reed against me. Only it didn't work. But suppose Ricky finds reason to believe I'm as bad as he said I was? Everything Reed refused to believe?''

Winslow sniggered. ''Fool that he was.''

Cheryl shot him a reproachful glance. ''I wasn't any of those things then. I knew when Reed married me he was leaving everything to Ricky. But after my uneventful life I was happy to grab Reed. And quite satisfied with him until you came along.''

''You haven't told me your idea.''

''Suppose I make a play for Ricky? He's sure to tattle to Reed. But Reed won't believe him this time either. And it'll look as if Ricky's change of heart is just a put-on. It might be all that's needed to stir them up again.''

Clay was skeptical. ''What if it doesn't work?''

''Then we try something else. But we've got to be extra careful now, love. If anyone suspected you and I were—''

''There's always the cabin,'' he reminded her, reaching for her again.

''We have to work fast,'' she said, succumbing to his embrace. ''We've only got two weeks.''

Fast, but with caution, she knew. She couldn't simply throw herself at Ricky. She had to work on him gradually. Not that she would actually seduce him, of course; she would just convey the message that she was interested. She smiled to herself. It might be fun. Clay would murder her if he could read some of her thoughts. For all her desire to acquire Reed's fortune,

Cheryl was a sensual creature to whom Ricky's combination of manly good looks and boyish innocence held a strong, if resistible, appeal. That she could bring the boy to the verge of seduction she had no doubt whatsoever. Her success with his father proved that—and *he* had had a wife.

Reed himself unwittingly cooperated with her plan, for although he would have preferred to spend every waking hour with Ricky he couldn't neglect his many duties and therefore passed much of the responsibility for entertaining his son to Cheryl. She went riding with him along the mountain trails, played tennis and golf with him, enjoyed the pool with him, at first with a good deal of circumspection in her behavior. Most of the time when they were alone together she talked lovingly about Reed and the plans they shared for Limberlost. But as the days passed she adopted a subtly flirtatious attitude, employing little smiles and casual touches that needn't necessarily be misconstrued. And her references to her married life projected a faintly plaintive tone of regret.

"Honestly, Ricky, I saw more of your father when I was his secretary than I do now. I really can't blame your mother for feeling neglected. Not that he *neglects* me—I don't mean that. I realize how much work he has to do. But it does get rather lonely at times. Your being here makes such a difference. I wish you could stay all summer."

"I wish I could too," he said. "You've been terrific. I was afraid you'd avoid me like the plague—and I wouldn't have blamed you."

They had paused to give the horses a rest in the dense pine-scented forest, and as she let him help her remount she managed to slip back into his arms. For a moment she clung to him, her breath warm on his neck, then—scolding herself for being clumsy—she tried again. Neither of them spoke as they made their way back along the trail to the lodge.

The following night Cheryl knocked on Ricky's door. For a moment she thought he wasn't going to let her in, but he quickly slipped his jeans on over his shorts and held open the door. "Is something wrong, Cheryl?"

She pretended a demure confusion as she stepped inside, her

fingers sketching little nervous gestures along the collar of her revealingly low-cut blouse. "No, nothing's wrong—I was just feeling lonely. Reed's working late again in his office."

He shut the door uncertainly. "You sound a little upset."

With her most beguilingly innocent look, she said quietly, "Last winter. What you told your father about us. It wasn't altogether a lie—in a way. You were only reading my mind."

"Cheryl—"

"Ricky—wasn't there maybe just a tiny bit of wishful thinking in it on your part?"

"What do you mean?"

She looked up at him, frankly enticing now. "You know what I mean."

The conflict apparent on his lean brown face amused Cheryl, but she knew she couldn't let things get out of hand. He took a step toward her and she moved around him, paused, came back, and planted a kiss lightly on his lips. "I just had to know where we stood, that's all. I'd better leave. Reed might be looking for me. Tomorrow? We could stop at that cabin on the North Trail. Nobody would see us there." Without giving him time to react, she opened the door and slipped away.

Back in her room she had bathed, washed her hair, and was propped up in bed reading a magazine when Reed came in. She yawned, stretched, and asked him about his work.

He told her. "And what have you been doing all evening?" he asked.

"I came up hours ago. Keeping up with that son of yours these past few days has been downright exhausting."

"I'm sorry, darling. You've been an angel. From now on I'm going to spend every minute I can with him."

"Good. He wants so much to make up for last winter. It's really touching."

She lay in bed the following morning, imagining the conversation between father and son at the breakfast table. When she got up she practiced her expression in the mirror, affecting a look of sorrowful disappointment. "Oh, darling," she would moan, "not again! You mean he's been pretending all this time? His attitude really *hasn't* changed?"

And that would be the beginning. She smiled, thinking of all the ways she could aggravate the friction and keep them sniping at each other. She dressed and started downstairs.

Clay intercepted her. "What the hell happened last night?"

"Nothing happened. I just did my little number. Now we have only to wait for the results."

He scowled at her. "They both looked happy as clams at breakfast."

Indeed, when she joined them—as they were just returning from nine holes of golf—neither seemed in any way perturbed. Reed's arm was slung affectionately around his son's shoulder and he gave Cheryl a quick kiss. "You want to come riding with us this afternoon?" he said.

Ricky's eyes seemed to avoid hers, his expression blandly detached. She guessed he hadn't said a word to his father about last night. Pre-med? He behaved as if he were majoring in diplomacy. The plan had obviously backfired.

"Thanks, but I'll pass," she murmured.

Ricky seemed to go out of his way thereafter to prevent being alone with her. Everything they did, they did as a threesome.

The days drifted by and she became desperate.

"O.K., O.K., I was wrong," she admitted, meeting Clay in the cabin near the top of the ski lift. "It was a good idea, but it didn't work."

"So that's it, sweet thing? We keep sneaking around like before? Till maybe you decide I'm not worth the effort?"

"Don't be dumb. We've still got five days."

"To do what?"

She ran her fingers through the thick mat of hair on his chest. "Use *your* imagination for a change. Maybe it was a stupid plan anyway. For all we know, a good lawyer might have got the kid off even if it did work."

But they had to do something. She couldn't face another winter stuck out here in the middle of nowhere. She thought a moment and then said brightly, "Why couldn't they have an accident? The two of them."

"What kind of accident?"

"Oh, Clay, what's the matter with you? *You* think of one."

•　　•　　•

Once a day Clay Winslow drove the jeep down to the village to pick up the mail. That afternoon it included a letter for Ricky.

"It's from Mom!" Ricky cried, tearing it open. He and Reed were sitting alone on the deck overlooking the valley.

"Everything O.K. at home?" Reed asked him after he'd read the letter.

"Yeah, everything's great. She misses me, says she hopes I'm having a good time. She asks about you."

Reed put his hand on his son's shoulder. "You are, aren't you? Having a good time?"

"Terrific—you know it. You and Cheryl have been super—considering."

"Hey, now, that's all forgotten."

They sat looking out at the view. Ricky said, "Mom would love this place."

"She was here once, you know. I brought her here on one of our anniversaries. I think that's when I first got the idea I'd like to own it."

Ricky watched his father's face. "Sometimes I wonder if you'd sold the business a long time ago, if you'd had more time to spend with Mom and me, maybe we'd all still be together."

A distant look settled on Reed's face. "Who knows, son?"

Ricky chose to discern a note of regret in his father's voice. "But if you had it all to do over again—would you have married Cheryl?"

A trace of irritation sharpened Reed's reply. "How the hell can I answer a question like that? It happened."

Ricky burst out, "I *know*. It's done, and we have to make the best of it—"

"I didn't say that."

"If I could just understand *why* it happened."

Reed shrugged, then pointed toward the right of the lodge where the tow lines of the ski lift crossed the ridge of pines. "You know what it's like up there, don't you, son? You're poised, ready to take off. For an instant or two you're scared, uncertain, wondering if you're going to make a fool of yourself or worse.

"But then you give yourself a push and it's too late to stop or turn back. All you feel is a marvelous sense of exhilaration. That's how it was for me with Cheryl—if it makes any sense to you.''

"Did you ever want to stop? Or turn back?''

Reed didn't answer. Giving his son a playful slap on the back, he sprang up and walked into the lodge.

Clay was again waiting in the cabin when Cheryl arrived next day. He seemed in a buoyant mood.

"You said it was important,'' she said.

"Not as important as this,'' he said, pulling her against him.

Later, pulling on his shirt, he said, "It'll have to be a last-minute move.''

"What?''

"The accident, sweet thing.''

Her flushed face beamed at him. "You've thought of something!''

"Something perfect—as long as you do your part.''

Her smile faltered. "My part?''

"Relax. All you have to do is make damn sure Reed drives the kid to the village when he leaves. Can you do that?''

"Yes.''

"I'll make sure I'm busy so he can't ask me.''

"It's all right, Clay, Reed will want to drive him. Why does it matter?''

"Because, sweet thing, they're not going to reach the village. A bit of sabotage to the brakes and they'll never make it around that hairpin curve. They'll end up in the gorge and never know what hit them.''

"Are you sure you can do it?''

"A cinch.''

She nodded approvingly. "I like it.''

"I thought you would.''

Suddenly she stiffened. "What was that?''

"What?''

She glanced toward the open window. "I thought I heard something. Look outside.''

He came back grinning. "Save your nerves for Saturday. If you heard anything it was a deer.''

She was still a bit on edge. "Sometimes I wonder if Reed suspects something."

"How could he? We've always played it safe."

"I don't mean 'suspects' exactly. It's just that he hasn't been himself these last few days."

He stroked her cheek with the back of his hand. "Maybe that's your fault, the two of us are more than you can handle?"

"I hate having him touch me any more. I try not to show it, but thank goodness it won't be for much longer."

"Two days, sweet thing, then it'll all be yours. And you'll be all mine." He looked at his watch. "I'd better get back. It's almost mail time." He grinned. "And I promised to do a little errand for Ricky-boy."

"Oh?"

"He asked me to pick up something in the village. A going-away present for you. Isn't that sweet?"

"Going away is the best present he could give me."

Ricky, wearing his backpack, intercepted Clay Winslow as he drove back from the village. "I'm bushed, Clay. Can I hitch a ride with you the rest of the way?"

"Hop in," Clay said. Then, handing Ricky the purchase he'd made, he added, "You're lucky. It was their last box."

Ricky stowed it away in his pack. "Thanks a lot. It's not much of a present, but I remember from last year how she likes these French creams."

Clay chuckled. "The little country chick in the store wanted to know who I was buying candy for. One of these days I'm going to give her what she's asking for."

"Did you tell her?"

"Yeah, I said I was buying it for my best girl."

"Clay, you've got it made up here. All these women—"

Clay winked at him. "It's all part of the job, buddy."

That evening Ricky sought out his father in his pine-paneled office and handed him a slim gift-wrapped package. "You can open it now if you want to," he said.

Reed's face expressed a mixture of surprise and embarrassment when he pulled off the wrappings. "Hey, boy, it's—it's really beautiful. Thanks."

Ricky smiled. "I don't expect you to keep it on your desk, or I'd have had it framed." His long fingers played with his gold neck chain. "I didn't tell Mom I was having a print made for you, but I wanted you to see how really super she looks."

Reed stared thoughtfully at the picture of Ricky and Joyce. "She looks—different. Younger."

"Yeah. I guess she'd really let herself go. But I kept teasing her until she had to do something to shut me up. Her figure's pure dynamite now, and she does her hair differently."

"It's the way she used to wear it," Reed said musingly.

"If I were you I wouldn't let Cheryl see it. She might not understand."

With another embarrassed smile Reed placed the photograph in his bottom desk drawer. "Did you get something for Cheryl? A token of appreciation of some kind?"

"I'll send her something from home," Ricky said. "I'm sorry—I was going to pick up a box of those French creams she likes but Clay beat me to it."

"Clay?" Reed looked puzzled.

"Yeah, he just bought her some."

"How do you know that?"

Ricky regarded him innocently. "He told me." He cracked a broad grin. "Hey, you aren't jealous of old Clay, are you, Dad?"

"Don't be silly."

"I'm only kidding you, Dad. I saw the box in the jeep when he picked me up today and asked him who he was buying candy for. He said Cheryl asked him to pick it up for her."

The day before Ricky was to leave he went to his room after lunch and wrote a couple of postcards to college friends. Not that it made much sense, he knew, but it might be worthwhile afterward to have proof that he *thought* they would reach the post office in the village. He carried the cards downstairs. It was about time for Clay's daily trip down the mountain.

His heartbeat quickened when he saw that the jeep was already gone. Then he heard his name called and when he turned around he saw his father waving to him. Clay was with him.

"You better come with us, Ricky. One of the guests was thrown from her horse on the North Trail. She may have a broken leg."

Ricky looked down at the cards in his hand. "Sure. I was just going to ask Clay to drop these off at the post office."

Clay said, "You're too late. Mrs. Terner's making the mail run. She's already gone. Sorry."

Ricky stood looking back down the mountain, then turned to follow the two men, stuffing the postcards in his jacket pocket.

As it turned out, the guest had suffered only a bad sprain. Reed was obviously concerned but relieved that it was nothing more serious. But when they came in sight of the lodge, his jaw tightened again as two staff members and a man in the uniform of the state police came hurrying to meet them.

Ricky hung back, watching as they spoke to his father. Then, steeling himself, he advanced to join them.

"Dad, what is it?"

Reed's face was white, his mouth trembling. "Something terrible's happened. The jeep missed the curve—It went into the gorge."

"But you said Cheryl was—Oh, God! Is she—"

Reed's voice broke. "Cheryl's dead, Ricky."

Later that afternoon Ricky went to his room, opened his suitcase, and put something in his pocket. Then he picked up the box of French creams, still not wrapped, and carrying it under his arm he walked down the corridor, up the stairs to a door leading into a patio off the gym, and across the patio into the woods beyond. He was conscious of a feeling of acute relief that it had happened the way it did, even if he hadn't planned it that way. Winslow was supposed to have been in the jeep, not Cheryl. It was Winslow who had given him the idea about the brakes when Ricky had followed Cheryl to the cabin and stood listening outside the window. But now he felt no rancor against the man. What chance did any guy have against Cheryl? What chance had his father had? What chance would he himself have had, for that matter, if she hadn't left his room the other night before anything had happened?

Deep in the woods he tossed the box of candy down a shallow ravine. Then he knelt on the ground and buried the little vial of clear liquid there would now be no reason to plant in Clay's room. He had retraced his steps almost to the trail before realizing his carelessness. Returning to the ravine, he scrambled down the slope, retrieved the box of candy, and spent the next few minutes burying that deeply as well.

The last thing he wanted to do was poison some innocent animal.

BILL PRONZINI & JEFFREY WALLMANN

COYOTE AND QUARTER MOON

In addition to his own fine novels and short stories, Bill Pronzini has probably collaborated with more writers than anyone else in the mystery field. Jeffrey Wallmann was the first of his collaborators, beginning in 1968, and many of their early stories appeared under the name of "William Jeffrey." Here they team up to present an appealing new detective, in what we can only hope will be the first of a series.

WITH THE LAUREL COUNTY DEPUTY SHERIFF beside her, Jill Quarter-Moon waited for the locksmith to finish unlatching the garage door. Inside, the dog—a good-sized Doberman; she had identified it through the window—continued its frantic barking.

The house to which the garage belonged was only a few years old, a big ranch-style set at the end of a cul-de-sac and somewhat removed from its neighbors in the expensive Oregon Estates development. Since it was a fair Friday morning in June, several of the neighbors were out and mingling in a wide crescent around the property; some of them Jill recognized from her previous visit here. Two little boys were chasing each other around her Animal Regulation Agency truck, stirring up a pair of other barking dogs nearby. It added to the din being raised by the Doberman.

At length the locksmith finished and stepped back. "It's all yours," he said.

"You'd better let me go in with you," the deputy said to Jill.

There was a taint of chauvinism in his offer, but she didn't let it upset her. She was a mature twenty-six, and a full-blooded Umatilla Indian, and she was comfortable with both her womanhood and her role in society. She was also strikingly attractive, in the light-skinned way of Pacific Northwest Indians, with hip-length brown hair and a long willowy body. Some men, the deputy being one of them, seemed to feel protective, if not downright chivalric, toward her. Nothing made her like a man less than being considered a pretty-and-helpless female.

She shook her head at him and said, "No thanks. I've got my tranquilizer dart gun."

"Suit yourself, then." The deputy gave her a disapproving frown and stepped back out of her way. "It's your throat."

Jill drew a heavy padded glove over her left hand, gripped the dart gun with her right. Then she caught hold of the door latch and depressed it. The Doberman stopped barking; all she could hear from inside were low growls. The dog sensed that someone was coming in, and when she opened the door it would do one of two things; back off and watch her, or attack. She had no way of telling beforehand which it would be.

The Doberman had been locked up inside the garage for at least thirty-six hours. That was how long ago it had first started howling and barking and upsetting the neighbors enough so that one of them had complained to the Agency. The owner of the house, Jill had learned in her capacity as field agent, was named Edward Benham; none of the neighbors knew him—he'd kept to himself during the six months he had lived here—and none of them knew anything at all about his dog. Benham hadn't answered his door, nor had she been able to reach him by telephone or track down any local relatives. Finally she had requested, through the Agency offices, a court order to enter the premises. A judge had granted it, and along with the deputy and the locksmith, here she was to release the animal.

She hesitated a moment longer with her hand on the door latch. If the Doberman backed off, she stood a good chance of gentling it enough to lead it out to the truck; she had a way with animals, dogs in particular—something else she could attribute to her Indian heritage. But if it attacked she would have no choice except to shoot it with the tranquilizer gun. An attack-trained, or even an untrained but high-strung, Doberman could tear your throat out in a matter of seconds.

Taking a breath, she opened the door and stepped just inside the entrance. She was careful to act natural, confident; too much caution could be as provoking to a nervous animal as movements too bold or too sudden. Black and short-haired, the Doberman was over near one of the walls—yellowish eyes staring at her, fangs bared and gleaming in the light from the open doorway and the single dusty window. But it stood its ground, forelegs spread, rear end flattened into a crouch.

"Easy," Jill said soothingly. "I'm not going to hurt you."

She started forward, extending her hand, murmuring the words of a lullabye in Shahaptian dialect. The dog cocked its head, ears perked, still growling, still tensed—but it continued to stay where it was and its snub of a tail began to quiver. That was a good sign, Jill knew. No dog wagged its tail before it attacked.

As her eyes became more accustomed to the half light, she could see that there were three small plastic bowls near the Doberman; each of them had been gnawed and deeply scratched. The condition of the bowls told her that the dog had not been fed or watered during the past thirty-six hours. She could also see that in one corner was a wicker sleeping basket about a foot and a half in diameter, and that on a nearby shelf lay a curry comb. These things told her something else, but just what it meant she had no way of knowing yet.

"Easy, boy . . . calm," she said. She was within a few paces of the dog now and it still showed no inclination to jump at her. Carefully she removed the thick glove, stretched her hand out so that the Doberman could better take her scent. "That's it, just stay easy, stay easy . . ."

The dog stopped growling. The tail stub began to quiver faster, the massive head came forward and she felt the dryness of its nose as it investigated her hand. The yellow eyes looked up at her with what she sensed was a wary acceptance.

Slowly she put away the tranquilizer gun and knelt beside the animal, murmuring the lullabye again, stroking her hand around its neck and ears. When she felt it was ready to trust her she straightened and patted the dog, took a step toward the entrance. The Doberman followed. And kept on following as she retraced her path toward the door.

They were halfway there when the deputy appeared in the doorway. "You all right in there, lady?" he called.

The Doberman bristled, snarled again low in its throat. Jill stopped and stood still. "Get away, will you?" she said to the deputy, using her normal voice, masking her annoyance so the dog wouldn't sense it. "Get out of sight. And find a hose or a faucet, get some water puddled close by. This animal is dehydrated."

The deputy retreated. Jill reached down to stroke the Doberman another time, then led it slowly out into the sunlight. When they emerged she saw that the deputy had turned on a faucet built into the garage wall; he was backed off to one side now, one hand on the weapon holstered at his side, like an actor in a B movie. The dog paid no attention to him or to anyone else. It went straight for the water and began to lap at it greedily. Jill went with it, again bent down to soothe it with her hands and voice.

While she was doing that she also checked the license and rabies tags attached to its collar, making a mental note of the numbers stamped into the thin aluminum. Now that the tenseness of the situation had eased, anger was building within her again at the way the dog had been abused. Edward Benham, whoever he was, would pay for that, she thought. She'd make certain of it.

The moment the Doberman finished drinking, Jill stood and faced the bystanders. "All of you move away from the truck," she told them. "And keep those other dogs quiet."

"You want me to get the back open for you?" the deputy asked.

"No. He goes up front with me."

"Up front? Are you crazy, lady?"

"This dog has been cooped up for a long time," Jill said. "If I put him back in the cage, he's liable to have a fit. And he might never trust me again. Up front I can open the window, talk to him, keep him calmed down.''

The deputy pursed his lips reprovingly. But as he had earlier, he said, ''It's your throat,'' and backed off with the others.

When the other dogs were still Jill caught hold of the Doberman's collar and led it down the driveway to the truck. She opened the passenger door, patted the seat. The Doberman didn't want to go in at first, but she talked to it, coaxing, and finally it obeyed. She shut the door and went around and slid in under the wheel.

''Good boy,'' she told the dog, smiling. ''We showed them, eh?''

Jill put the truck in gear, turned it around, and waved at the scowling deputy as she passed him by.

At the Agency—a massive old brick building not far from the university—she turned the Doberman over to Sam Wyatt, the resident veterinarian, for examination and treatment. Then she went to her desk in the office area reserved for field agents and sat down with the Benham case file.

The initial report form had been filled out by the dispatcher who had logged the complaint from one of Benham's neighbors. That report listed the breed of Benham's dog as an Alaskan husky, female—not a Doberman, male. Jill had been mildly surprised when she went out to the house and discovered that the trapped dog was a Doberman. But then, the Agency was a bureaucratic organization, and like all bureaucratic organizations it made mistakes in paperwork more often than it ought to. It was likely that the dispatcher, in checking the registry files for the Benham name, had either pulled the wrong card or miscopied the information from the right one.

But Jill kept thinking about the sleeping basket and the curry comb inside the garage. The basket had been too small for the Doberman but about the right size for a female husky. And curry combs were made for long-haired, not short-haired dogs.

The situation puzzled as well as angered her. And made her more than a little curious. One of the primary character traits of the Umatilla was inquisitiveness, and Jill had inherited it along with her self-reliance and her way with animals. She had her grandmother to thank for honing her curiosity, though, for teaching her never to accept any half-truth or partial answer. She could also thank her grandmother, who had been born in the days when the tribe lived not on the reservation in northeastern Oregon but along the Umatilla River—the name itself meant "many rocks" or "water rippling over sand"—for nurturing her love for animals and leading her into her present job with the Agency. As far back as Jill could remember, the old woman had told and retold the ancient legends about "the people"—the giant creatures, Salmon and Eagle and Fox and the greatest of all, Coyote, the battler of monsters, who ruled the earth before human beings were created, before all animals shrank to their present size.

But she was not just curious about Benham for her own satisfaction; she had to have the proper data for her report. If the Agency pressed charges for animal abuse, which was what she wanted to see happen, and a heavy fine was to be levied against Benham, all pertinent information had to be correct.

She went to the registry files and pulled the card on Edward Benham. The dispatcher, it turned out, *hadn't* made a mistake after all: the breed of dog listed as being owned by Benham was an Alaskan husky, female. Also, the license and rabies tag numbers on the card were different from those she had copied down from the Doberman's collar.

One good thing about bureaucratic organizations, she thought, was that they had their filing systems cross-referenced. So she went to the files arranged according to tag numbers and looked up the listed owner of the Doberman.

The card said: *Fox Hollow Kennels, 1423 Canyon Road, Laurel County, Oregon.*

Jill had heard of Fox Hollow Kennels; it was a fairly large place some distance outside the city, operated by a man named Largo or Fargo, which specialized in raising a variety of pure-bred dogs. She had been there once on a field investigation that had only peripherally concerned the kennel. She was going to make her second visit, she decided, within the next hour.

The only problem with that decision was that her supervisor, Lloyd Mortisse, vetoed it when she went in to tell him where she was going. Mortisse was a lean, mournful-looking man in his

late forties, with wild gray hair that reminded Jill of the dried
reeds her grandmother had strung into ornamental baskets. He
was also a confirmed bureaucrat, which meant that he loved
paperwork, hated anything that upset the routine, and was
suspicious of the agents' motives every time they went out into
the field.

"Call up Fox Hollow," he told her. "You don't need to go
out there; the matter doesn't warrant it."

"I think it does."

"You have other work to do, Ms. Quarter-Moon."

"Not as important as this, Mr. Mortisse."

She and Mortisse were constantly at odds. There was a mutual
animosity, albeit low-key, based on his part by a certain con-
descension—either because she was a woman or an Indian, or
maybe both—and on her part by a lack of respect. It made for
less than ideal working conditions.

He said, "And I say it's not important enough for you to
neglect your other duties."

"Ask that poor Doberman how important it is."

"I repeat, you're not to pursue the matter beyond a routine
telephone call," Mortisse told her sententiously. "Now is that
understood?"

"Yes. It's understood."

Jill pivoted, stalked out of the office, and kept right on
stalking through the rear entrance and out to her truck. Twenty
minutes later she was turning onto the long gravel drive, bor-
dered by pine and Douglas fir, that led to the Fox Hollow Kennels.

She was still so annoyed at Mortisse, and preoccupied with
Edward Benham, that she almost didn't see the large truck that
came barreling toward her along the drive until it was too late.
As it was, she managed to swerve off onto the soft shoulder just
in time, and to answer the truck's horn blast with one of her
own. It was an old Ford stakebed, she saw as it passed her and
braked for the turn onto Canyon Road, with the words *Fox
Hollow Kennels* on the driver's door. Three slat-and-wire crates
were tied together on the bed, each of which contained what
appeared to be a mongrel dog. The dogs had begun barking at

the sound of the horns and she could see two of them pawing at the wire mesh.

Again she felt both her curiosity and her anger aroused. Transporting dogs in bunches via truck wasn't exactly inhuman treatment, but it was still a damned poor way to handle animals. And what was an American Kennel Club-registered outfit which specialized in purebreds doing with mongrels?

Jill drove up the access drive and emerged into a wide gravel parking area. The long whitewashed building that housed Fox Hollow's office was on her right, with a horseshoe arrangement of some thirty kennels and an exercise yard behind it. Pine woods surrounded the complex, giving it a rustic atmosphere.

When she parked and got out, the sound of more barking came to her from the vicinity of the exercise yard. She glanced inside the office, saw that it was empty, and went through a swing-gate that led to the back. There, beside a low fence, a man stood tossing dog biscuits into the concrete run on the other side, where half a dozen dogs—all of these purebred setters—crowded and barked together. He was in his late thirties, average-sized, with bald head and nondescript features, wearing Levi's and a University of Oregon sweatshirt. Jill recognized him as the owner, Largo or Fargo.

"Mr. Largo?" she said.

He turned, saying, "The name is Fargo." Then he set the food sack down and wiped his hands on his Levi's. His eyes were speculative as he studied both her and her tan Agency uniform. "Something I can do for you, miss?"

Jill identified herself. "I'm here about a dog," she said, "a male Doberman, about three years old. It was abandoned inside a house in Oregon Estates at least two days ago; we went in and released it this morning. The house belongs to a man named Benham, Edward Benham, but the Doberman is registered to Fox Hollow."

Fargo's brows pulled down. "Benham, did you say?"

"That's right. Edward Benham. Do you know him?"

"Well, I don't recognize the name."

"Is it possible you sold him the Doberman?"

"I suppose it is," Fargo said. "Some people don't bother to

change the registration. Makes a lot of trouble for all of us when they don't.''

"Yes, it does. Would you mind checking your records?''

"Not at all.''

He led her around and inside the kennel office. It was a cluttered room that smelled peculiarly of dog, dust and cheap men's cologne. An open door on the far side led to an attached work room; Jill could see a bench littered with tools, stacks of lumber, and several slat-and-wire crates of the kind she had noticed on the truck, some finished and some under construction.

Along one wall was a filing cabinet and Fargo crossed to it, began to rummage inside. After a time he came out with a folder, opened it, consulted the papers it held, and put it away again. He turned to face Jill.

"Yep,'' he said. "Edward Benham. He bought the Doberman about three weeks ago. I didn't handle the sale myself; one of my assistants took care of it. That's why I didn't recognize the name.''

"Is your assistant here now?''

"No, I gave him a three-day weekend to go fishing.''

"Is the Doberman the only animal Benham has bought from you?''

"As far as the records show, it is.''

"Benham is the registered owner of a female Alaskan husky,'' Jill said. "Do you know anyone who specializes in that breed?''

"Not offhand. Check with the American Kennel Club; they might be able to help you.''

"I'll do that.'' Jill paused. "I passed your truck on the way in, Mr. Fargo. Do you do a lot of shipping of dogs?''

"Some, yes. Why?''

"Just curious. Where are those three today bound?''

"Portland.'' Fargo made a deliberate point of looking at his watch. "If you'll excuse me, I've got work to do . . .''

"Just one more thing. I'd like to see your American Kennel Club registration on the Doberman you sold Benham.''

"Can't help you there, I'm afraid,'' Fargo said. "There wasn't any AKC registration on that Doberman.''

"No? Why not? He's certainly a purebred."

"Maybe so, but the animal wasn't bred here. We bought it from a private party who didn't even know the AKC existed."

"What was this private party's name?"

"Adams. Charles Adams. From out of state—California. That's why Fox Hollow was the first to register the dog with you people."

Jill decided not to press the matter, at least not with Fargo personally. She had other ways of finding out information about him, about Fox Hollow, and about Edward Benham. She thanked Fargo for his time, left the office, and headed her truck back to the Agency.

When she got there she went first to see Sam Wyatt, to check on the Doberman's health. There was nothing wrong with the animal, Wyatt told her, except for minor malnutrition and dehydration. It had been fed, exercised, and put into one of the larger cages.

She looked in on it. The dog seemed glad to see her; the stub of a tail began to wag when she approached the cage. She played her fingers through the mesh grille, let the Doberman nuzzle them.

While she was doing that the kennel attendant, a young redhead named Lena Stark, came out of the dispensary. "Hi, Jill," she said. "The patient looks pretty good, doesn't he?"

"He'll look a lot better when we find him a decent owner."

"That's for sure."

"Funny thing—he's registered to the Fox Hollow Kennels, but they say he was sold to one Edward Benham. It was Benham's garage he was locked up in."

"Why is that funny?"

"Well, purebred Dobermans don't come cheap. Why would anybody who'd pay for one suddenly go off and desert him?"

"I guess that is kind of odd," Lena admitted. "Unless Benham was called out of town on an urgent matter or something. That would explain it."

"Maybe," Jill said.

"Some people should never own pets, you know? Benham should have left the dog at Fox Hollow; at least they care about the welfare of animals."

"Why do you say that?"

"Because every now and then one of their guys comes in and takes most of our strays."

"Oh? For what reason?"

"They train them and then find homes for them in other parts of the state. A pretty nice gesture, don't you think?"

"Yes," Jill said thoughtfully. "A pretty nice gesture."

She went inside and straight to the filing room, where she pulled the Fox Hollow folder. At her desk she spread out the kennel's animal licensing applications and studied them. It stood to reason that there would be a large number and there were; but as she sifted through them Jill was struck by a peculiarity. Not counting the strays Fox Hollow had "adopted" from the Agency, which by law had to be vaccinated and licensed before being released, there were less than a dozen dogs brought in and registered over the past twelve months. For a kennel which claimed to specialize in purebreds, this was suspiciously odd. Yet no one else had noticed it in the normal bureaucratic shuffle, just as no one had paid much attention to Fox Hollow's gathering of Agency strays.

And why *was* Fox Hollow in the market for so many stray dogs? Having met Fargo, she doubted that he was the humanitarian type motivated by a desire to save mongrels from euthanasia, a dog's fate if kept unclaimed at the Agency for more than four days. No, it sounded as if he were in some sort of strange wholesale pet business—as if the rest of the state, not to mention the rest of the country, didn't have their own animal overpopulation problems.

But where did Edward Benham, and the Doberman, fit in? Jill reviewed the Benham file again, but it had nothing new to tell her. She wished she knew where he'd gone, or of some way to get in touch with him. The obvious way, of course, was through his place of employment; unfortunately, however, pet license applications did not list employment of owners, only home address and telephone number. Nor had any of his neighbors known where he worked.

Briefly she considered trying to bluff information out of one of the credit-reporting companies in the city. Benham had bought rather than rented or leased his house, which meant that he probably carried a mortgage, which meant credit, which meant an application listing his employment. The problem was that legitimate members of such credit companies used special secret numbers to identify themselves when requesting information, so any ruse she might attempt would no doubt fail, and might even backfire and land her in trouble with Mortisse.

Then she thought of Pete Olafson, the office manager for Mid-Valley Adjustment Bureau, a local bad-debt collection service. Mid-Valley could certainly belong to a credit-reporting company. And she knew Pete pretty well, had dated him a few times in recent months. There wasn't any torrid romance brewing between her and the sandy-haired bachelor, but she knew he liked her a good deal—maybe enough to bend the rules a little and check Benham's credit as a favor.

She looked up Mid-Valley's number, dialed it, and was talking to Pete fifteen seconds later. "You must be a mind-reader, Jill," he said after she identified herself. "I was going to call you later. The University Theater is putting on 'Our Town' tomorrow night and I've wangled a couple of free passes. Would you like to go?"

"Sure. If you'll do me a favor in return."

Pete sighed dramatically. "Nothing is free these days, it seems. Okay, what is it?"

"I want to know where a man named Edward Benham is employed. Could you track down his credit applications and find out from them?"

"I can if he's got credit somewhere."

"Well, he owns his own home, out in Oregon Estates. The name is Benham. B-e-n-h-a-m, Edward. How fast can you find out for me?"

"It shouldn't take long. Sit tight; I'll get back to you."

Jill replaced the handset and sat with her chin propped in one palm brooding. If the lead to Edward Benham through Pete didn't pan out, then what? Talk to his neighbors again? Through them she could find out the name of the real estate agent who had sold Benham his home . . . but it was unlikely that they would divulge personal information about him, since she had no official capacity. Talk to Fargo again? That probably wouldn't do her any good either. . . .

The door to Lloyd Mortisse's private office opened; Jill saw him thrust his wild-maned head out and look in her direction. It was not a look of pleasure. "Ms. Quarter-Moon," he said. "Come into my office, please."

Jill complied. Mortisse shut the door behind her, sat down at his desk, and glared at her. "I thought," he said stiffly, "that I told you not to go out to Fox Hollow Kennels."

Surprised, Jill asked, "How did you know about that?"

"Mr. Fargo called me. He wanted to know why you were out there asking all sorts of questions. He wasn't pleased by your visit; neither am I. Why did you disobey me?"

"I felt the trip was necessary."

"Oh, you felt it was necessary. I see. That makes it all right, I suppose."

"Look, Mr. Mortisse—"

"I do not like disobedience," Mortisse said. "I won't stand for it again, is that clear? Nor will I stand for you harassing private facilities like Fox Hollow. This Agency's sole concern in the Benham matter is to house the Doberman for ninety-six hours or until it is claimed. And I'll be the one, not you, to decide if any misdemeanor animal-abuse charges are to be filed against Mr. Benham."

Jill thought that it was too bad these weren't the old days, when one of the Umatilla customs in tribal disputes was to hold a potlatch—a fierce social competition at which rival chiefs gave away or destroyed large numbers of blankets, coppers, and slaves in an effort to outdo and therefore vanquish each other. She would have liked nothing better than to challenge Mortisse in this sort of duel, using bureaucratic attitudes and red tape as the throwaway material. She also decided there was no point in trying to explain her suspicions to him; he would only have said in his supercilious way that none of it was Agency business. If she was going to get to the bottom of what was going on at Fox Hollow, she would have to do it on her own.

"Do you understand?" Mortisse was saying. "You're to drop this matter and attend to your assigned duties. And you're not to disobey a direct order again, under any circumstances."

"I understand," Jill said thinly. "Is that all?"

"That's all."

She stood and left the office, resisting an impulse to slam the door. The wall clock said that it was 4:10—less than an hour until quitting time for the weekend. All right, she thought as she crossed to her desk. I'll drop the matter while I'm on Agency time. But what I do and where I go on my own time is *my* business. Mortisse or no Mortisse.

It was another ten minutes, during which time she typed up a pair of two-day-old reports, before Pete Olafson called her back. "Got what you asked for, Jill," he said. "Edward Benham has a pretty fair credit rating, considering he's modestly employed."

"What does he do?"

"He's a deliveryman, it says here. For a kennel."

Jill sat up straight. "Kennel?"

"That's right," Pete said. "Place called Fox Hollow outside the city. Is that what you're after?"

"It's a lot more than I expected," Jill told him. Quickly she arranged tomorrow night's date with him, then replaced the receiver and sat mulling over this latest bit of news.

If she had needed anything more to convince her that something was amiss at Fox Hollow, this was it. Fargo had claimed he didn't know Edward Benham; now it turned out that Benham worked for Fargo. Why had he lied? What was he trying to cover up? And where was Benham? And where did the Doberman fit in?

She spent another half hour at her desk, keeping one eye on the clock and pretending to work while she sorted through questions, facts, and options in her mind. At ten minutes of five, when she couldn't take any more of the inactivity, she went out into the kennel area to see Lena Stark.

"Release the Doberman to me, will you, Lena?" she asked. "I'll bring him back later tonight and check him in with the night attendant."

"Why do you want him?"

"I like his looks and I want to get better acquainted. If it turns out neither Fox Hollow nor Benham decides to claim him, I may just adopt him myself."

"I don't know, Jill . . ."

"He's all right, isn't he? Sam Wyatt said he was."

"Sure, he's fine. But the rules—"

"Oh, hang the rules. Nobody has to know except you and me and the night attendant. I'll take full responsibility."

"Well . . . okay, I guess you know what you're doing."

Lena opened the cage and the Doberman came out, stubby tail quivering, and nuzzled Jill's hand. She led it out through the rear door, into the parking lot to where her compact was parked. Obediently, as if delighted to be free and in her company, the dog jumped onto the front seat and sat down with an expectant look.

Jill stroked its ears as she drove out of the lot. "I don't want to keep calling you 'boy'," she said. "I think I'll give you a name, even if it's only temporary. How about Tyee?" In the old Chinook jargon, the mixed trade language of Indians and whites in frontier days, *tyee* was the word for chief. "You like that? Tyee?"

The dog cocked its head and made a rumbly sound in its throat.

"Good," Jill said. "Tyee it is."

She drove across the city and into Oregon Estates. Edward Benham's house, she saw when she braked at the end of the cul-de-sac, looked as deserted as it had this morning. This was confirmed when she went up and rang the doorbell several times without getting a response.

She took Tyee with her and let him sniff around both front and back. The Doberman showed none of the easy familiarity of a dog on its own turf; rather, she sensed a wary tenseness in the way he moved and keened the air. And when she led him near the garage he bristled, made low growling noises. He was as much a stranger here as she was, Jill thought. But then why had he been locked in Benham's garage?

She would have liked to go inside for a better look around, but the locksmith had relocked the doors, as dictated by law, before leaving the premises that morning. The house was securely locked too, as were each of the windows. And drawn drapes and blinds made it impossible to see into any of the rooms from outside.

Jill took Tyee back to her compact. She sat for a time, considering. Then she started the engine and pointed the car in an easterly direction.

It was just seven o'clock when she came up the access drive to Fox Hollow Kennels and coasted to a stop on the gravel parking area near the main building. There were no other vehicles around, a *Closed* sign was propped in one dusty pane of the front door, and the complex had a deserted aura; even the dogs in the near kennels were quiet.

She got out, motioning for Tyee to stay where he was on the front seat. The setting sun hung above the tops of the pines straight ahead, bathing everything in a dark-orange radiance. Jill judged that there was about an hour of daylight left, which meant that an hour was all she would have to look around. Prowling in daylight was risky enough, though if she were seen she might be able to bluff her way out of trouble by claiming she had brought Tyee back to his registered owner. If she were caught here after dark, no kind of bluff would be worth much.

The office door was locked, but when she shook it, it rattled loosely in its frame. Jill bent for a closer look at the latch. It was a spring-type lock, rather than a deadbolt. She straightened again, gnawing at her lower lip. Detectives in movies and on TV were forever opening spring locks with credit cards or pieces of celluloid; there was no reason why she couldn't do the same thing. No reason, that was, except that it was illegal and would cost her her job, if not a prison term, were she to be caught. She could imagine Lloyd Mortisse smiling like the Cheshire Cat at news of her arrest.

But she was already here, and the need to sate her curiosity was overpowering. The debate with her better judgment lasted all of ten seconds. Then she thought: Well, fools rush in—and she went back to the car to get a credit card from her purse.

Less than a minute of maneuvering with the card rewarded her with a sharp click as the lock snapped free. The door opened under her hand. Enough of the waning orange sunlight penetrated through the windows, she saw when she stepped inside, so that she didn't need any other kind of light. She went straight to the filing cabinets, began to shuffle through the folders inside.

The kennel records were in something of a shambles; Jill realized quickly that it would take hours, maybe even days, to sort through all the receipts, partial entries, and scraps of paper. But one file was complete enough to hold her attention and to prove interesting. It consisted of truck expenses—repair bills, oil company credit card receipts, and the like—and what intrigued her was that, taken together, they showed that the Fox Hollow delivery truck consistently traveled to certain towns in Oregon, northern California, and southern Washington. Forest Grove, Corvallis, Portland, McMinnville, Ashland, La Grande, Arcata, Kirkland.   . These, and a few others, comprised a regular route.

Which might explain why Edward Benham was nowhere to be found at the moment; some of the towns were at least an overnight's drive away, and it was Benham's signature that was on most of the receipts. But the evident truck route also raised more questions. Why such long hauls for a small kennel? Why to some points out of state? And why to these particular towns, when there were numerous others of similar size along the way?

"Curiouser and curiouser," Jill murmured to herself.

She shut the file drawers and turned to the desk. Two of the drawers were locked; she decided it would be best not to try forcing them. None of the other drawers, nor any of the clutter spread across the top, told her anything incriminating or enlightening.

The door to the adjacent workroom was closed, but when she tried the knob it opened right up. That room was dimmer but there was still enough daylight filtering in to let her see the tools, workbench, stacks of lumber, finished and unfinished crates. She picked through the farrago of items on the bench; caught up slats and corner posts of an unassembled cage, started to put them down again. Then, frowning, she studied one of the wooden posts more carefully.

The post was hollow. So were the others; the inner lengths of all four had been bored out by a large drill bit. When fitted into the frame of a fully constructed cage the posts would appear solid, their holes concealed by the top and bottom sections. Only when the cage was apart, like now, would the secret compartments be exposed, to be filled or emptied.

Of what?

Jill renewed her search. In a back corner were three rolls of cage wire—and caught on a snag of mesh on one roll was a small cellophane bag. The bag was out of easy sight and difficult to reach, but she managed to retrieve it. It looked new, unopened, and it was maybe 3 x 5 inches in size. The kind of bag—

And then she knew. What the bag was for, why the corner posts were hollowed out, what Fox Hollow was involved in. And it was ugly enough and frightening enough to make her feel a chill of apprehension, make her want to get away from there in a hurry. It was more than she had bargained for—considerably more.

She ran out of the workroom, still clutching the cellophane bag in her left hand. At the office door she peered through the glass before letting herself out, to make sure the parking area remained deserted. Then she set the button-lock on the knob, stepped outside, pulled the door shut, and started across to her compact.

Tyee was gone.

She stopped, staring in at the empty front seat. She had left the driver's window all the way down and he must have jumped out. Turning, she peered through gathering shadows toward the kennels. But the dogs were still quiet back there, and they wouldn't be if the Doberman had gone prowling in that direction. Where, then? Back down the drive? The pine woods somewhere?

Jill hesitated. The sense of urgency and apprehension demanded that she climb into the car, Tyee or no Tyee, and drive away pronto. But she couldn't just leave him here while she went to tell her suspicions to the county sheriff. The law would not come out here tonight no matter what she told them; they'd wait until tomorrow, when the kennel was open for business and when they could obtain a search warrant. And once she left here herself she had no intention of coming back again after dark.

She moved away from the car, toward the dark line of evergreens beyond. It was quiet here, with dust settling, and sounds carried some distance; the scratching noises reached her ears when she was still twenty paces from the woods. She'd heard enough dogs digging into soft earth to recognize the sound and she quickened her pace. Off to one side was a beaten-down area, not quite a path, and she went into the trees at that point. The digging sounds grew louder. Then she saw Tyee, over behind a decayed moss-festooned log, making earth and dry needles fly out behind him with his forepaws.

"What are you doing?" she called to him. "Come here, Tyee."

The Doberman kept on digging, paying no attention to her. She hurried over to him, around the bulky shape of the log. And then she stopped abruptly, made a startled gasping sound.

A man's arm and clenched hand lay partially uncovered in the soft ground.

Tyee was still digging, still scattering dirt and pine needles. Jill stood frozen, watching part of a broad back encased in a khaki shirt appear.

Now she knew what had happened to Edward Benham.

She made herself move, step forward and catch hold of the Doberman's collar. He resisted at first when she tried to tug him away from the shallow grave and what was in it; but she got a firmer grip and pulled harder, and finally he quit struggling. She dragged him around the log, back out of the trees.

Most of the daylight was gone now; the sky was grayish, streaked with red, like bloody fingermarks on faded cloth. A light wind had come up and she felt herself shiver as she took the Doberman toward her compact. She was anything but a shrinking violet, but what she had found at Fox Hollow tonight was enough to frighten Old Chief Joseph or any of the other venerable Shahaptian warriors. The sooner she was sitting in the safety of the Laurel County Sheriff's office, the better she—

And the figure of a man came out from behind her car.

She was ten feet from the driver's door, her right hand on Tyee's collar, when the man rose up into view like Nashlah, the legendary monster of the Columbia River. Jill made an involuntary cry, stiffened into a standstill. The Doberman seemed to go as tense as she did; a low rumble sounded in his throat as the man came toward them.

Fargo. With a gun in his hand.

"You just keep on holding that dog," he said. He stopped fifteen feet away, holding the gun out at arm's length. "You're both dead if you let go his collar."

She was incapable of speech for five or six seconds. Then she made herself say, "There's no need for that gun, Mr. Fargo. I'm only here to return the Doberman . . . ."

"Sure you are. Let's not play games. You're here because you're a damned snoop. And I'm here because you tripped a silent alarm connected to my house when you broke into the office."

It was not in Jill's nature to panic in a crisis; she got a grip on her fear and held it down, smothered it. "The office door was unlocked," she said. "Maybe you think you locked it when you left but you didn't. I just glanced inside."

"I don't buy that either," Fargo said. "I saw you come out of the office; I left my car down the road and walked up here through the trees. I saw you go into the woods over there, too."

"I went to find the dog, that's all."

"But that's not what you found, right? He's got dirt all over his forepaws—he's been doing some digging. You found Benham. And now you know too much about everything."

"I don't know what you're talking about."

"I say you do. So does that cellophane bag you're carrying."

Jill looked down at her left hand; she had forgotten all about the bag. And she had never even considered the possibility of a silent alarm system. She had a lot to learn about being a detective—if she survived to profit by her mistakes.

"All right," she said. "It's drugs, isn't it? That's the filthy business you're in."

"You got it."

"Selling drugs to college kids all over the Pacific Northwest," she said. That was the significance of the towns on the Fox Hollow shipping route: they were all college or university towns. Humboldt State in Arcata, Lewis & Clark in Portland, Linfield College in McMinnville, Eastern Oregon College in La Grande. And the state university right here in this city. That was also why Fox Hollow had taken so many stray dogs from the Agency; they needed a constant supply to cover their shipment of drugs—cocaine and heroin, probably, the kind usually packaged and shipped in small cellophane bags—to the various suppliers along their network. "Where does it come from? Canada?"

"Mexico," Fargo said. "They bring it up by ship, we cut and package and distribute it."

"To kennels in those other cities, I suppose."

"That's right. They make a nice cover."

"What happens to the dogs you ship?"

"What do you think happens to them? Dogs don't matter when you're running a multi-million-dollar operation. Neither do snoops like you. Nobody fouls up this kind of operation and gets away with it."

Tyee growled again, shifted his weight; Jill tightened her grip on his collar. "Did Benham foul it up? Is that why he's dead?"

"He tried to. His percentage wasn't enough for him and he got greedy; he decided to hijack a shipment for himself —substitute milk sugar and then make off with the real stuff. When he left here on Wednesday for Corvallis he detoured over to his house and made the switch. Only one of the crates had the drugs in it, like always; he had to let the dog out of that one to get at the shipment and it turned on him, tried to bite him."

"This dog, the Doberman."

"Yeah. He managed to lock it up inside his garage, but that left him with an empty crate and he couldn't deliver an empty, not without making the Corvallis contact suspicious. So he loaded his own dog, the husky, inside the crate and delivered it instead. But our man checked the dope anyway, discovered the switch, and called me. I was waiting for Benham when he got back here."

"And you killed him."

Fargo shrugged. "I had no choice."

"Like you've got no choice with me?"

He shrugged again. "I forgot all about the Doberman, that was my mistake. If I hadn't, I wouldn't have you on my hands. But it just didn't occur to me the dog would raise a ruckus and a nosy Agency worker would decide to investigate."

"Why did you lie to me before about knowing Benham?"

"I didn't want you doing any more snooping. I figured if I gave you that story about selling him the Doberman, you'd come up against a dead-end and drop the whole thing. Same reason I called your supervisor: I thought he'd make you drop it. Besides, you had no official capacity. It was your word against mine."

"Lying to me was your second mistake," Jill said. "If you kill me, it'll be your third."

"How do you figure that?"

"I told somebody I came out here tonight. He'll go to the county sheriff if I disappear, and they'll come straight to you."

"That's a bluff," Fargo said. "And I don't bluff. You didn't tell anybody about coming here; nobody knows but you and me. And pretty soon it'll just be me." He made a gesture with the gun. "Look at it this way. You're only one person, but I got a lot of people depending on me: others in the operation, all those kids we supply."

All those kids, Jill thought, and there was a good hot rage inside her now. College kids, some of them still in their teens. White kids, black kids—Indian kids. She had seen too many Indian youths with drug habits; she had talked to the parents of a sixteen-year-old boy who had died from an overdose of heroin on the Umatilla reservation, of a seventeen-year-old girl, an honor student, killed in a drug raid at Trout Lake near the Warm Springs development. Any minority, especially its restless and sometimes disenchanted youth, was susceptible to drug exploitation; and Indians were a minority long oppressed in their own country. That was why she hated drugs, and hated these new oppressors, the drug dealers like Fargo, even more.

Fargo said, "Okay, we've done enough talking—no use in prolonging things. Turn around, walk into the woods."

"So you can bury me next to Benham?"

"Never mind that. Just move."

"No," she said, and she let her body go limp, sank onto her knees. She dropped the cellophane bag as she did so and then put that hand flat on the gravel beside her, keeping her other hand on Tyee's collar. The Doberman, sensing the increase of tension between her and Fargo, had his fangs bared now, growling steadily.

"What the hell?" Fargo said. "Get up."

Jill lowered her chin to her chest and began to chant in a soft voice—a Shahaptian prayer.

"I said get up!"

She kept on chanting.

Fargo took two steps toward her, a third, a fourth. That put less than five feet of ground between them. "I'll shoot you right where you are, I mean it—"

She swept up a handful of gravel, hurled it at his face, let go of Tyee's collar, and flung herself to one side.

The gun went off and she heard the bullet strike the ground near her head, felt the sting of a pebble kicked up against her cheek. Then Fargo screamed, and when Jill rolled over she saw that Tyee had done what she'd prayed he would—attacked Fargo the instant he was released. He had driven the man backward and knocked him down and was shaking his captured wrist as if it were a stick; the gun had popped loose and sailed off to one side. Fargo cried out again, tried to club the Doberman with his free hand. Blood from where Tyee's teeth had bitten into his wrist flowed down along his right arm.

Jill scrambled to her feet, ran to where the gun lay and scooped it up. But before she could level it at Fargo, he jacknifed his body backwards, trying to escape from the Doberman, and cracked his head against the front bumper of her compact; she heard the thunking sound it made in the stillness, saw him go limp. Tyee still straddled the inert form, growling, shaking the bloody wrist.

She went over there, caught the dog's collar again, talked to him until he let go of Fargo and backed off with her. But he stood close, alert, alternately looking at the unconscious man and up at her. She knelt and hugged him, and there were tears in her eyes. She disliked women who cried, particularly self-sufficient Indian women, but sometimes . . . sometimes it was a necessary release.

"You know who you are?" she said to him. "You're not Tyee, you're Coyote. You do battle with monsters and evil beings and you save Indians from harm."

The Doberman licked her hand.

"The Great One isn't supposed to return until the year 2000, when the world changes again and all darkness is gone; but you're here already and I won't let you go away. You're mine and I'm yours from now on—Coyote and Quarter-Moon."

Then she stood, shaky but smiling, and went to re-pick the lock on the office door so she could call the Laurel County sheriff.

JACK RITCHIE

THE ABSENCE OF EMILY

As readers of previous best mystery anthologies know, there's rarely been a year when Jack Ritchie hasn't been represented with one of his distinctive short stories. Though he can be unusually serious at times, his detective and crime tales are more likely to have a certain zany quality about them that has become Ritchie's trademark. This story was judged the best of the year by Mystery Writers of America, and it won Ritchie an Edgar that's been long overdue.

THE PHONE RANG AND I PICKED UP THE RE-ceiver. "Yes?"

"Hello, darling, this is Emily."

I hesitated. "Emily who?"

She laughed lightly. "Oh, come now, darling. Emily, your wife."

"I'm sorry, you must have a wrong number." I hung up, fumbling a bit as I cradled the phone.

Millicent, Emily's cousin, had been watching me. "You look white as a sheet."

I glanced covertly at a mirror.

"I don't mean in actual *color*, Albert. I mean figuratively. In attitude. You seem frightened. Shocked."

"Nonsense."

"Who phoned?"

"It was a wrong number."

Millicent sipped her coffee. "By the way, Albert, I thought I saw Emily in town yesterday, but, of course, that was impossible."

"Of course it was impossible. Emily is in San Francisco."

"Yes, but *where* in San Francisco?"

"She didn't say. Just visiting friends."

"I've known Emily all her life. She has very few secrets from me. She doesn't *know* anybody in San Francisco. When will she be back?"

"She might be gone a rather long time."

"How long?"

"She didn't know."

Millicent smiled. "You have been married before, haven't you, Albert?"

"Yes."

"As a matter of fact, you were a widower when you met Emily?"

"I didn't try to keep that fact a secret."

"Your first wife met her death in a boating accident five years ago? She fell overboard and drowned?"

"I'm afraid so. She couldn't swim a stroke."

"Wasn't she wearing a life preserver?"

"No. She claimed they hindered her movements."

"It appears that you were the only witness to the accident."

"I believe so. At least no one else ever came forward."

"Did she leave you any money, Albert?"

"That's none of your business, Millicent."

Cynthia's estate had consisted of a fifty-thousand-dollar life-insurance policy, of which I was the sole beneficiary, some forty-thousand dollars in sundry stocks and bonds, and one small sailboat.

I stirred my coffee. "Millicent, I thought I'd give you first crack at the house."

"First crack?"

"Yes. We've decided to sell this place. It's really too big for just the two of us. We'll get something smaller. Perhaps even an apartment. I thought you might like to pick up a bargain. I'm certain we can come to satisfactory terms."

She blinked. "Emily would never sell this place. It's her home. I'd have to hear the words from her in person."

"There's no need for that. I have her power of attorney. She has no head for business, you know, but she trusts me implicitly. It's all quite legal and aboveboard."

"I'll think it over." She put down her cup. "Albert, what

did you do for a living before you met Emily? Or Cynthia, for
that matter?''

"I managed.''

When Millicent was gone, I went for my walk on the back
grounds of the estate. I went once again to the dell and
sat down on the fallen log. How peaceful it was here. Quiet.
A place to rest. I had been coming here often in the last few
days.

Millicent and Emily. Cousins. They occupied almost identical large homes on spacious grounds next to each other. And,
considering that fact, one might reasonably have supposed that
they were equally wealthy. Such, however, was not the case, as I
discovered after my marriage to Emily.

Millicent's holdings must certainly reach far into seven
figures, since they require the full-time administrative services
of Amos Eberly, her attorney and financial advisor.

Emily, on the other hand, owned very little more than the
house and the grounds themselves and she had borrowed
heavily to keep them going. She had been reduced to two servants, the Brewsters. Mrs. Brewster, a surly creature, did the
cooking and desultory dusting, while her husband, formerly the
butler, had been reduced to a man-of-all-work, who pottered
inadequately about the grounds. The place really required the
services of two gardeners.

Millicent and Emily. Cousins. Yet it was difficult to imagine
two people more dissimilar in either appearance or nature.

Millicent is rather tall, spare, and determined. She fancies
herself an intellect and she has the tendency to rule and
dominate all those about her, and that had certainly included
Emily. It is obvious to me that Millicent deeply resents the fact
that I removed Emily from under her thumb.

Emily. Shorter than average. Perhaps twenty-five pounds
overweight. An amiable disposition. No claim to blazing intelligence. Easily dominated, yes, though she had a surprising
stubborn streak when she set her mind to something.

When I returned to the house, I found Amos Eberly waiting.
He is a man in his fifties and partial to gray suits.

"Where is Emily?'' he asked.

"In Oakland.'' He gave that thought.

"I meant San Francisco. Oakland is just across the bay, isn't it? I usually think of them as one, which, I suppose, is unfair to both."

He frowned. "San Francisco? But I saw her in town just this morning. She was looking quite well."

"Impossible."

"Impossible for her to be looking well?"

"Impossible for you to have seen her. She is still in San Francisco."

He sipped his drink. "I know Emily when I see her. She wore a lilac dress with a belt. And a sort of gauzy light-blue scarf."

"You were mistaken. Besides, women don't wear gauzy light-blue scarves these days."

"Emily did. Couldn't she have come back without letting you know?"

"No."

Eberly studied me. "Are you ill or something, Albert? Your hands seem to be shaking."

"Touch of the flu," I said quickly. "Brings out the jitters in me. What brings you here anyway, Amos?"

"Nothing in particular, Albert. I just happened to be in the neighborhood and thought I'd drop in and see Emily."

"Damn it, I told you she isn't here."

"All right, Albert," he said soothingly. "Why should I doubt you? If you say she isn't here, she isn't here."

It has become my habit on Tuesday and Thursday afternoons to do the household food shopping, a task which I pre-empted from Mrs. Brewster when I began to suspect her arithmetic.

As usual, I parked in the supermarket lot and locked the car. When I looked up, I saw a small, slightly stout woman across the street walking toward the farther end of the block. She wore a lilac dress and a light-blue scarf. It was the fourth time I'd seen her in the last ten days.

I hurried across the street. I was still some seventy-five yards behind her when she turned the corner.

Resisting the temptation to shout at her to stop, I broke into a trot.

When I reached the corner, she was nowhere in sight. She could have disappeared into any one of a dozen shop fronts.

I stood there, trying to regain my breath, when a car pulled to the curb.

It was Millicent. "Is that you, Albert?"

I regarded her without enthusiasm. "Yes."

"What in the world are you doing? I saw you running and I've never seen you run before."

"I was *not* running. I was merely trotting to get my blood circulating. A bit of jogging is supposed to be healthy, you know."

I volunteered my adieu and strode back to the supermarket.

The next morning when I returned from my walk to the dell, I found Millicent in the drawing room, pouring herself coffee and otherwise making herself at home—a habit from the days when only Emily occupied the house.

"I've been upstairs looking over Emily's wardrobe," Millicent said. "I didn't see anything missing."

"Why should anything be missing? Has there been a thief in the house? I suppose you know every bit and parcel of her wardrobe?"

"Not every bit and parcel, but almost. Almost. And very little, if anything, seems to be missing. Don't tell me that Emily went off to San Francisco without any luggage."

"She had luggage. Though not very much."

"What was she wearing when she left?"

Millicent had asked that question before. This time I said, "I don't remember."

Millicent raised an eyebrow. "You don't remember?" She put down her cup. "Albert, I'm holding a seance at my place tonight. I thought perhaps you'd like to come."

"I will not go to any damn seance."

"Don't you want to communicate with any of your beloved dead?"

"I believe in letting the dead rest. Why bother them with every trifling matter back here."

"Wouldn't you want to speak to your first wife?"

"Why the devil would I want to communicate with Cynthia? I have absolutely nothing to say to her anyway."

"But perhaps she has something to say to you."

I wiped my forehead. "I'm not going to your stupid seance and that's final."

That evening, as I prepared for bed, I surveyed the contents of Emily's closet. How would I dispose of her clothes? Probably donate them to some worthy charity, I thought.

I was awakened at two A.M. by the sound of music.

I listened. Yes, it was plainly Emily's favorite sonata being played on the piano downstairs.

I stepped into my slippers and donned my dressing robe. In the hall, I snapped on the lights.

I was halfway down the stairs when the piano-playing ceased. I completed my descent and stopped at the music room doors. I put my ear to one of them. Nothing. I slowly opened the door and peered inside.

There was no one at the piano. However, two candles in holders flickered on its top. The room seemed chilly. Quite chilly.

I found the source of the draft behind some drapes and closed the French doors to the terrace. I snuffed out the candles and left the room.

I met Brewster at the head of the stairs.

"I thought I heard a piano being played, sir," he said. "Was that you?"

I wiped the palms of my hands on my robe. "Of course."

"I didn't know you played the piano, sir."

"Brewster, there are a lot of things you don't know about me and never will."

I went back to my room, waited half an hour, and then dressed. In the bright moonlight outside, I made my way to the garden shed. I unbolted its door, switched on the lights, and surveyed the gardening equipment. My eyes went to the tools in the wall racks.

I pulled down a long-handled irrigating shovel and knocked a bit of dried mud from its tip. I slung the implement over my shoulder and began walking toward the dell.

I was nearly there when I stopped and sighed heavily. I shook my head and returned to the shed. I put the shovel back into its place on the rack, switched off the lights, and returned to bed.

The next morning, Millicent dropped in as I was having breakfast.

"How are you this morning, Albert?"

"I have felt better."

Millicent sat down at the table and waited for Mrs. Brewster to bring her a cup.

Mrs. Brewster also brought the morning mail. It included a number of advertising fliers, a few bills, and one small blue envelope addressed to me.

I examined it. The handwriting seemed familiar and so did the scent. The postmark was town.

I slit open the envelope and pulled out a single sheet of notepaper.

> Dear Albert:
> You have no idea how much I miss you. I shall return home soon, Albert. Soon.
> Emily

I put the note back into the envelope and slipped both into my pocket.

"Well?" Millicent asked.

"Well, what?"

"I thought I recognized Emily's handwriting on the envelope. Did she say when she'd be back?"

"That is *not* Emily's handwriting. It is a note from my aunt in Chicago."

"I didn't know you had an aunt in Chicago."

"Millicent, rest assured. I *do* have an aunt in Chicago."

That night I was in bed, but awake, when the phone on my night table rang. I picked up the receiver.

"Hello, darling. This is Emily."

I let five seconds pass. "You are *not* Emily. You are an impostor."

"Now, Albert, why are you being so stubborn? Of course this is me. Emily."

"You couldn't be."

"Why couldn't I be?"

"Because."

"Because why?"

"Where are you calling from?"

She laughed. "I think you'd be surprised."

"You couldn't be Emily. I *know* where she is and she couldn't—*wouldn't*—make a phone call at this hour of the night just to say hello. It's well past midnight."

"You think you know where I am, Albert? No, I'm not there any more. It was so uncomfortable, so dreadfully uncomfortable. And so I left, Albert. I left."

I raised my voice. "Damn you, I can *prove* you're still there."

She laughed. "Prove? How can you prove anything like that, Albert? Good night." She hung up.

I got out of bed and dressed. I made my way downstairs and detoured into the study. I made myself a drink, consumed it slowly, and then made another.

When I consulted my watch for the last time it was nearly one A.M. I put on a light jacket against the chill of the night and made my way to the garden shed. I opened the doors, turned on the lights, and pulled the long-handled shovel from the rack.

This time I went all the way to the dell. I paused beside a huge oak and stared at the moonlit clearing.

I counted as I began pacing. "One, two, three, four—" I stopped at sixteen, turned ninety degrees, and then paced off eighteen more steps.

I began digging.

I had been at it for nearly five minutes when suddenly I heard the piercing blast of a whistle and immediately I became the focus of perhaps a dozen flashlight beams and approaching voices.

I shielded my eyes against the glare and recognized Millicent. "What the devil is this?"

She showed cruel teeth. "You had to make sure she was really dead, didn't you, Albert? And the only way you could do that was to return to her grave."

I drew myself up. "I am looking for Indian arrowheads. There's an ancient superstition that if one is found under the

light of the moon it will bring luck for the finder for several
weeks.''

Millicent introduced the people gathered about me. ''Ever
since I began suspecting what really has happened to Emily
you've been under twenty-four-hour surveillance by private
detectives.''

She indicated the others. ''Miss Peters. She is quite a clever
mimic and was the voice of Emily you heard over the phone.
She also plays piano. And Mrs. McMillan. She reproduced
Emily's handwriting and was the woman in the lilac dress and
the blue scarf.''

Millicent's entire household staff seemed to be present. I also
recognized Amos Eberly and the Brewsters. I would fire them
tomorrow.

The detectives had brought along their own shovels and
spades, and two of them superseded me in my shallow de-
pression. They began digging.

''See here,'' I said, exhibiting indignation. ''You have no
right to do that. This is *my* property. At the very least you need
a search warrant.''

Millicent found that amusing. ''This is *not* your property,
Albert. It is *mine*. You stepped over the dividing line six paces
back.''

I wiped my forehead. ''I'm going back to the house.''

''You are under arrest, Albert.''

''Nonsense, Millicent. I do not see a *proper* uniformed
policeman among these people. And in this state private detectives do not have the right to arrest anyone at all.''

For a moment she seemed stymied, but then saw light. ''You
are under *citizen's* arrest, Albert. Any citizen has the power to
make a citizen's arrest and I am a citizen.''

Millicent twirled the whistle on its chain. ''We knew we were
getting to you, Albert. You almost dug her up last night,
didn't you? But then you changed your mind. But that was just
as well. Last night I couldn't have produced as many witnesses.
Tonight we were ready and waiting.''

The detectives dug for some fifteen minutes and then paused
for a rest. One of them frowned. ''You'd think the digging

would be easier. This ground looks like it's never been dug up before.''

They resumed their work and eventually reached a depth of six feet before they gave up. The spade man climbed out of the excavation. "Hell, nothing's been buried here. The only thing we found was an Indian arrowhead.''

Millicent had been glaring at me for the last half hour.

I smiled. "Millicent, what makes you think that I *buried* Emily?''

With that I left them and returned to the house.

When had I first become aware of Millicent's magnificent maneuverings and the twenty-four-hour surveillance? Almost from the very beginning, I suspect. I'm rather quick on the up-take.

What had been Millicent's objective? I suppose she envisioned reducing me to such a state of fear that eventually I'd break down and confess to the murder of Emily.

Frankly, I would have regarded the success of such a scheme as farfetched, to say the least. However, once I was aware of what Millicent was attempting, I got into the spirit of the venture.

Millicent may have initiated the enterprise, the play, but it is I who led her to the dell.

There were times when I thought I overdid it just a bit—wiping at nonexistent perspiration, trotting after the elusive woman in the lilac dress, that sort of thing—but on the other hand I suppose these reactions were rather expected of me and I didn't want to disappoint any eager watchers.

Those brooding trips to the dell had been quite a good touch, I thought. And the previous night's halfway journey there, with the shovel over my shoulder, had been intended to assure a large audience at the finale twenty-four hours later.

I had counted eighteen witnesses, excluding Millicent.

I pondered. Defamation of character? Slander? Conspiracy? False arrest? Probably a good deal more.

I would threaten to sue for a large and unrealistic amount. That was the fashion nowadays, wasn't it? Twenty million? It didn't really matter, of course, because I doubted very much if the matter would ever reach court.

No, Millicent wouldn't be able to endure the publicity. She couldn't let the world know what a total fool she'd made of herself. She couldn't bear to be the laughingstock of her circle, her peers.

She would, of course, attempt to hush it up as best she could. A few dollars here and a few there to buy the silence of the witnesses. But could one seriously hope to buy the total silence of eighteen individual people? Probably not. However, when the whispers began to circulate, it would be a considerable help to Millicent if the principal player involved would join her in vehemently denying that any such ridiculous event had ever taken place at all.

And I would do that for Millicent. For a consideration. A *large* consideration.

At the end of the week, my phone rang.

"This is Emily. I'm coming home now, dear."

"Wonderful."

"Did anyone miss me?"

"You have no idea."

"You haven't told anyone where I've been these last four weeks, have you, Albert? Especially not Millicent?"

"Especially not Millicent."

"What *did* you tell her?"

"I said you were visiting friends in San Francisco."

"Oh, dear. I don't *know* anybody in San Francisco. Do you suppose she got suspicious?"

"Well, maybe just a little bit."

"She thinks I have absolutely no will power, but I really have. But just the same, I didn't want her laughing at me if I didn't stick it out. Oh, I suppose going to a health farm is cheating, in a way. I mean you can't be tempted because they control all of the food. But I really stuck it out. I could have come home any time I wanted to."

"You have marvelous will power, Emily."

"I've lost *thirty* pounds, Albert! And it's going to *stay* off. I'll bet I'm every bit as slim now as Cynthia ever was."

I sighed. There was absolutely no reason for Emily to keep comparing herself to my first wife. The two of them are separate entities and each has her secure compartment in my affections.

Poor Cynthia. She had insisted on going off by herself in that small craft. I had been at the yacht-club window sipping a martini and watching the cold gray harbor.

Cynthia's boat seemed to have been the only one on the water on that inhospitable day and there had apparently been an unexpected gust of wind. I had seen the boat heel over sharply and Cynthia thrown overboard. I'd raised the alarm immediately, but by the time we got out there it had been too late.

Emily sighed too. "I suppose I'll have to get an entire new wardrobe. Do you think we can really afford one, Albert?"

We could now. And then some.

DONALD E. WESTLAKE

ASK A SILLY QUESTION

Donald E. Westlake is one of the most popular of today's crime writers, whether he's writing about the inept thief Dortmunder in The Hot Rock *or* Bank Shot, *or the cold-blooded Parker in the "Richard Stark" series of novels. He has produced more than fifty books since 1960, which unfortunately leaves him little time for short stories like the following—a Dortmunder caper with all the fun and plot twists of a Westlake novel.*

"ART THEFT, OF COURSE," SAID THE ELEGANT MAN, "has been overdone. By now it's thoroughly boring."

Dortmunder didn't say anything. His business was theft, of art or whatever else had value, and he'd never supposed it was meant to be exciting. Nor, while tiptoeing around darkened halls in guarded buildings with his pockets full of stolen goods, had he ever found boredom much of a problem.

The elegant man sighed. "What do people of your sort drink?" he asked.

"Bourbon," Dortmunder said. "Water. Coca-Cola. Orange juice. Beer."

"Bourbon," the elegant man told one of the plug-uglies who'd brought Dortmunder here. "And sherry for me."

"Coffee," Dortmunder went on. "Sometimes Gallo Burgundy. Vodka. Seven-Up. Milk."

"How do you prefer your bourbon?" the elegant man asked.

"With ice and water. People of my sort also drink Hi-C, Scotch, lemonade, Nyquil——"

"Do you drink Perrier?"

"No," said Dortmunder.

"Ah," said the elegant man, closing the subject with his preconceptions intact. "Now," he said, "I suppose you're wondering why we all gathered you here."

"I got an appointment uptown," Dortmunder answered. He was feeling mulish. When a simple walk to the subway turns into an incident with two plug-uglies, a gun in the back, a shoving into a limousine outfitted with liveried chauffeur beyond the closed glass partition, a run up the stocking of Manhattan to the East Sixties, a swallowing up into a town house *with* a garage *with* an electronically operated door, and an interview at gunpoint with a tall, slender, painfully well-dressed, 60ish, white-haired, white-mustached elegant man in a beautifully appointed and very masculine den imported intact from Bloomingdale's, a person has a right to feel mulish. "I'm already late for my appointment," Dortmunder pointed out.

"I'll try to be brief," the elegant man promised. "My father—who, by the way, was once Secretary of the Treasury of this great land, under Teddy Roosevelt—always impressed upon me the wisdom of obtaining expert advice before undertaking any project, of whatever size or scope. I have always followed that injunction."

"Uh-huh," said Dortmunder.

"The exigencies of life having made it necessary for me," the elegant man continued, "to engage for once in the practice of grand larceny, in the form of burglary, I immediately sought out a professional in the field to advise me. You."

"I reformed," Dortmunder said. "I made some mistakes in my youth, but I paid my debt to society and now I'm reformed."

"Of course," said the elegant man. "Ah, here are our drinks. Come along, I have something to show you."

It was a dark and lumpy statue, about four feet tall, of a moody teenaged girl dressed in curtains and sitting on a tree trunk. "Beautiful, isn't it?" the elegant man said, gazing fondly at the thing.

Beauty was outside Dortmunder's visual spectrum. "Yeah," he said, and looked around this subterranean room, which had been fitted out like a cross between a den and a museum. Bookcases alternated with paintings on the walls, and antique furniture shared the polished wood floor with statuary, some on pedestals, some, like this bronze of a young girl, on low platforms. Dortmunder and the elegant man and the armed pluguglies had come down here by elevator; apparently, the only route in and out. There were no windows and the air had the flat blanketlike quality of tight temperature and humidity control.

"It's a Rodin," the elegant man was saying. "One of my wiser acquisitions, in my youth." His mouth forming a practiced *moue*, he said, "One of my *less* wise acquisitions, more recently, was a flesh-and-blood young woman who did me the disservice of becoming my wife."

"I really got an appointment uptown," Dortmunder said.

"More recently still," the elegant man persisted, "we came to a particularly bitter and unpleasant parting of the ways, Moira and I. As a part of the resulting settlement, the little bitch got this nymph here. But she *didn't* get it."

"Uh-huh," Dortmunder said.

"I have friends in the art world," the elegant man went on, "and all men have sympathizers where grasping ex-wives are concerned. Several years earlier, I'd had a mold made of this piece, and from it an exact copy had been cast in the same grade of bronze. A virtually identical copy; not quite museum quality, of course, but aesthetically just as pleasing as the original."

"Sure," said Dortmunder.

"It was that copy I gave to Moira; having, of course, first bribed the expert she'd brought in to appraise the objects she was looting from me. The other pieces I gave her with scarcely a murmur, but my nymph? Never!"

"Ah," said Dortmunder.

"All was well," the elegant man said. "I kept my nymph, the one and only true original from Rodin's plaster form, with the touch of the sculptor's hand full upon it. Moira had the copy, pleased with the thought of its being the original, cheered by the memory of having done me in the eye. A happy ending for everyone, you might have said.''

"Uh-huh," said Dortmunder.

"But not an ending at all, unfortunately." The elegant man shook his head. "It has come to my attention, *very* belatedly, that tax problems have forced Moira to make a gift of the Rodin nymph to the Museum of Modern Art. Perhaps I ought to explain that even I cannot with any certainty bribe an appraiser from the Museum of Modern Art.''

"He'll tell," Dortmunder said.

"He will, in the argot of the underworld," the elegant man said, "spill the beans.''

"That isn't the argot of the underworld," Dortmunder told him.

"No matter. The point is, my only recourse, it seems to me, is to enter Moira's town house and make off with the copy.''

"Makes sense," Dortmunder agreed.

The elegant man pointed at his nymph. "Pick that up," he said.

Dortmunder frowned, looking for the butcher's thumb.

"Go ahead," the elegant man insisted. "It won't bite.''

Dortmunder handed his bourbon and water to one of the plug-uglies; then, hesitant, unfamiliar with the process of lifting teenaged girls dressed in curtains—whether of bronze or anything else—he grasped this one by the chin and one elbow and lifted . . . and it didn't move. "Uh," said Dortmunder, visions of hernias blooming in his head.

"You see the problem," the elegant man said, while the muscles in Dortmunder's arms and shoulders and back and groin all quivered from the unexpected shock. "My nymph weighs five hundred twenty-six pounds. As does Moira's copy, give or take a few ounces.''

"Heavy," agreed Dortmunder. He took back his drink and drank.

"The museum's expert arrives tomorrow afternoon," the elegant man said, touching his white mustache. "If I am to avoid discomfort—possibly even public disgrace—I must remove Moira's copy from her possession tonight.''

Dortmunder said, "And you want me to do it?''

"No, no, not at all." The elegant man waved his elegant fingers. "My associates"—meaning the plug-uglies—"and I will, as you would say, pull the scam."

"That's not what I'd say," Dortmunder told him.

"No matter, no matter. What we wish from you, Mr. Dortmunder, is simply your expertise. Your professional opinion. Come along." The elevator doors opened to his elegant touch. "Care for another bourbon? Of course you do."

"Fortunately," the elegant man said, "I kept the architect's plans and models, even though I lost the town house itself to Moira."

Dortmunder and his host and one plug-ugly (the other was off getting more bourbon and sherry) stood now in a softly glowing dining room overlooking a formal brick-and-greenery rear garden. On the antique refectory table dominating the room stood two model houses, next to a roll of blue prints. The tinier model, barely six inches tall and built solid of balsa wood with windows and other details painted on, was placed on an aerial photograph to the same scale, apparently illustrating the block in which the finished house would stand. The larger, like a child's dollhouse, was over two feet tall, with what looked like real glass in its windows and even some furniture in the rooms within. Both models were of a large, nearly square house with a high front stoop, four stories tall, with a big square many-paned skylight in the center of the roof.

Dortmunder looked at the big model, then at the small, then at the photograph of the street. "This is in New York?"

"Just a few blocks from here."

"Huh," said Dortmunder, thinking of his own apartment.

"You see the skylight," suggested the elegant man.

"Yeah."

"It can be opened in good weather. There's an atrium on the second level. You know what an atrium is?"

"No."

"It's a kind of garden, within the house. Here, let me show you."

The larger model was build in pieces, which could be disassembled. The roof came off first, showing bedrooms and baths all around a big square opening coinciding with the skylight. The top floor came off, was set aside and showed a third floor given over to a master bedroom suite and a bookcase-lined den, around the continuing square atrium hole. The details impressed even Dortmunder. "This thing must have cost as much as the real house," he said.

The elegant man smiled. "Not quite," he said, lifting off the third floor. And here was the bottom of the atrium—fancy word for air shaft, Dortmunder decided—a formal garden like the one outside these real-life dining-room windows, with a fountain and stone paths. The living and dining rooms in the model were open to the atrium. "Moira's copy," the elegant man said, pointing at the garden, "is just about there."

"Tricky," Dortmunder commented.

"There are twelve steps down from the atrium level to the sidewalk in front. The rear garden is sunk deeper, below ground level."

"Very tricky."

"Ah, our drinks," the elegant man said, taking his, "and not a moment too soon." He sipped elegantly and said, "Mr. Dortmunder, the workman is worthy of his hire. I shall now outline to you our plans and our reasoning. I ask you to give us your careful attention, to advise us of any flaws in our thinking and to suggest whatever improvements come to your professional mind. In return, I will pay you—in cash, of course—one thousand dollars."

"And drive me uptown," Dortmunder said. "I'm really late for my appointment."

"Agreed."

"OK, then," Dortmunder said, and looked around for a place to sit down.

"Oh, come along," said the elegant man. "We might as well be comfortable."

Tall, narrow windows in the living room overlooked a tree-lined expensive block. Long sofas in ecru crushed velvet faced each other on the Persian carpet, amid glass-topped tables, modern lamps and antique bric-a-brac. In a Millet over the mantel, a French farmer of the last century endlessly pushed his barrowload of hay through a narrow barn door. The elegant man might have lost his atriummed town house to the scheming Moira, but he was still doing OK. No welfare housing necessary.

With a fresh drink to hand, Dortmunder sat on a sofa and listened. "We've made three plans," the elegant man said, as Dortmunder wondered who this "we" was he kept talking about; surely not the plug-uglies, giants with the brains of two-by-fours, sitting around now on chair arms like a rock star's bodyguards. "Our first plan, perhaps still feasible, involves that skylight and a helicopter. I have access to a heli——"

"Loud," Dortmunder said.

The elegant man paused, as though surprised, then smiled. "That's right," he said.

Dortmunder gave him a flat look. "Was that a test? You wanna see if I'll just say, 'Yeah, yeah, that's fine, give me my grand and take me uptown,' is that it?"

"To some extent," agreed the elegant man placidly. "Of course, apart from the noise—a dead giveaway to the entire neighborhood, naturally, the house would swarm with police before we'd so much as attached the grapple—still, apart from that noise problem, a helicopter *is* quite an attractive solution. At night, from above——"

"Illegal," interrupted Dortmunder.

"Eh?"

"You can't fly a helicopter over Manhattan after dark. There's a law. Never break a law you don't intend to break; people get grabbed for a traffic violation, and what they're really doing is robbing a bank. That kind of thing. It happens all the time."

"I see." The elegant man looked thoughtful. Smoothing back his silver locks, he said, "Every trade is more complicated than it appears, isn't it?"

"Yeah," said Dortmunder. "What's plan number two?"

"Ah, yes." The elegant man regained his pleased look. "This involves the front door."

"How many people in this house?"

"None." Then the elegant man made a dismissing finger wave, saying, "The staff, of course. But they're all downstairs.

It's soundproofed down there and servants sleep like the dead, anyway.''

"If you say so. Where's this Moira?''

"She *should* be in England, mired on the M four,'' the elegant man said, looking extremely irritated, ''but the delay I'd arranged for her to undergo didn't quite take place. As a result, she is probably at this very moment boarding her flight to New York. She'll be here sometime early tomorrow morning.'' Shrugging away his annoyance, he said, ''Nevertheless, we still have all of tonight. Plan number two, as I started to say, has us forcing entry through the front door. Three strong men''—with a graceful hand gesture to include both himself and the silent plug-uglies—''with some difficulty, can jog the statue onto a low wheeled dolly. Out front, we shall have a truck equipped with a winch, whose long cable will reach as far as the atrium. The winch can pull the statue on the dolly through the house and down a metal ramp from the head of the stairs to the interior of the truck.''

"That sounds OK,'' said Dortmunder. ''What's the problem?''

"The guard,'' the elegant man explained, ''outside the embassy next door.''

"Oh,'' said Dortmunder. ''And if you get rid of the guard. . . .''

"We create an international incident. A side effect even more severe than the breaking of helicopter-at-night laws.''

Dortmunder shook his head. ''Tell me about plan number three.''

"We effect entry through the rear, from the house on the next block. We set various incendiary devices and we burn the place down.''

Dortmunder frowned. ''Metal doesn't burn,'' he objected.

"A flaw we'd noticed ourselves,'' the elegant man admitted.

Dortmunder drank bourbon and gave his host a look of disgust. ''You don't have any plan at all,'' he said.

"We have no *good* plans,'' the elegant man said. ''Would you have a suggestion of your own?''

"For a thousand dollars?'' Dortmunder sipped bourbon and looked patiently at the elegant man.

Who smiled, a bit sadly. "I see what you mean," he said. "Say two thousand."

"Say ten thousand," Dortmunder suggested.

"I couldn't possibly say ten thousand. I might find it possible to say twenty-five hundred."

It took three minutes and many little delicate silences before Dortmunder and the elegant man reached the $5000 honorarium both had settled on in advance.

The interior ladder down from the skylight had been so cunningly integrated into the decor of the house that it was practically useless; tiny rungs, irregularly spaced, far too narrow and curving frighteningly down the inside of the domed ceiling. Dortmunder, who had a perfectly rational fear of heights, inched his way downward, prodded by the plug-ugly behind him and encouraged by the plug-ugly ahead, while trying not to look between his shoes at the tiny shrubbery and statuary and ornamental fountain three long stories below.

What a lot of air there is in an atrium!

Attaining the safety of the top-floor floor, Dortmunder turned to the elegant man, who had come first down the ladder with an astonishing spryness and lack of apprehension, and told him, "This isn't fair, that's all. I'm here under protest."

"Of course you are," the elegant man said. "That's why my associates had to show you their revolvers. But surely for five thousand dollars, we can expect you to be present while your rather ingenious scheme is being worked out."

A black satchel, tied about with a hairy thick yellow rope, descended past in small spasms, lowered by the plug-ugly who was remaining on the roof. "I never been so late for an appointment in my life," Dortmunder said. "I should of been uptown hours ago."

"Come along," the elegant man said, "we'll find you a phone, you can call and explain. But please invent an explanation; the truth should not be telephoned."

Dortmunder, who had never telephoned the truth and who hardly ever even presented the truth in person, made no reply, but followed the elegant man and the other plug-ugly down the winding staircase to the main floor, where the plug-ugly with muttered curses removed the black satchel from the ornamental fountain. "You shouldn't get that stuff wet," Dortmunder pointed out.

"Accidents will happen," the elegant man said carelessly, while the plug-ugly continued to mutter. "Let's find you a telephone."

They found it in the living room, near the tall front windows, on a charming antique desk inlaid with green leather. Seated at this, Dortmunder could look diagonally out the window and see the guard strolling in front of the embassy next door. An empty cab drifted by, between the lines of parked cars. The elegant man went back to the atrium and Dortmunder picked up the phone and dialed.

"O. J. Bar and Grill, Rollo speaking."

"This is Dortmunder."

"Who?"

"The bourbon and water."

"Oh, yeah. Say, your pals are in the back. They're waiting for you, huh?"

"Yeah," Dortmunder said. "Let me talk to Ke——The other bourbon and water."

"Sure."

A police car oozed by; the embassy guard waved at it. Opening the desk drawer, Dortmunder found a gold bracelet set with emeralds and rubies; he put it in his pocket. Behind him, a sudden loud mechanical rasping sound began; he put his thumb in his other ear.

"Hello? Dortmunder?" Kelp's voice.

"Yeah," Dortmunder said.

"You're late."

"I got tied up. With some people."

"Something going on?"

"I'll tell you later."

"You sound like you're in a body shop."

"A what?"

"Where they fix cars. You don't have a car, do you?"

"No," Dortmunder said. The rasping sound was *very* loud.

"That's very sensible," Kelp said. "What with the energy crisis, and inflation, and being in a city with first-rate mass transportation, it doesn't make any sense to own your own car."

"Sure," Dortmunder said. "What I'm calling about——"

"Any time you need a car," Kelp said, "you can just go pick one up."

"That's right," Dortmunder said. "About tonight——"

"So what are you doing in a body shop?"

The rasping sound, or something, was getting on Dortmunder's nerves. "I'll tell you later," he said.

"You'll be along soon?"

"No. I might be stuck here a couple hours. Maybe we should make the meet tomorrow night."

"No problem," Kelp said. "And if you break loose, we can still do it tonight."

"You guys don't have to hang around," Dortmunder told him.

"That's OK. We're having a nice discussion on religion and politics. See you later."

"Right," said Dortmunder.

In the atrium, they were cutting the nymph's head off. As Dortmunder came back from his phone call, the girl's head nodded once, then fell with a splash into the fountain. As the plug-ugly switched off the saw, the elegant man turned toward Dortmunder a face of anguish, saying, "It's like seeing a human being cut up before your eyes. Worse. Were she flesh and blood, I could at least imagine she was Moira."

"That thing's loud," Dortmunder said.

"Not outside," the elegant man assured him. "Because of traffic noise, the façade was soundproofed. Also the floor; the servants won't hear a thing."

The plug-ugly having wrapped the decapitated head in rope, he switched on his saw again and attacked the nymph, this time at her waistline. The head, meantime, peering raffishly through circlets of yellow rope, rose slowly roofward, hauled from above.

Dortmunder, having pointed out to the elegant man that *removal* of this statue was all that mattered, that its postoperative condition was unimportant, had for his $5000 suggested they cut it into totable chunks and remove it via the roof. Since, like most castbronze statues, it was hollow rather than solid, the dismembering was certainly within the range of the possible.

Dortmunder had first thought in terms of an industrial laser, which would make a fast, clean and absolutely silent cut, but the elegant man's elegant contacts did not include access to a laser, so Dortmunder had fallen back on the notion of an acetylene torch. (Everybody in Dortmunder's circle had an acetylene torch.) But there, too, the elegant man had turned out to be deficient, and it was only after exhaustive search of the garage that this large saber saw and several metal-cutting blades had been found. Well, it was better than a pocketknife, though not so quiet.

The head fell from the sky into the fountain, splashing everybody with water.

The plug-ugly with the saw turned it off, lifted his head and spoke disparagingly to his partner on the roof, who replied in kind. The elegant man raised his own voice, in French, and when the plug-uglies ceased maligning each other, he said, "*I shall bind the parts.*"

The nearer plug-ugly gave him a sullen look. "That's brain-work, *I* guess," he said, switched on the saber saw and stabbed the nymph in the belly with it. Renewed racket buried the elegant man's response.

It was too loud here. From Dortmunder's memory of the model of this house, the kitchen should be through the dining room and turn right. While the elegant man fumbled with the bronze head, Dortmunder strolled away. Passing through the dining room, he pocketed an antique oval ivory cameo frame.

Dortmunder paused in the preparation of his second *pâté* and swiss on rye with Dijon mustard—this kitchen contained neither peanut butter *nor* jelly—when the racket of saber saw was abruptly replaced by the racket of angry voices. Among them was a voice undoubtedly female. Dortmunder sighed, closed the sandwich, carried it in his left hand and went through to the atrium, where a woman surrounded by Louis Vuitton suitcases was yelling at the top of her voice at the elegant man, who was yelling just as loudly right back. The plug-ugly stood to one side, openmouthed but silent, the saber saw also silent in his hand, hovering over the statue stub, now reduced to tree trunk, knees, shins, feet, toes, base and a bit of curtain hem.

This was clearly the ex-wife, home ahead of schedule. The elegant man seemed unable to do *anything* right. In the semidarkness of the dining-room doorway, Dortmunder ate his sandwich and listened and watched.

The screaming was merely that at first, screaming, with barely any rational words identifiable in the mix, but the ex-wife's first impulse to make lots of noise was soon overtaken by the full realization that her statue was *all cut to pieces;* gradually, her shrieks faded away to gasps and then to mere panting, until at last she merely stood in stunned silence, staring at the destruction, while the elegant man also ceased to bray. Regaining his composure and his elegance, he readjusted his cuffs and, with barely a tremor in his voice, he said, "Moira, I admit you have me at a disadvantage."

"You—you——" But she wasn't capable of description, not yet, not with the butchery right here in front of her.

"An explanation is in order," the elegant man acknowledged, "but first let me reassure you on one point: The Rodin has not been destroyed. You will still, I'm afraid, be able to turn it over to the populace."

"You bluh—you——"

"My presence here," the elegant man continued, as though his ex-wife's paralysis were an invitation to go on, "is the result of an earlier deception, at the time of our separation. I'm afraid I must admit to you now that I bribed Grindle at that time to accept on your behalf not the original but a copy of the Rodin—this copy, in fact."

The ex-wife took a deep breath. She looked away from the bronze carnage and gazed at the elegant man. "You bloody fool," she said, having at last recaptured her voice, and speaking now almost in a conversational tone. "You bloody self-satisfied fool, do you think you *invented* bribery?"

A slight frown wrinkled the elegant man's features. "I beg your pardon?"

"Beg Rodin's," she told him. "*You* could only bribe Grindle with cash. When he told me your proposition, I saw no reason why he shouldn't take it."

"You—you——" Now it was the elegant man who was losing the power of speech.

"And, having taken your bribe *and* mine," she went inexorably on, "he pronounced the false true before reversing the statues. *That*," pointing at the shins and tree trunk, "was the original."

"Impossible!" The elegant man had begun to blink. His tie was askew. "Grindle wouldn't——I've kept the——"

"*You bloody* FOOL!" And the woman reached for a handy piece of luggage—toilet case, swamp-colored, speckled with someone else's initials, retail $364.50—and hurled it at her ex-husband, who ducked, bellowed and reached for the late nymph's bronze thigh with which to riposte. The woman side-stepped and the thigh rolled across the atrium, coming to a stop at Dortmunder's feet. He looked down at it, saw the glint of something shiny on the rough inside surface and hunkered down for a closer look. At the foundry, when they'd covered the removable plaster interior with wax prior to pouring the bronze, maybe some French coin, now old and valuable, had got stuck in the wax and then transferred to the bronze. Dortmunder peered in at the thing, reaching out one hand to turn the thigh slightly to improve the light, then running his finger tips over the shiny thing, testing to see if it would come loose. But it was well and firmly fixed in place.

The rasp of the saber saw once more snarled: Dortmunder, looking up, saw that the woman had it now, and was chasing her ex-husband around the plants and flowers with it, while the plug-ugly stood frozen, pretending to be a floor lamp. Dortmunder stood, mouthed the last of his sandwich, retraced his steps to the kitchen and went out the window.

The far-off sound of sirens was just audible when he reached the pay phone at the corner and called again the O.J. Bar and Grill. When Kelp came on the phone, Dortmunder said, "The guys still there?"

"Sure. You on your way?"

"No. I got a new thing over here on the East Side. You and the guys meet me at Park and Sixty-fifth."

"Sure. What's up?"

"Just a little breaking and entering."

"The place is empty?"

Down the block, police cars were massing in front of Moira's house. "Oh, yeah," Dortmunder said, "it's empty. I don't think the owner's gonna be back for years."

"Something valuable?"

There weren't two copies of the Rodin, no; there was one original, one copy. And the elegant man had been right about ex-husbands' getting the sympathy vote. The hired expert had accepted bribes from both parties, but he'd made his own decision when it came to distributing the real and the fake Rodins. In Dortmunder's mind's eye, he saw again the shiny thing hidden within the nymph's thigh. It was the flip-off ring from a thoroughly modern beer can. "It's valuable OK," he said. "But it's kind of heavy. On the way over, steal a truck."

THE YEARBOOK OF THE MYSTERY & SUSPENSE STORY

THE YEAR'S BEST MYSTERY AND SUSPENSE NOVELS

Chosen by Martin H. Greenberg

Eric Ambler: *The Care of Time* (Farrar, Straus & Giroux)
Marian Babson: *Line Up for Murder* (Walker)
Beryl Bainbridge: *Winter Garden* (Braziller)
Robert Barnard: *Death of a Literary Widow* (Scribner)
Tony Cohan: *Canary* (Doubleday)
E. V. Cunningham (Howard Fast): *The Case of the Sliding Pool* (Delacorte)
Nelson DeMille: *Cathedral* (Delacorte)
Wessel Ebersohn: *Divide the Night* (Pantheon)
Dick Francis: *Reflex* (Putnam)
Stephen Greenleaf: *Death Red* (Dial)
Frederic Vincent Huber: *Apple Crunch* (Seaview)
Tony Hillerman: *People of Darkness* (Harper & Row)
Richard Hugo: *Death and the Good Life* (St. Martin's)
William X. Kienzle: *Mind Over Murder* (Andrews & McMeel)
Ernest Larsen: *Not a Through Street* (Random House)
Emma Lathen: *Going for the Gold* (Simon & Schuster)
Michael Z. Lewin: *Missing Woman* (Knopf)
John D. MacDonald: *Free Fall in Crimson* (Harper & Row)
Ngaio Marsh: *Photo Finish* (Little, Brown)
Ed McBain: *Heat* (Viking)
Patrick McGinley: *Bogmail* (Ticknor & Fields)

Herbert Mitgang: *The Montauk Fault* (Arbor House)
Bill Pronzini: *Hoodwink* (St. Martin's)
Ruth Rendell: *Death Notes* (Pantheon)
Richard Rhodes: *Sons of Earth* (Coward, McCann and Geoghegan)
Gerald Seymour: *The Contract* (Holt, Rinehart and Winston)
Martin Cruz Smith: *Gorky Park* (Random House)
Ross H. Spencer: *Echoes of Zero* (St. Martin's)
Ross Thomas: *The Mordida Man* (Simon & Schuster)
Gene Thompson: *Murder Mystery* (Random House)
Dorothy Uhnak: *False Witness* (Simon & Schuster)
Joseph Wambaugh: *The Glitter Dome* (Perigord Press / William
    Morrow)

BIBLIOGRAPHY

I. Collections

1. Borges, Jorge Luis & Bioy-Casares, Adolfo. *Six Problems for Don Isidro Parodi*. New York: Dutton. First American edition of a 1942 collection published in Argentina as by "H. Bustos Domecq." Number 96 in *Queen's Quorum*, Ellery Queen's list of the 125 most important books of detective-crime short stories.
2. Cain, James M. *The Baby in the Icebox*. New York: Holt, Rinehart & Winston. A novelette and 19 stories and sketches, some criminous.
3. Doyle, Sir Arthur Conan. *The Final Adventures of Sherlock Holmes*. Secaucus, NJ: Castle Books. A dozen stories, parodies, articles and plays in which Holmes appears or is alluded to, all introduced by Peter Haining. Nine of the items may also be found in *Sherlock Holmes: The Published Apocrypha* (1980), edited by Jack Tracy.
4. Gardner, Erle Stanley. *The Human Zero*. New York: Morrow. Seven science fiction novelettes from *Argosy*, 1928–1932, some criminous. Edited by Martin Greenberg and Charles Waugh.
5. Garfield, Brian. *Checkpoint Charlie*. New York (129 E. 56 St.): The Mysterious Press. Twelve stories about aging spy Charlie Dark, one of them new.
6. Garrett, Randall. *Lord Darcy Investigates*. New York: Ace Books.

Four detective novelettes set in an alternate universe where magic flourishes in a modern Anglo-French Empire. Despite the fantasy element, the impossible crime puzzles are logically resolved.

7. Gibson, Walter. *The Shadow: Jade Dragon & House of Ghosts.* New York: Doubleday. Two short novels from *The Shadow* magazine, 1942–43.

8. Mortimer, John. *The Trials of Rumpole.* New York: Penguin Books. Six new stories about a British barrister.

9. Simenon, Georges. *The Little Doctor.* New York: Harcourt Brace Jovanovich. Thirteen detective stories from the 1940s, all solved by the title character.

10. Sladek, John. *The Best of John Sladek.* New York: Pocket Books. Twenty-six stories and parodies first published in England, mainly fantasy but a few criminous.

11. Treat, Lawrence. *Crime & Puzzlement.* Boston: David R. Godine. Twenty-four brief picture mysteries, illustrated by Leslie Cabarga.

12. Wodehouse, P.G. *Wodehouse on Crime.* New York: Ticknor & Fields. Twelve crime stories by the noted British humorist, edited by D.R. Bensen and introduced by Isaac Asimov.

13. Woolrich, Cornell. *The Fantastic Stories of Cornell Woolrich.* Carbondale, IL: Southern Illinois University Press. Eight fantasies, all criminous, edited by Charles G. Waugh and Martin H. Greenberg, with an introduction by Francis M. Nevins Jr. and an afterword by Barry N. Malzberg.

II. Anthologies

1. Asimov, Isaac; Greenburg, Martin H.; & Olander, Joseph D., editors. *Miniature Mysteries.* New York: Taplinger. One hundred short-short mystery and crime stories.

2. Coffey, Frank, ed. *Modern Masters of Horror.* New York: Coward, McCann & Geoghegan. Fifteen stories, six of them new, some criminous.

3. *Crime Wave.* London: Collins. Eighteen prize-winning stories in a contest sponsored by the Third Crime Writers' International Congress, Introduction by Desmond Bagley.

4. Hale, James, ed. *The After Midnight Ghost Book.* New York: Franklin Watts. Twenty-four new stories, some criminous.

5. Hardinge, George, ed. *Winter's Crimes 13.* London: Macmillan. Eleven new stories by British writers.

6. Harris, Herbert, ed. *John Creasey's Crime Collection 1981.* London: Gollancz. Sixteen stories, five of them new, in the annual

anthology of the Crime Writers' Association. American edition published by St. Martin's Press.

7. Hoch, Edward D., ed. *All But Impossible!* New York: Ticknor & Fields. Twenty stories of locked rooms and impossible crimes by members of the Mystery Writers of America.

8. _____. *Best Detective Stories of the Year 1981*. New York: E.P. Dutton. Sixteen of the best short stories published during 1980.

9. Pronzini, Bill; Malzberg, Barry; & Greenberg, Martin H., eds. *The Arbor House Treasury of Horror and the Supernatural*. New York: Arbor House. Forty-one stories, many criminous.

10. Queen, Ellery, ed. *Crime Cruise Round the World*. New York: Dial. Twenty-six stories from *EQMM*.

11. _____. *Doors to Mystery*. New York: Dial. A short novel and 18 stories from *EQMM*.

12. _____. *Eyes of Mystery*. New York: Dial. Five novelettes and 16 stories from *EQMM*.

13. Sullivan, Eleanor, ed. *Alfred Hitchcock's Tales to Make Your Hair Stand on End*. New York: Dial. Twenty-four stories from *AHMM*.

14. _____. *Alfred Hitchcock's Tales to Make You Weak in the Knees*. New York: Dial. Twenty-six stories from *AHMM*.

15. Van Thal, Herbert, ed. *The Fifth Bedside Book of Great Detective Stories*. London: Arthur Barker. Twelve stories, one of them new.

16. Waugh, Carol-Lynn Rossel; Greenberg, Martin H.; & Asimov, Isaac, eds. *The Twelve Crimes of Christmas*. New York: Avon. Twelve mysteries with a Christmas setting.

III. *Biographical, Critical & General Nonfiction*

1. Adams, Tom. *Agatha Christie: The Art of Her Crimes*. New York: Everest House. Tom Adams's cover art for all the Christie books, with text by the artist and additional commentary by Julian Symons. Introduction by John Fowles.

2. Baird, Newton. *A Key to Fredric Brown's Wonderland*. Georgetown, CA: Talisman Literary Research, Inc. An annotated bibliography of Brown's novels and short stories, with reminiscences by Elizabeth Brown and Harry Altshuler, and a brief essay by Brown himself.

3. Bargainner, Earl F. *The Gentle Art of Murder*. Bowling Green, Ohio: Bowling Green University Popular Press. A study of Agatha Christie's work.

4. _____, ed. *Ten Women of Mystery*. Bowling Green, Ohio: Bowling Green University Popular Press. Ten critical essays on Dorothy L. Sayers, Josephine Tey, Ngaio Marsh, P.D. James, Ruth Rendell, Anna Katherine Green, Mary Roberts Rinehart, Margaret Millar, Emma Lathen and Amanda Cross.

5. Benvenuti, Stefano & Rizzoni, Gianni. *The Whodunit: An Informal History of Detective Fiction*. New York: Macmillan. An illustrated history, translated from the Italian, with an added chapter on modern writers by Edward D. Hoch.

6. Blackbeard, Bill. *Sherlock Holmes in America*. New York: Abrams. A collection of essays, illustrations, cartoons, reviews and pastiches. Foreword by Dean Dickensheet.

7. Bilgrey, Marc. *The Sherlock Holmes Cartoon Book*. New York (Box 501, Ansonia Station): Cuckoo Bird Press. One hundred cartoons about Holmes, Watson and their adventures.

8. Brabazon, James. *Dorothy L. Sayers*. New York: Scribners. The first Sayers biography written with access to her letters and private papers.

9. Breen, Jon L. *What About Murder?* Metuchen, NJ: The Scarecrow Press. An annotated bibliography of 239 books about mystery and detective fiction, with critical evaluations of each title.

10. Chandler, Raymond. *Selected Letters of Raymond Chandler*. New York: Columbia University Press. Edited by Chandler biographer Frank MacShane.

11. Corsaut, Aneta; Singer, Muff; & Wagner, Robert. *The Mystery Reader's Quiz Book*. New York: Evans. Questions and answers.

12. De Waal, Ronald Burt. *The International Sherlock Holmes*. Hamden, CT: Archon Books. A companion volume to *The World Bibliography of Sherlock Holmes and Dr. Watson*, annotating all Sherlockiana appearing between 1971 and 1978, with additions to the pre-1972 entries in the previous volume.

13. Gaillard, Dawson. *Dorothy L. Sayers*. New York: Unger. A critical study.

14. Haining, Peter. *Mystery! An Illustrated History of Crime and Detective Fiction*. New York: Stein and Day. A brief history up to World War II, with numerous illustrations from early magazines.

15. _____, ed. *A Sherlock Holmes Compendium*. Secaucus, NJ: Castle Books. Thirty-seven Sherlockian essays, quizzes, etc.

16. Hubin, Allen J., ed. *The Armchair Detective, Volume One*. Madison, IN: Brownstone Books. Hardbound edition of the first four issues of a popular mystery fan magazine.

17. Johnson, Timothy W. & Julia, eds. *Crime Fiction Criticism*. New York: Garland. An annotated bibliography of books and magazine articles on mystery fiction.

18. Keating, H.R.F. *Murder Must Appetize*. New York (129 W. 56 St.): The Mysterious Press. Revised American edition of a brief 1975 study of British mystery writers of the Golden Age.

19. Layman, Richard. *Shadow Man*. New York: Harcourt Brace Jovanovich. A biography of Dashiell Hammett.

20. Macdonald, Ross. *Self-Portrait: Ceaselessly into the Past*. Santa Barbara, CA (Box 2068): Capra Press. Twenty-one essays, introductions and interviews in which Macdonald examines his life and writing. Foreword by Eudora Welty.

21. Mann, Jessica. *Deadlier Than the Male*. New York: Macmillan. A study of feminine crime writing, with emphasis on Christie, Sayers, Allingham, Tey and Marsh.

22. O'Brien, Geoffrey. *Hardboiled America*. New York: Van Nostrand Reinhold. A study of paperbacks' "lurid years," their covers and contents, with emphasis on hardboiled mystery writers.

23. Porter, Dennis. *The Pursuit of Crime*. New Haven, CT: Yale University Press. The art of the detective story, focusing on Doyle, Christie, Hammett, Chandler and Simenon.

24. Ryan, Elizabeth Bond & Eakins, William J. *The Lord Peter Wimsey Cookbook*. New York: Ticknor & Fields. Recipes and information about food and drink in Dorothy L. Sayers's mysteries.

25. Shine, Walter & Jean. *A Bibliography of the Published Works of John D. MacDonald*. Gainesville, FL: Patrons of the Libraries, University of Florida. Includes biographical material.

26. Siebenheller, Norma. *P.D. James*. New York: Unger. A critical study.

27. Speir, Jerry. *Raymond Chandler*. New York: Unger. A Critical study.

28. Symons, Julian. *Critical Observations*. New York: Ticknor & Fields. Twenty-two literary essays, some criminous.

29. _____. *Great Detectives*. New York: Abrams. Seven essays about possible events in the lives of Sherlock Holmes, Nero Wolfe, Philip Marlowe, Miss Marple, Hercule Poirot, Ellery Queen and Maigret. Illustrated by Tom Adams.

AWARDS

Mystery Writers of America
> Best novel — William Bayer, *Peregrine* (Congdon & Lattès/St. Martin's Press)
> Best first novel — Stuart Woods, *Chiefs* (Norton)
> Best paperback novel — L. A. Morse, *The Old Dick* (Avon)
> Best short story — Jack Ritchie, "The Absence of Emily" (*Ellery Queen's Mystery Magazine*)
> Best critical/biographical study — Jon L. Breen, *What About Murder?* (Scarecrow Press)
> Grand master award — Julian Symons

Crime Writers Association (London)

> Gold Dagger — Martin Cruz Smith, *Gorky Park* (Collins; U.S. edition, Random House)
> Silver Dagger — Colin Dexter, *The Dead of Jericho* (Macmillan)
> John Creasey Award (first novel) — James Leigh, *The Ludi Victor* (Bodley Head)
> Nonfiction Gold Dagger — Jacobo Timerman, *Prisoner Without a Name, Cell Without a Number* (Weidenfeld & Nicolson; U.S. edition, Alfred A. Knopf)

NECROLOGY

1. Martha Albrand (1914–1981). Pseudonym of Heidi Huberta Freybe, German-American author of spy novels, beginning with *No Surrender* (1942).
2. John Franklin Bardin (1916–1981). Author of four mystery novels, notably *Devil Take the Blue-Tail Fly* (1948), plus four others published under the pseudonyms of "Douglas Ashe" and "Gregory Tree."
3. Eleanor Rosenfeld Bayer (1908–1981). Author, with her husband Leo, of four 1940s mystery novels under the joint pseudonym of "Oliver Weld Bayer."
4. Nathaniel Benchley (1915–1981). Well-known novelist who

authored two suspense books, *Catch a Falling Spy* (1963) and *The Hunter's Moon* (1972).

5. Raymond T. Bond (1893?–1981). Former president of Dodd, Mead publishers and editor of two mystery anthologies, *Famous Stories of Code and Cipher* (1947) and *Handbook for Poisoners* (1951).

6. Nellise Child (ca. 1902–1981). Author of two novels, *Murder Comes Home* (1933) and *The Diamond Ransom Murders* (1935).

7. Edwin (Ray) Corley (1931–1981). Author of a suspense novel *The Jesus Factor* (1970), and other mysteries under the pseudonyms "David Harper" and "William Judson." With Jack Murphy he published four mysteries under the joint pseudonym "Patrick Buchanan," notably *A Requiem of Sharks* (1973).

8. A. J. Cronin (1896–1981). Distinguished Scottish-American novelist whose works included a suspense novel, *Beyond This Place* (1953).

9. Hildegarde Dolson (1908–1981). Author of four novels, 1971–1977, about detective Lucy Ramsdale.

10. Robert L. Fish (1912–1981). Well-known author of the "Schlock Homes" parodies and ten novels about Captain Jose da Silva of the Brazilian police, beginning with *The Fugitive* (1962), an MWA Edgar winner. Also published a score of other mystery and suspense novels, some under the pseudonym of "Robert L. Pike," one of which, *Mute Witness* (1963), became the popular film *Bullitt*. Past president of Mystery Writers of America.

11. Douglas Fisher (1902–1981). British author of more than twenty mystery novels, many under the pseudonym of "George Douglas," unpublished in America.

12. David Garnett (1892–1981). British novelist best known for his fantasy *Lady Into Fox* (1922), who published one suspense novel *Dope-Darling* (1919) under the pseudonym of "Leda Burke."

13. Lee Hays (1914?–1981). Co-founder of "The Weavers" singing group, who published three short mysteries in *EQMM*, 1948–1954.

14. James D. Horan (1914–1981). Author of a suspense novel *The New Vigilantes* (1975).

15. Pamela Hansford Johnson (1912–1981). Well-known novelist who published two 1940s mysteries with Neil Stewart under the joint pseudonym of "Nap Lombard."

16. Lawrence Lariar (1908–1981). Author of some twenty detective novels, notably *The Girl With the Frightened Eyes* (1945), some published under the pseudonyms "Adam Knight," "Michael Lawrence" and "Michael Stark."

17. Meyer Levin (1905–1981). Best-selling author of *Compulsion* (1956).
18. Victoria Lincoln (1904–1981). Author of *The Swan Island Murders* (1930).
19. Philip MacDonald (1896-1981). Anglo-American mystery novelist and screenwriter, best known for *The Rasp* (1924), *Warrant for X* (1938) and *The List of Adrian Messenger* (1959). Some of his novels such as *The Mystery of the Dead Police* (1933) were first published under the pseudonym of "Martin Porlock," and his first two novels, in collaboration with Ronald MacDonald, appeared as bv "Oliver Fleming." He also wrote as "Anthony Lawless."
20. Robin Maugham (1916–1981). Author of several suspense novels including *The Link: A Victorian Mystery* (1969).
21. Robert A. Simon (1897–1981). Author of a single crime novel, *The Weekend Mystery* (1926).
22. Harrison R. Steeves (1881–1981). Former head of Columbia College's English Department and author of a single well-regarded mystery novel, *Good Night, Sheriff* (1941).

HONOR ROLL

Abbreviations:
EQMM—Ellery Queen's Mystery Magazine
AHMM—Alfred Hitchcock's Mystery Magazine
MSMM—Mike Shayne Mystery Magazine

(Starred stories are included in this volume. All stories from 1981.)

Alexander, Gary, "The Confession," *AHMM*, April 29
_____, "A Matter of Conscience," *EQMM*, March 25
Asimov, Isaac, "The Gilbert and Sullivan Mystery," *EQMM*, January 1
*Baber, Asa, "The French Lesson," *Playboy*, March
Backus, Jean L., "A Hearse Is Not a Home," *EQMM*, May 20
Bankier, William, "Happiness You Can Count On," *EQMM*, January 1
_____, "Marti Roch," *AHMM*, May 27
_____, "A Woman Waits For Me," *EQMM*, March 25
Baxt, George, "Show Me a Hero," *EQMM*, July 15

* _____, "What Have You Been Up to Lately?" *EQMM*, January 28

Blau, Kelly H., "Services," *AHMM*, December 9

Block, Lawrence, "Going Through the Motions," *EQMM*, August 12

Bloomfield, Anthony, "How Does Your Garden Grow?" *EQMM*, June 17

Boland, John C., "Reunion in Baineville," *EQMM*, August 12

Booker, Lionel, "The Dubbing Clue," *EQMM*, May 20

Brand, Christianna, "The Hand of God," *EQMM*, March 25

Breen, Jon L., "Mourning Noon at Night," *MSMM*, July

Bretnor, Reg, "Wonder Cure," *EQMM*, March 25

Brett, Simon, "Metaphor for Murder," *EQMM*, February 25

Brittain, William, "Mr. Strang Interprets a Picture," *EQMM*, August 12

Buck, Anita, "The Way You See It," *EQMM*, October 7

Chesmore, Robert, "The Long Ball," *MSMM*, March

Chi, Ta Huang, "The Foreign Devil," *AHMM*, August 19

_____, "The Shanghai Gold Bars," *EQMM*, March 25

Crawford, Barbara, "The Unbidden Thought," *EQMM*, January 1

*Curtiss, Ursula, "The House on Plymouth Street," *Cosmopolitan*, June

Dale, Celia, "What a Treasure!" *EQMM*, September 9

Davis, Dorothy Salisbury, "The Devil and His Due," *EQMM*, April 22

Dirckx, John H., "Eyes That See, Ears That Hear," *EQMM*, September 9

Dwyer, Thomas, "Wait For Me," *MSMM*, November

Fieldhouse, W.L., "Ape Murder," *MSMM*, August

_____, "Murder in Bonn," *MSMM*, February

Fish, Robert L., "The Adventure of the Pie-eyed Piper," *EQMM*, June 17

_____, "The Adventure of the Ukrainian Foundling Orphans," *EQMM*, January 28

Francis, Dick, "The Day of the Losers," *EQMM*, September 9

Fremlin, Celia, "Anything May Happen," *EQMM*, July 15

*Garfield, Brian, "The Chalk Outline," *EQMM*, May 20

_____, "The Shopping List," *EQMM*, December 2

*Gash, Jonathan, "The Hours of Angelus," *The Fifth Bedside Book of Great Detective Stories*

*Gilbert, Michael, "Camford Cottage," *The After Midnight Ghost Book*

_____, "The Last Reunion," *EQMM*, December 2

_____, "Source Seven," *EQMM*, July 15

_____, "The Violence Peddlers," *EQMM*, February 25

Goulart, Ron, "The Rise and Fall of Norbert Tuffy," *EQMM*, June 17
* _____, "Suspense," *AHMM*, July 22
Grant, Richard, "Commute to Murder," *EQMM*, July 15
Hamilton, Nan, "Seeds of Murder," *AHMM*, December 9
Harrington, Joyce, "Dispatching Bootsie," *EQMM*, January 28
* _____, "Sweet Baby Jenny," *EQMM*, May 20
Henle, Theda O., "A Harmless Vanity," *EQMM*, March 25
Hoch, Edward D., "The Bad Samaritan," *AHMM*, December 9
_____, "Captain Leopold and the Silver Foxes," *EQMM*, January 1
* _____, "The Problem of the Octagon Room," *EQMM*, October 7
_____, "The Spy and the Walrus Cipher," *EQMM*, March 25
Holding, James, "The Only One of Its Kind," *EQMM*, February 25
_____, "The Search for Tamberlane," *EQMM*, May 20
_____, "Work of Art," *AHMM*, February 4
Holm, Janet, "A Pocket of Gold," *EQMM*, April 22
Howard, Clark, "Hit and Run," *AHMM*, September 16
* _____, "Mexican Triangle," *EQMM*, October 7
_____, "Top Con," *EQMM*, March 25
Jordan, Clements, "Come to Me, Tessie," *EQMM*. April 22
_____, "Has Anyone Seen Joey?" *EQMM*, November 4
* _____, "Won't Daddy Be Surprised?" *EQMM*, June 17
Keating, H.R.F., "Mrs. Craggs and a Certain Lady's Townhouse," *Mystery*, July
Laymon, Richard, "Blarney," *MSMM*, September
Legru, Seiko, "Inspector Saito and the Fox Girl," *AHMM*, February 4
Lopresti, Robert, "The Dear Departed," *AHMM*, June 24
Lovesey, Peter, "A Bride in the Bath," *EQMM*, August 12
Martin, Carol Myers, "Diamonds in the Rough," *AHMM*, December 9
Mayberry, Florence V., "The Girl Downstairs," *EQMM*, January 28
McGerr, Patricia, "Every Litter Bit Helps," *EQMM*, September 9
Natsuki, Shizuko, "The Sole of the Foot," *EQMM*, September 9
Olson, Donald, "A Friend Who Understands," *EQMM*, June 17
_____, "Indian Summer," *EQMM*, October 7
* _____, "A Token of Appreciation," *AHMM*, June 24
Owens, Barbara, "The Music in His Veins," *EQMM*, January 1
Panzran, Carl, "Counselor at Law," *MSMM*, September
Parry, Henry T., "The Black Stain," *EQMM*, January 28
_____, "The Final Secret," *EQMM*, July 15
_____, "Paris Green," *EQMM*, November 4
Perowne, Barry, "Raffles and Operation Champagne," *EQMM*, November 4

_____, "Raffles and the Box 4 Drama," *EQMM*, January 28

Powell, James, "Blind Man's Cuff," *EQMM*, July 15

_____, "The Notorious Snowman," *EQMM*, October 7

Powell, Talmadge, "The Beacon," *MSMM*, April

_____, "Night of the Goblin," *MSMM*, October

Pronzini, Bill, "The Terrarium Principle, *EQMM*, April 22

* _____ & Wallmann, Jeffrey, "Coyote and Quarter Moon," *MSMM*, October

Rafferty, S.S., "The Incomplete Salmagundi," *AHMM*, November 11

Rathjen, Carl Henry, "Not in the Script," *MSMM*, January

Rendell, Ruth, "The Boy Who Collected Poisons," *EQMM*, February 25

_____, "The Green Road," *EQMM*, January 1

Richter, Joan, "The House That Jill Built," *EQMM*, May 20

*Ritchie, Jack, "The Absence of Emily," *EQMM*, January 28

_____, "Body Check," *EQMM*, July 15

_____, "The Connecting Link," *EQMM*, October 7

Romun, Isak, "The Message," *AHMM*, September 16

Savage, Ernest, "The Best Man in Town," *EQMM*, July 15

_____, "Dangerous Ground," *EQMM*, May 20

Schraff, A.E., "Lost Causes," *AHMM*, April 1

Scott, Jeffry, "In the Eye of the Beholder," *EQMM*, November 4

_____, "Now You See It," *AHMM*, February 4

Seidman, Michael, "Perchance to Dream," *Mystery*, March

Sisk, Frank, "A Visit With Montezuma," *Crime Wave*

Smith, Pauline C., "The Plough Horse," *AHMM*, November 11

Sorrels, Roy, "Like a Million Bucks," *EQMM*, October 7

Stephenson, Michael, "Neatness Doesn't Count," *MSMM*, March

Steward, Dwight, "Genesis," *Crime Wave*

Suter, John F., "Dead Man's Honor," *EQMM*, April 22

_____, "Nine Strokes of the Bell," *EQMM*, September 9

_____, "The Power of the Tongue," *EQMM*, December 2

Symons, Julian, "The Dupe," *EQMM*, May 20

Townley, Mark, "The Hundred-Thousand-Dollar Wall," *AHMM*, March 4

Treat, Lawrence, "M As in Mayhem," *EQMM*, June 17

Twohy, Robert, "Mousie," *EQMM*, November 4

Underwood, Michael, "Death at the Opera," *EQMM*, May 20

Walker, Dale L., "Death of an Old Man," *AHMM*, January 7

Walsh, Thomas, "Leon's Last Job," *EQMM*, October 7

Wasylyk, Stephen, "Death of an Englishman," *AHMM*, January 7

————, "The Runaways," *AHMM*, April 29
————, "The Timetable," *AHMM*, June 24
————, "The Vindication of Pharo Grindle," *AHMM*, February 4
Wellen, Edward, "The Payoff," *MSMM*, June
*Westlake, Donald E., "Ask a Silly Question," *Playboy*, February

About the Editor

Edward D. Hoch, winner of an Edgar Award for his short story "The Oblong Room," is President of the Mystery Writers of America. He is a full-time writer and editor, mainly of mystery fiction, and his stories appear regularly in leading mystery magazines. He is probably best known as the creator of detective/thief Nick Velvet, whose exploits were collected in *The Thefts of Nick Velvet* and have been dramatized on French television. In addition to nearly 600 published short stories, his eighteen books include four novels—*The Shattered Raven, The Transvection Machine, The Fellowship of the Hand* and *The Frankenstein Factory*—four short story collections, nine anthologies and a children's book. Hoch and his wife, Patricia, reside in Rochester, N.Y., where he is a trustee of the Rochester Public Library.